WHISPERS OF SPRING

SEASON OF CHANGE SERIES BOOK 2

ANNEMARIE BREAR

CHAPTER 1

*H*opewood Farm
Yorkshire, England
July 1853

CAROLINE LAWSON TIPPED the bucket of food scraps into the trough and watched the sow and her fat piglets rush to delve their snouts into the offerings, squealing and grunting. Recent rain had muddied their stall and Caroline wrinkled her nose at the smell of dung. Fresh straw needed to be spread.

She gazed beyond the pigsty to the field behind where a small herd of cattle grazed. She silently prayed they would remain healthy and grow large for the market. Much depended on the cattle sale at the end of summer, and that of the sheep roaming the hills, stock all bought by her friend, Mr Bent, a butcher in York, and her business partner. He'd invested in buying the animals and she would be fattening them on her land before they went to market.

She turned and surveyed the outbuildings and cobbled

yard of Hopewood Farm, her late husband's boyhood home. She had taken it on to run after her father-in-law's death a few months ago and, with the help of her friends, she was determined to show everyone that a woman could manage a farm successfully. It wouldn't be easy, of course, she knew that. However, the alternative of failing and moving away was something she refused to think about. She'd only just returned to the countryside after some difficult months of living rough in the bleak slums of York.

The very thought of leaving the farm and perhaps once again living in a harsh city somewhere filled her with horror. Cities, York in particular, held no interest for her. The time she spent there showed her a different way of life than the gentle existence she enjoyed with her husband. The wild streets, filled with desperate people all trying to survive poverty and disease, was a world away from the quiet countryside. Caroline had found it difficult to adjust to the cramped unsavoury conditions of the city and wouldn't have made it if it wasn't for several people who became her dear friends, like Septimus Casey, who everyone fondly called, Mussy, and Trixie Wilkes and Trixie's two little sisters, Elsie and Bertha, people she cherished. However, the squalor, the danger, the risk of being homeless and the struggle to find work made York a place to avoid. Those reasons and the evil threat of the criminal Victor Dolan, a man who pretended to be a landlord, but who kept her prisoner and attacked her, were enough to keep Caroline in the countryside.

Leaning on the fence, she shivered, remembering her terrifying ordeal at the hands of Victor Dolan. Trixie had helped her escape him, but not before Caroline raked her nails down his face, scaring him for life. She later learned Dolan wanted to sell her as a prostitute, one of the illegal businesses he ran. Trixie's involvement in helping Caroline nearly killed her, as Dolan and his men gave Trixie a beating that she nearly died from. In fear, Caroline had taken Trixie, Elsie and Bertha and fled York to Hopewood Farm, the only place she knew that was safe.

A man's sharp curse interrupted her thoughts. Mussy. Her dear friend had no head for farming, having been raised as a gentleman in Manchester, yet he was living with her to escape the torment of a dark and secretive past. He, too, found it necessary to leave the city and forge a new life.

Caroline rounded the side of the barn and entered the stable where Mussy was trying and failing to harness Dossy, the horse, to the gig. 'Would you care for some help?'

He looked up, his overlong salt-and-pepper coloured hair falling over his eyes, as he wrestled with a strap. 'I was going to venture into the village, but I didn't want to walk and get my boots covered in mud. I polished them this morning.'

Threading the harness through the rings on the gig, Caroline tightened the straps. 'What do you need in the village?'

'Trixie asked for some more thread, and I want to check at the general store for the book I ordered, an atlas. I have been teaching Elsie and Bertha about different countries. The book should have arrived by now.' Mussy straightened his tall, thin frame. Today, he wore a bright red waistcoat under a blue pinstriped suit with a yellow silk cravat. His extravagant clothes used to match his flamboyant manner, but his time in prison for committing an indecent act with another man had curbed his natural outgoing character, that and the illness which still plagued him from his time incarcerated. 'Do you need me to get anything for you?'

'No, thank you.' Caroline adjusted another strap and

patted Dossy's neck. 'If you buy any more books, we'll need to start housing them in the barn. Your bedroom is full.'

He smiled sheepishly and smoothed his thin moustache he'd grown back after having it shaved off in prison. 'Books are my passion. I must have something to be enthusiastic about.'

'It's an obsession that's taken you over.' She couldn't blame him for escaping into the pages of the hundreds of books he'd accumulated. She knew he still suffered from the months he spent in jail. She often attended to him in the night when he cried out, lost in a nightmare. In jail, he'd wanted to die and had stopped eating. His gaunt features and lingering cough were a testament to the hardship of the ordeal.

'I was grateful my father sent me the books from my old home. I didn't expect him to. I fully believed he would have removed all traces of me from the house the moment I was sentenced.' Mussy ran a hand over Dossy's rump. The hurt of his family's rejection stamped on his thin face.

'One day they might visit. They have this address. Don't give up hope.'

'My dear Caro, I gave up hope years ago of my family understanding the person that I am. They will not visit.' Mussy led the horse out of the barn and climbed up onto the seat. With a wave, he guided Dossy across the yard and down the drive.

Turning, she walked towards the fields where she'd sown turnips and potatoes and, further afield, were acres of hay growing strong and green in the sunshine. A wistful smile lingered when she looked at those fields. Long days of manning the plough, churning up the ground, tilling and seeding had produced the beginnings of a future. Crops would give them food and income and feed for the stock over winter if the summer weather behaved and disease didn't ravish yield.

She'd not done all this work by herself. Jacob Adams had been a neighbour in the York slums, a man who helped them escape and who had also received a near fatal beating at the hands of Victor Dolan. Like Mussy, Jacob now called the farm home.

Caroline's other champion was Maxwell Cavendish, who had ploughed and sown the hay. In the last few months, he'd become a valued friend, someone she could discuss farming with and learn from. He was the estate land agent for her landlord, and his uncle, Lord Stockton-Lee, who owned thousands of acres locally and most of Melliton, the village a few miles away. Maxwell Cavendish and his younger brother Thomas were often visitors to her farm. She enjoyed having them as her friends, but sometimes the way Mr Cavendish looked at her, she felt he wanted more.

Mr Cavendish's assistance had saved her time and from breaking her own back working such hard toil, but the rewards wouldn't be until harvest, and she desperately needed a good harvest. Money was tight, worryingly tight. On a market stall each week, she sold her dairy products, cheese and butter, made from her own cows' milk in her dairy and Trixie sold her loaves of bread she was becoming increasingly good at baking. Mussy gave Caroline some of his allowance he received from his family, but other than that, there was little income, and Caroline's small hoard of coins was dwindling fast as she improved the farm. They ate the food they grew in the vegetable garden, eggs from the chickens and geese. Jacob had learnt to trap rabbits and often shot the odd pheasant. They got by as long as they worked hard, but poverty was never far away.

Smothering a yawn, for she'd been awake since four that morning to milk the cows, Caroline headed across the yard, then spotted Jacob pushing a wheelbarrow full of sawn logs up the hill and waited for him to reach her.

'I'll help you unload,' Caroline said to him as he reached her.

Jacob had recovered from his beating, thanks to Trixie and her devoted care. Plenty of bed rest and nourishing food had changed Jacob. Away from the dirty slums, the coal smoke city air and poor diet, Jacob had altered, gained a little weight and more muscle as he began working about the farm. For a man who'd never lived outside of a city, Jacob had soon learned the ways of farm life, and more importantly, he thrived on it.

'I've cleared that fallen tree from over the stream.' Jacob wheeled the barrow around to the back of the barn and to the chopping block. 'The water is running free now and shouldn't get blocked when it rains.'

'You mustn't push yourself. It's only been a few weeks since you left your sickbed,' she warned. Jacob was one of those rare men you knew you could trust with your life or your greatest secrets.

'I'm fine, honestly. I've eaten well and my strength is back.' He gave a shy smile from an ordinary face, but his kindness and goodness gave him an extra quality that shone from his eyes. 'The care you and Trixie have given me has brought me back from death's door.'

'Well, just don't undo all Trixie's care and attention to make you better by becoming ill from doing too much too soon.'

'This farm has given me a new lease on life, Caroline.' Jacob looked about, taking in the surroundings of the woodshed, the barns, and beyond. 'I can never thank you enough for letting me call this place home. The only way I can repay you is by working hard.'

'I don't need repaying, Jacob. You helped save Trixie and me from Dolan. All debts are paid. I just wished I could pay you a wage for your work, but until we sell the beasts in the autumn, I have little to spare.'

'You're putting a roof over my head and food in my belly. That's enough for me, for now.' He lifted up one foot, showing his boot was tied together with string. 'Although I'll be needing new boots before winter.' He laughed in the light-hearted way he had that brought a smile to Caroline's face.

'I think we'll be able to get you some boots and a good coat.' Then she had a thought. 'Oh, there are some of Howard's boots in the cupboard in the scullery. You should wear them if they fit.'

'You don't mind?'

'Not at all. Howard would want his things used and not go to waste. I'll look through the cupboards, for I know he had a good thick coat you could wear in the winter.' Caroline thought of her dear father-in-law, who died soon after she arrived at the farm. He'd been planning to marry Annie Aspall, but his health had failed, that and the loss of two sons, one in death and the other to Canada, gave him little to live for. She missed him terribly.

Inspecting the sawn branches, Caroline picked up one of the smaller ones. 'It'll take some months for the wood to dry out.'

'I'll stack it in the barn out of the weather.' Jacob pulled out a longer branch. 'I'll cut them up smaller, and they'll be grand by winter.'

Elsie and Bertha came running around the side of the barn, calling for Caroline.

Jacob threw the log on the ground. 'Here comes the little imps,' he joked.

The two girls ran up to them, pushing at each other and both talking at once.

'Stop that. Calm down,' Caroline told them.

'The Misters Cavendish are here,' Elsie, the eldest aged eight, blurted out. 'And they've brought a present for you, for us!'

'You're not to tell!' Bertha pushed at her sister.

'Enough.' Caroline held up her hand. 'This is not how we behave, is it? We act with dignity, not like urchins in the street.' Having grown up in a convent, the nuns' teachings had instilled lady-like behaviour in Caroline that she was trying to teach Elsie and Bertha.

She walked with them back to the house, ignoring the way her stomach fluttered at the mention of Mr Cavendish.

Maxwell Cavendish was becoming important to her, and that alarmed her. The first anniversary of Hugh's death was coming up soon, and she still missed her husband keenly, but Hugh was gone and since his death last year, her world had been turned upside down. She'd lost not only Hugh but everything she had, her farm, her belongings and the life she thought she'd live forever. She hadn't had the time back then to grieve for him properly. Surviving was the only way forward. After his death, she'd suffered so much in the few months she lived in York alone and poor. Now she was safe and back in the country and starting again with her friends, so did she want to complicate things by letting her emotions run towards Maxwell Cavendish?

Hugh would want her to be happy and secure, she knew

that, yet there was a part of her which enjoyed the freedom of being a widow, of running the farm in the way she wanted, of being answerable to no one. She'd been lucky enough to marry a wonderful man once. Was it tempting fate to even consider doing it again? Could she be that fortunate? She didn't think so. Mr Cavendish was a nephew to a lord and lived a life of mixing with gentlemen. Although employed as an estate land agent, he was also family to a wealthy man and moved within those circles. Maxwell Cavendish would set his sights higher than her when he came to selecting a wife. No, she was doing well enough on her own. She didn't need a man to complicate her life.

Entering the sunny, clean kitchen, Caroline smiled a welcome to the two handsome brothers, who were chatting to Trixie.

Maxwell, older and wiser than his brother, Thomas, gave her a half-smile in return, one she was beginning to recognise meant many things. He was a quiet man, not talkative like Thomas. Mr Cavendish was happy to observe, think deeply about a subject before speaking.

'Look!' Bertha ran to the small straw-filled crate near the table and inside it, two fat black and white puppies rolled playfully with each other.

'They are for the farm,' Elsie piped up, kneeling next to the crate.

Caroline stared at the scrapping puppies and then at the brothers. 'They are fine puppies.' She didn't know how to respond and hoped they weren't for her, but instead the dogs belonged to the brothers.

Max knelt and rubbed their ears while looking up at her. 'I thought you could use some dogs for the sheep and cattle. Every farm should have good working dogs.'

She inwardly groaned at the responsibility. She had enough to do getting the farm profitable without this added commitment. 'I don't know how to train dogs to work with animals. I've never owned a dog before.'

'I will help you.' Max gave her an apologetic shrug. 'I thought, in time, they will be a great help to you, but if I have made a mistake, I can take them back.'

Thomas took out a chair and sat down as Trixie poured out tea for them all. 'My brother also has a puppy from the same litter. If I wasn't going back to university in the autumn, I'd have bought one as well.'

'You bought them?' Caroline's heart sank. She didn't have spare money to repay him for puppies she didn't even want.

'Please,' Max said, holding up his hand, 'they are at no cost to you. Mr Purcell, from High Ridge Farm, wanted them gone to a good home. It is a large littler of eight pups and he has only sold four. Mr Purcell was going to keep the four remaining, but his wife told him otherwise.'

'I don't blame her,' Caroline muttered.

'Mr Purcell is a fine dog trainer and has started the puppies' training around stock. He has offered to continue to help teach them if I took them off his hands at a low cost. They are six months old and can sit at command and return.' He gave her another smile. 'I will assist you, too.'

'Max has trained sheep dogs before,' Thomas added, tucking into a slice of the sponge cake Trixie placed next to his tea. 'What names will you call them?'

'We can't accept them without payment,' Caroline uttered, thinking quickly about how much she could afford.

'No, I will not take a penny for them,' Mr Cavendish was adamant. 'They are a gift.'

Bertha and Elsie started shouting out names such as Spot

and Petal, but they quietened down when Max lifted one of the puppies out and handed it to Caroline.

She took the soft ball of fur, which was heavier than she expected, and held the pup against her chest, grinning when it licked her chin. They were adorable for sure, but such a commitment.

'They are both boys,' Max told her, grabbing the other one and coming to stand close to her so she could see both puppies side by side. 'They are from a good mother who has a solid Welsh Sheepdog breeding background and is a prized sheepdog. These pups will be very useful to you.'

She should have been angry with him. Dogs were the last thing she wanted, but when she gazed into Max's blue eyes, she couldn't resist. He was kind and generous and such a good friend. 'Very well…' She snuggled the puppy she held closer while reaching out to fondle the other one Max held. She smiled at Max. 'Since you believe they will be good for the farm.'

He watched her carefully, waiting.

Caroline turned away from him, breaking the contact and the acute awareness she experienced whenever he was near for it unnerved her and she wasn't ready to acknowledge it. 'They are fine-looking puppies,' she spoke to Elsie and Bertha. 'They need strong names.'

'Blackie,' Elsie suggested.

Caroline studied the puppy in her arms. He looked at her quizzically and gave her another lick. His black and white markings were similar to his brother's, but this one had more white fur on his chest. 'This one will be called Prince.'

'Prince!' Elsie and Bertha clapped, and the puppy wiggled in excitement.

'And this one?' Max held him out and Caroline swapped

puppies with him. Their hands touched, and she glanced at Max to see if he felt the same reaction as she did. His eyes narrowed, his stare intense.

She sucked in a shallow breath and stroked the soft black fur as the puppy rested his head on her chest. 'This one will be called Duke.'

'Splendid names,' Max murmured, placing Prince in the crate. 'That's settled then. Prince and Duke are the new inhabitants of Hopewood Farm.'

The girls knelt by the crate and played with the puppies.

'Have some tea, Mr Cavendish,' Trixie offered, glancing at Caroline. Trixie knew she'd be hesitant to take on more obligations.

'The summer fair is on in a couple of weeks, so I'm told. Being new to the area, I'd like to attend,' Thomas said, crossing one leg over the other. He was at ease in their company, more so than his brother. 'I think we should all go. What do you say?' he spoke directly to Trixie, who blushed.

'I say you should spend more time on your farm,' Max said quietly. 'The whole purpose for you to live on Springwood Farm was to learn the hands-on approach to farming before you go away and recommence your studies.'

'I'm involved in every aspect of that farm, Maxwell. I am learning a great deal which will improve my knowledge and my studies when I return to university,' Thomas replied tightly, his handsome face showing his annoyance. 'I'm allowed to have a day off now and then.'

'You have more days away from the farm than you do on it.' Max sipped his tea.

'That is untrue, and you know it,' Thomas said. 'But we shall discuss that later.'

'Can we go to the fair?' Elsie asked. 'Annie is having a stall there to sell her candles.' Elsie spoke of Annie Aspall, a widow and friend, who lived in the village. Annie had become a type of grandmother to the girls.

'We'll see,' Trixie answered.

'Perhaps take the puppies outside, girls,' Caroline suggested. 'They may need to relieve themselves.'

With the girls carrying a puppy each, they ran outside and the adults could hear them squealing and laughing with excitement in the yard.

'We should be taking our leave.' Max placed his hat on his head and turned to Caroline. 'I shall return in a few days, and we can start the pups' training out in the fields.'

'Yes, thank you, and thank you for considering us regarding the puppies.'

'My intentions are well intended. I hope I do not live to regret buying one myself.' Max raised his eyebrows in mock horror.

Reluctantly, Thomas followed Max out and Caroline stood in the doorway and waved them off.

Trixie stood beside her as the two men rode out of the yard. 'That was kind of Mr Cavendish to give you two dogs, but it's two more mouths to feed when we're struggling to feed ourselves.'

'He doesn't know that, though.'

'What do you make of him and Thomas having words? They are never like that.'

Caroline looked at Trixie. 'I think Mr Cavendish was hinting that Thomas spends too much time at *this* farm and not at his own.'

'He is here a lot.'

'And we know why.' She nudged Trixie playfully.

'Not for me, Caroline. I'm not worthy of someone like

Thomas, of anyone really, not with my past.' Trixie turned away and went back to the range where the pot of stew simmered.

'Your past is behind you,' Caroline said, seeing the wounded gaze haunting Trixie's eyes.

'No, it isn't. It lives with me, every day. It's who I am or was.' Trixie stirred the stew with a wooden spoon.

'You are the person we love. You're kind and thoughtful and caring. That's all that matters.'

'Really? Maybe to you and the girls, but not to a potential husband. Thomas Cavendish is a gentleman. He'd never look twice in my direction if he knew I'd been a prostitute.'

A sound in the doorway had them turning. Max Cavendish stood there and, by the look on his face, he'd heard every word.

CHAPTER 2

'*M*r Cavendish!' Trixie jerked in surprise and horror at what he had heard. Embarrassed, she felt her cheeks burn and her stomach clenched in dread.

'I returned because I forgot to tell you that there is a farming machinery auction on Thursday in Boroughbridge.' He looked only at Caroline. 'Did you wish to attend? I am happy to collect you at eight?'

'Thank you, but no, I don't think I will go. We don't have the money to purchase machinery at the moment,' Caroline spoke quickly, also blushing.

Trixie's guilt deepened. She understood Maxwell was keen on Caroline. A blind man could see it, even if Caroline wasn't fully aware, and now with him hearing about her past, Trixie knew it would change everything. The Cavendish brothers would keep their distance now, and any silly feelings she held for Thomas would be ashes once Maxwell told him about her. She bowed her head in shame and sadness.

'You heard us talking?' Caroline confronted Cavendish, her head held high.

Trixie's head shot up, and she stared at Caroline in shock.

'I did,' he acknowledged. 'Forgive me for interrupting. I did not realise it was a conversation about such an intimate subject.'

'Nevertheless, you've heard it now. You know of Trixie's past.'

'It is none of my business.' A muscle pulsed in his strong jaw.

Trixie wanted to escape, to not see the condemnation in his face, but Caroline was holding her ground, refusing to allow him to walk away.

'Will you tell Thomas?' Caroline demanded to know.

'You are asking me to keep this from my brother?' Cavendish seemed put out by the request.

'Thomas is our friend,' Caroline continued. 'I'd hate to see him think differently about Trixie now and perhaps not visit anymore.'

'That would be up to my brother.' Cavendish looked at Trixie. 'I cannot keep this from him. I fear he has developed some sort of admiration towards you.'

'You fear it?' Trixie took a deep breath. Cavendish didn't approve of her, but would he have anyway? She was a nobody from the slums of York, worse she was a prostitute from the slums of York. That he confirmed Thomas felt some emotion for her was exciting, for she respected Thomas greatly. Thomas was handsome and funny and took time out of his day to come and see her, and she knew it was her he wanted to be with, for he never left her side when he visited, but she was far below Thomas in every way.

Cavendish gripped his hat tightly. 'My brother cannot marry for years yet. He has to prove himself. He has to finish university, obtain a position somewhere on a grand estate.

Thomas cannot support a wife. He can barely support himself without me.'

'Thank you, Mr Cavendish, for making that clear,' Caroline said stiffly.

He tapped his hat against his leg. 'I will not tell my brother of your past, Miss Wilkes. It is not my business.'

'Thank you.'

'Good day to you both.' With a last look at Caroline, Cavendish left the kitchen.

Trixie, her knees wobbly, and sat at the table. 'I'm so sorry.'

'Whatever for?' Caroline joined her and took her fingers in hers.

'I've ruined any chance you had with Maxwell Cavendish.'

'Stuff and nonsense,' Caroline declared. 'I don't want him, and even if I did, if he refused me because of your past, then he isn't the man I think he is, and I wouldn't want him, anyway.'

'Thomas… I hate to think of him knowing about me.' Trixie bowed her head. Her chest tightened at the humiliation of Thomas being told about her. She imagined his reaction of shock and revulsion.

'Again, the same thing, if Thomas finds out and shuns you, then he was never a true friend.'

'And that is all he could ever have been, only a friend, never a suitor.' Of course, she understood he would never have been hers. He was too far above her, but she liked to dream about the idea of him loving her. One look from him and her knees went weak. It was a strange sensation because when she lived in York, doing what she did, she never looked at a man with desire or yearning. They used her body, never touching her mind or her heart, and paid her for that service.

'You don't know that.'

Trixie tutted. 'I do. Why would he want someone like me? I'd only be an embarrassment to him. I'm not worthy of him. How can I be? I can't even read or write, and he attends university! Nor am I any great beauty, unlike you.'

'You are beautiful, Trixie,' Caroline declared fiercely. 'You've those large eyes and delicate features. Any man would be honoured to have you as his wife.'

'Not a Cavendish.'

'You can't speak for Thomas.'

'Thomas will listen to his brother.'

'I'm sorry Mr Cavendish overheard us, but he won't tell him. He'll keep his word.'

'What does it matter? Thomas is far above me.'

'But you'd want him as a husband, if it were possible?'

'It'd be hard not to. Thomas is handsome and funny and nice…' Trixie wished she'd lived a different life, one that was clean and honest. Thomas was everything she wanted and everything she could never have.

'Forget the Cavendish brothers for now.' Caroline embraced her. 'You have me, and the girls, Mussy and Annie and, of course, Jacob, who adores you.'

Frowning, confused, Trixie reared back a little. What was Caroline saying? 'Jacob?'

'Yes, Jacob. How have you not seen it?' Caroline grinned. 'You might have feelings for Thomas, but Jacob shares the same feelings for you.'

'Jacob is a friend. He has been for years, since we were kids. We've lived in the same building all our lives. He is like a brother of sorts to me, always looking out for me and the girls in our lane. You've got it wrong, Caroline. Jacob doesn't think of me in *that* way.'

Caroline stood as the girls came in, carrying the puppies.

'Are you sure about that? He risked his life to save you from Dolan.'

Trixie stood and began to clear away the tea things from the table, her mind whirling. Jacob? Jacob desired her? She wanted to laugh it off, but couldn't. It was too unbelievable.

In York, Jacob had seen her leave their dilapidated tenement building every night to go and earn money walking the streets, selling her body. He'd seen her at her worst, poor, cold and hungry, living in a squalid room with nothing to her name, trying to survive and feed her sisters. He'd seen her broken and bleeding, beaten by Dolan, left for dead in the snowy backstreets. No man would want someone like her. And who could blame them?

Yet, now that Caroline had planted the seed, she thought back to all the weeks she'd nursed Jacob back to health after he arrived at the farm nearly dead from Dolan's henchmen. She spent hours caring for his wounds, feeding him broth from a spoon when his swollen face was unable to handle chewing and his hands were too damaged to fend for himself. She'd talked quietly to him when he drifted in and out of sleep, praying to a God she wasn't sure she had faith in to let him live. She'd done all that because he was her oldest friend, because Jacob knew first-hand how they survived in the slums, he knew *her*.

So, what Caroline said, was it true? Did he have feelings for her? Or was Caroline wrong and misconstruing what was simply just friendship?

She didn't know what to think.

Needing a distraction, Trixie went into the scullery and changed her house shoes for boots and, gathering her garden apron and gloves, walked outside. The sun shone from a clear blue sky and swallows and other birds flittered from the large pear tree to the rooftops of the house and barns, their chatter filling the air along with the scent of flowers she didn't know the names of.

Walking around the side of the house, Trixie entered the broken gate of the kitchen garden, which was in a sorry state. Once it would have been a neat and productive garden near the house, but years of neglect had given the weeds and self-sown vegetables the chance to take over the garden beds and paths.

Trixie had been spending any spare moment to sort it out and with the girls' help, they were making progress. The paths were weeded, and the pebbles raked. Jacob had straightened and staked the wooden planks edging each bed so now Trixie could dig the soil over and add manure to it, ready for the winter vegetables. Some of the beds held summer crops, self-sown, and herbs ran riot in places. Trixie would like to have known more about growing produce, but she couldn't read or write very well even with Caroline's teachings, and so the farming manuals were useless to her. However, instinct came to the fore as she worked, and she realised with great surprise that she had a knack for growing plants, she, Trixie Wilkes, the slum girl, who'd never work with soil or plants, found a great satisfaction in growing things. The notion was ridiculous.

'Do you need a hand?' Jacob came to stand opposite her across one of the long beds she was digging over.

'I've more lettuce seeds to plant. Annie says we need to keep a rotating crop, planting at different times, so we always have continued growth through summer or something like that. We've eaten many lettuces already,' Trixie said, keeping her head down. She didn't want to look into his face and see something there to confirm Caroline's words. Jacob wasn't someone to consider as a husband, not when her heart had already been given to Thomas.

'I can dig, and you plant if you want?' Jacob offered, picking up the spade.

'Yes, all right then. The tomatoes are growing well. I'm surprised.' She kept the conversation light.

'You shouldn't be surprised. You and Annie have done well growing them.'

'I couldn't have done any of this without Annie, and you, of course.' Trixie kept her eyes on the soil, positioning the seeds with care.

'We make a good team,' Jacob said happily. 'Who'd have thought it, hey? Us city urchins growing food.'

'It is mad to think about.' It truly was. Living and working on a farm was something she'd never have thought would happen to her. Until she met Caroline, she believed her life path had already been set out and would never change. 'I'm pleased Elsie and Bertha will grow up out here on the farm and not in those filthy streets as we did.'

'Where are the girls? They should be helping.' Jacob began digging the soil, turning it over.

'They won't leave the puppies alone. They can have today playing with them but tomorrow they will be back working.' She watched a butterfly hover about a plant at the end of the row. 'I wish I knew if that was a vegetable or a weed,' she murmured.

'We need to ask Caroline. She'd know. She said she used to work in the garden at the convent where she grew up.'

'Caroline is too busy. She's got enough to do.' Trixie used a small garden fork to make lines in the dirt. Carefully, she placed the lettuce seeds from her pocket into the lines and gently covered the dirt over them. 'Annie'll be here later, I'll ask her.'

They worked side by side for an hour, clearing beds and turning the soil over and weeding between the vegetables already growing that Trixie and Annie had planted a month earlier.

Jacob rested his arms on the top of the spade handle. 'You're quiet. Anything the matter?'

Trixie glanced at him, and his warm smile made her smile back. 'No, nowt.' At that moment in time, she was happy and content.

'We've weeded a lot.' Jacob wiped the sweat from his forehead under his hat, gazing at the long rows of carrots, onions, leeks and the staked tomatoes and cucumbers.

'I'm so pleased.' Trixie raked a pile of weeds to join the other pile Jacob had made.

'I'll burn it.' He forked the weeds into a wheelbarrow. 'What more do you want to do?'

Trixie bent and inspected the ripening tomatoes, thrilled at their progress and what she'd created. 'That's enough for today. Annie will be here soon to give me a baking lesson.'

'What are you making?'

'Meat and potato pie and a lemon curd tart. I can never get the curd right,' Trixie mused, annoyed at her failings. She plucked a caterpillar from near a radish and trod on it.

'I don't like those.' Jacob nodded to the plant.

'The radish or caterpillar?' She laughed.

'Both.' Jacob chuckled. 'I remember taking one of those radishes from beneath a stall in the market back home. I was only a kid. It tasted awful.'

'Aye, I remember taking a tomato from the market, though it was overripe and bruised and had fallen onto the cobbles...

It was disgusting.' Trixie sighed at the sharp pang of home-sickness for York. Sometimes it surprised her, the longing to be amongst the old buildings, smelling the smut from coal fires, the noise of hundreds of boots on cobbles, the factory whistles, the boat horns blaring in the fog.

'Do you miss York?' Jacob asked, as if reading her mind.

'Sometimes. Not the awful room we lived in or the filthy Water Lanes, but I miss watching the river flow past and hearing the cathedral bells tolling.'

'I miss being able to get a pint of ale on any street corner.' He chuckled. 'I miss me mates and Sarah and the kiddies.'

'You should get Caroline to write again to Sarah, to let her know you're still well.'

'We don't even know if the first letter reached Sarah.' Jacob scratched the stubble on his chin. 'I'd like to go and see me sister to make sure she's doing fine.'

'Return to York?' Trixie stared at him. 'What if Dolan sees you?'

'I'll go early one morning, slip through the streets while everyone sleeps. Dolan can't be everywhere all the time.'

'But his men might be. Dolan hates us. He wants revenge on Caroline for escaping him and disfiguring his face.'

'He got his revenge by beating you and me.' Jacob dug the fork into the pile with more force, taking his frustrations out on the weeds. 'Dolan would've forgotten us all by now.'

'That's what we thought in York, but he hadn't. Every time he looks in the mirror, he is reminded of Caroline by the ugly scars on his face.'

'He is *ugly*.' Jacob nodded. 'His face must have got infected when she scratched him and didn't heal properly. He looks like a monster.'

'Exactly, and that is why we can never return home.' Trixie

dusted off her gloves, sad that she'd never be able to walk the streets of York again. Although, she liked the country, the fresh air and how her sisters were thriving, she did miss the noise, the familiar streets she knew so well. The country was so spacious, and quiet.

'I've brought you both a drink,' Caroline declared, walking through the gate carrying a tray. 'Elderberry cordial and some bread and cheese.'

Subdued, Trixie and Jacob joined her and took a glass of cordial.

'I've managed to get the girls away from the puppies, finally, and sent them to the stable to muck out Dossy's stall,' Caroline told them, leaning against the fence post. 'The puppies fell asleep the minute the girls were out the door.'

Jacob sat on the grass eating the bread and cheese. 'Mr Cavendish is a good friend to you, Caroline. Those dogs will save you paying a man's labour to round up the sheep and cattle.'

At the mention of the name of Cavendish, Trixie put down her glass and focused on the garden beds. She hoped Thomas wouldn't turn his back on their friendship when he found out about her, but she had to be prepared for it to happen.

She heard the sound of the cart as Mussy drove up the long drive from the village road. Annie was with him. Before long, they were at the gate, talking to Caroline and Jacob.

'Trixie,' Mussy walked between the beds towards her. 'I have something for you.'

'My thread?' She straightened and pulled off her gloves. 'That's kind of you to fetch it for me.'

'I did get your thread but also this.' He handed her a large book bound in green leather, coughing as he did so.

'A book?' She scowled. 'Why?'

Mussy pointed to the words on the front. '*Gardening for Ladies* by Mrs Loudon.' He smiled that cheeky smile they all adored. 'There are wonderful illustrations inside. Look.' He opened the book to show her artwork of gardening implements. 'The names are underneath, see?'

Trixie gazed in awe at the artwork. 'I can't read, Mussy.'

'You cannot read *yet*, but I shall help you. We will go through the book together and soon you shall have a whole new understanding and knowledge of gardening. Annie also brought you a cookbook as well. I will teach you to be reading both by the end of the year.'

She gazed up at him, for he was so much taller than her, and noticed his pale face, the dark shadows under his eyes. 'I'll treasure this always.'

He looked pleased with himself as he walked back towards the gate. 'We can start reading it this evening, if you would like?'

'Aye, I would,' she called after him. Caroline was right. No matter what the Cavendish brothers thought of her, or anyone else for that matter, she had her sisters and her dear friends here who cared for her and that was worth a great deal. And if Thomas's face lingered in her mind for a moment, she quickly pushed it away.

CHAPTER 3

Maxwell sat at his desk in the steward's office in the west wing of Misterton Abbey writing a letter to his uncle Richard, Lord Stockton-Lee, who was currently in India. Further along the corridor were the service areas that operated the efficient workings of the large country house, but his door was closed, minimising the noise of passing servants. He had, however, opened both of the tall sash windows and the warm July breeze gently lifted the curtains and birds twittering on the rooftops was a pleasant sound.

Once he'd finished the letter, he'd go for a ride and possibly call in at Hopewood Farm to see Mrs Lawson. Pen poised, his thoughts drifted to Caroline. What a fine woman she was. Strong-minded, determined to make the farm a success, hard-working, loving and caring to the unique circle of friends she'd taken under her wing and protected at the farm. All that and beautiful with it. Her hair, the colours of roasted chestnuts, those green eyes he could stare into for the rest of his life. Caroline was the woman for him, of that he had no doubts, but he had to tread carefully, slowly. She was a recent widow and had been through a great deal since her husband's death last year. Max had to be patient and wait for the time to be perfect before he declared himself.

The idea of taking a wife brought a smile to his lips. He thought one day he'd marry, but that was always in the distant future. Since meeting Caroline, his plans had changed, grown and revolved around her.

A knock on the door brought him out of his thoughts. 'Yes?'

Alfred, the upper footman entered. 'Sorry to disturb you, Mr Cavendish, but you're wanted in the drawing room by Lord Stockton-Lee.'

'My *uncle* has arrived?' Shocked, Max stood abruptly. He'd had no correspondence informing him of such an event. His uncle last wrote that he would not be returning from India for some years yet.

'No, sir, your cousin, Wayland Stockton-Lee has arrived.'

Even more intrigued that his cousin had ventured this far north, Max replaced his pen in the stand and pulled on his jacket, his movement unhurried. He nodded to Alfred as he passed, not mentioning the footman's slip of calling Wayland, Lord, and took a deep breath to prepare himself to face his cousin, a man he didn't like nor respected. He hoped it was to be a short visit and Wayland would soon be gone again.

Since his uncle and aunt's departure for India, Max inspected all the abbey's rooms, from attics to cellars, once a month in the company of Mr Reeves, the butler and Mrs Hoskins, the housekeeper, to make sure the building, originally built in late Tudor times, was still watertight and in good condition. Therefore, Max was ready for Wayland should his cousin ask him questions about the house or estate.

The first thing Max noted was that his cousin was wearing severe black with a brilliant white shirt, his receding black hair was lavishly oiled flat to his head. 'Wayland, this is a surprise.'

'I imagine it is.' Wayland, tall, lanky and with small eyes that narrowed a lot, shook Max's hand. The cousins looked nothing alike.

'What brings you this far north?' Max couldn't remember the last time he saw his cousin, but it was many years ago when they were at university, for they were of similar age. One thing he did remember was his uncle saying that Wayland hated Yorkshire. Anywhere further north than Oxford and Wayland believed the country to be dirty and uncivilised and not worth his time visiting. His base was his father's London townhouse in Mayfair or at the family's delightful little manor on the Sussex coast and sometimes the apartment in Paris.

'Grave news, Max.' Wayland glanced around the drawing room as if seeing it for the first time. His eyebrows knotted together as he stared at the framed country scenes hanging on the wall. 'I received the terrible news two days ago that my father has died.'

'Uncle Richard is dead?' Max rocked back on his heels, disbelieving what he'd heard. The blow was difficult to absorb for he admired his uncle a great deal and now he was dead? 'Dear God! How?'

'Some revolting disease, apparently. You know what the Indian sub-continent is like, a hideous pot of sickness, disorder and filth.'

'I am floored by this news, Wayland, truly. You must be distraught.' Max rubbed his forehead, dismayed and terribly saddened.

Wayland sat on one of the green velvet sofas positioned at right angles to the large marble fireplace. 'It isn't ideal timing, to be certain.'

Max frowned. 'Not ideal timing?' Was there ever such a thing as good timing for a death?

'Well, I am not ready to take over Father's vast empire. I am a *Lord* now, for heaven's sake and all the duties that requires. I loathe parliament.'

'Yes, of course, but you have been knowing all that responsibly would one day be yours.'

'I did not believe that day would come so soon.' Wayland inspected his clean-cut fingernails.

Max's mind whirled. He would now report to his cousin. Wayland was the new Lord Stockton-Lee, owner of the estate and village. Would he want things to change? Did he even want Max in this position anymore?

The door opened and refreshments were brought in by two maids with Mr Reeves assisting.

'Ah, about time.' Wayland sat forward and suspiciously eyed the tea tray of the abbey's finest silver and the dainty china holding a selection of cakes. 'Not quite London's standards, but pleasant enough it seems.' He waved the maids away. 'I shall serve myself as I doubt you could make my tea the way I like it.'

Max watched the maids scurry away and Reeves stand to attention.

'Will there be anything else, sir?' Reeves asked Wayland.

'Yes, you are to address me as *my lord* from now on, Reeves, and inform the staff of the news that my father is dead. I am the new Lord Stockton-Lee.' Wayland didn't even bother to look in the butler's direction as he added milk to his teacup.

Max winced at the blunt announcement.

'Yes, certainly, my lord.' Reeves stood as straight as a rod, only his eyes betraying his emotions.

Wayland sniffed the tea as if it stank. 'I shall be staying for a week, possibly two. Make sure my valet has everything he needs. I shall stay in my old bedroom until you have organised the removal of my father's belongings from his suite.'

'Very good, my lord.' Reeves swallowed. 'May I, on behalf of all the staff, give you our deepest condolences on the loss of your excellent father.'

'Yes, yes.' Wayland waved him away like a bothersome fly and took a small apple cinnamon tart from the plate. When the butler had closed the door behind him, Wayland glanced at Max. 'I spent all day yesterday with father's solicitors and, to be honest, by the end of the afternoon, my head was spinning, and I had to leave their office for the sake of my own sanity. We had hardly broken the surface of all my father's land holdings and business enterprises. Mother's interests are just as complicated!'

'How is your mother faring?' He should have asked about her earlier, but this news had shocked him enormously. His thoughts went to his dear aunt Lucille, his mother's sister, a tender woman of high intelligence. A sincere woman who took him and Thomas under her care when their parents died, even though they were grown men. He would write to her as soon as he returned to his desk, and he must inform Thomas.

'Mother is bereft but writes that she is to stay on at the tea plantation. She has a great many friends out there. Naturally, Mother wants me to visit, but I have no interest in suffering the heat of India. Besides, I have much to deal with here now.' Wayland ate three tarts. 'These kinds of pastries are passable.

Provincial, but edible. Thank goodness I am not entertaining here.'

'So, you are staying only a week or two?' Max sat down, unable to stand for a moment longer.

'Less if I can.' Wayland sipped his tea. 'That depends on you, of course.'

'On me?'

'Why yes, you manage the abbey, the estate and the concerns of the village, do you not?'

'I do.' Max held his breath.

'Are you willing to continue in that role?'

'I am.'

'Excellent. That is what I wanted to hear.' Wayland poured more tea, but noticed Max hadn't touched his cup. 'Drink up, Cousin. Unless we should have something stronger?'

'Tea is fine.' Max picked up his cup and saucer but simply held it. 'So, I shall send reports to you each month as I have been doing with your father? Naturally, more often if there is something serious to discuss.'

Wayland groaned. 'Gracious, I do not have the time with reports, Max. I shall be travelling to Paris and Rome at the end of August. No, I trust you implicitly. I will write to you when I return to London at Christmas, and you can journey down to see me, and we shall talk then. Morcombe, father's solicitor told me that you have full access to a bank account in the estate's name for all income and expenditure for the abbey?'

'Indeed. Your father arranged for me to have access to funds for improvements to the estate and such things. I always corresponded with him over what was spent.'

'If my father trusted you, then so shall I.' Wayland stood. 'I fancy a ride after days of being in the carriage.'

'You did not journey by train?'

'And be covered in soot? I think not. There is no privacy on trains. Other passengers feel inclined to talk to you constantly. In my own carriage I can stop when I like, where I like. Besides, staying at inns along the way I get to taste the delights of the local women, who will oblige a man anything for a few shillings. Do you not agree?' Wayland smirked slyly.

'I would not know,' Max replied stiffly.

'What say we take a ride about the village? I need to be introduced to people, inform them of who I am.'

Max rose and pulled the bell pull by the fireplace. When Reeves entered Max asked him to send word to the stables to have his horse saddled and one for his lordship. Just saying those words, *his lordship*, felt uncomfortable on Max's tongue. He believed his cousin hadn't earned or deserved them.

'Which horse will I be riding?' Wayland held up his hand to stop Reeves leaving and stared at Max.

'Your father's horse, Lucifer,' Max answered, giving the nod to Reeves to leave.

'Lucifer? My father had a horse named Lucifer?'

'Lucifer acquired the name as a young colt who misbehaved a lot. Your father thought it a fine name that suited him. Did he never speak of his horse to you?'

'No.' Wayland snorted. 'Why would we have ever talked about horses on this estate? I loathed it here as a child and I made sure as a grown man I would stay away.'

'And now it is all yours, to be passed on to your own children one day.'

'Huh, that shan't be for some time. I refuse to be tied to a whining wife just yet. I must change my clothes.'

Max walked with him to the door. 'We should stop by the church in the village. Your father must be buried in India by now, but we should have a service for him, and a plaque erected inside the church.'

Shrugging one shoulder, Wayland headed for the staircase. 'Fine. Surely the local vicar can prepare something for Sunday's service?'

'I am certain it can be arranged. I shall wait for you on the drive.'

Max walked down the front steps and onto the white gravelled drive. The sky shone blue, and a warm breeze whistled through the highest branches of the chestnut trees lining the parkland in front of the abbey. He loved the abbey as though it was his own. Thank God his cousin didn't care for the place and was happy to leave it in his care.

'Mr Cavendish.' Reeves came out carrying a black armband. 'I thought you should have this. I've instructed the staff to wear one as well. They are all very upset.'

'Thank you, Reeves.' Max took the armband and pulled it on. 'Could the laundry women press my black suit before Sunday? I will leave it out for them.'

'Certainly, sir.' Reeves nodded sadly. 'May I say again how sorry I am. My lord was a good and kind man to me for the last twenty-five years I've been here at the abbey.'

'We shall miss him.' Max couldn't grieve for his uncle yet, that would come later. 'When my cousin has returned to London, I feel we should have a small gathering to honour my uncle. Perhaps the stone mason could carve something, if not a headstone, perhaps a statue? We could place it in the garden in honour of my uncle.'

'I think that would be a perfect mark of respect, sir.' Reeves took a step back. 'I expect you will be dining in the abbey tonight with your lordship?'

'I expect I shall be, and possibly my brother as well. My

cousin is not one for his own company if I remember correctly, and especially here where he knows no one.'

'Very good, sir.' Reeves returned inside as the sound of horses' hooves crunched on the drive.

Max smiled at the groom who led the two horses along the path from the stables to the front of the house. 'Everything is well with Lucifer, John?'

'Aye, sir, but he'll be a bit fidgety. He'll want a good canter. He's been in the short field for the past week after getting new shoes, as you're aware.'

'I had meant to take him out yesterday, but time got away from me.' Max rubbed Lucifer's black nose, before turning to his own horse, a dun-coloured mare called Queenie. 'There's my girl.' He gave her a piece of carrot he always kept in his coat pocket just for her.

'Is it true, sir, that your uncle has died?' John shook his head sorrowfully.

Max mounted Queenie. 'Unfortunately, yes.'

They spoke no more as Wayland came down the steps pulling on his leather gloves. 'So, this is Lucifer?' He checked the horse over and then quickly mounted, surprising the animal.

'He's a bit spirited, my lord,' John said, dodging out of the way of Lucifer as he sidestepped.

'I am certain I can handle him.' Wayland kicked his heels into the horse's side and Lucifer's hooves scattered gravel as he raced up the drive.

Sighing, Max urged Queenie on at a trot, not inclined to copy his cousin.

On the road to the village, Max only caught glimpses of Wayland. Lucifer was given his head and galloped along the winding narrow road. At one corner Wayland had to pull up sharply to avoid colliding with a farmer's cart. The farmer waved his fist in annoyance.

'Did ye see that, Mr Cavendish?' the old farmer asked when Max drew level with him.

'I did, Mr Riley.'

'Who the 'ell is 'e?'

'The new Lord Stockton-Lee,' Max said gravely.

'Nay, it never is. Ye mean ye uncle is dead?'

'He is. Good day, Mr Riley.' Max rode on, still unable to come to terms with his uncle's death. They didn't always see eye to eye on estate business, but they respected each other's opinions and had built a bonding friendship since Max and Thomas came to live in Yorkshire.

Thomas. Max realised he'd have to tell Thomas and quickly, before his brother heard it from village gossip.

When Max caught up with Wayland, his cousin was outside the Fox and Hound, the village inn, sipping a glass of ale and reading the poster for the upcoming summer fair. Lucifer was blowing from the fast ride.

'You took your time!' Wayland nodded to a second glass of ale beside him.

'I did not see what the hurry was.' Max dismounted and led both horses over to the trough at the side of the road and left the animals to drink. He ran a quick eye over Lucifer's legs, hoping he'd not gone lame in the mad dash.

Wayland grinned. 'You are a funny fellow, Max. Such a serious man. No wonder my father liked you.'

'The feeling was mutual. Uncle Richard was very good to me.'

'Really? He barely had time for me.' Scanning the narrow village High Street, Wayland grimaced. 'I had forgotten just how small this place was. How do you stand living here?'

Max raised his hand to another farmer passing them in his cart before answering. 'I enjoy the quietness.'

'But there is nothing to do here. No gambling dens, no theatre, no parties, and no brothels or high-class drinking establishments, no clubs.'

'I experienced my fair share of all of that when I lived in Lincoln.' Max smiled wistfully.

Wayland grimaced as a young woman walked past, a crying baby on her hip and a little boy hanging onto her skirts, his nose running. 'And you do not miss any of it?'

'No, not really.'

'You must be mad. This little backwater is dreadful. You could do a lot better than this, Max. I could easily put in another manager at the abbey, and you could find a better suited position closer to a city or somewhere down south and less provincial.'

Max's stomach clenched. 'There is no need for you to find someone else for the abbey. It has become my home. I want to stay.'

Wayland watched the blacksmith, wearing a stained leather apron, come out into his yard and dip a wooden bucket into a barrel of water. 'The estate is not entailed, I could sell the lot of it for I have no use for it. I would buy a smaller estate closer to London, or maybe not. I have no keen interest in estates. I prefer London or Paris.'

'Sell the abbey?' Max sucked in a breath. 'You would not do such a thing? It has been in your family for generations.'

'And yet, I care nothing for it. I would be happy to never see it again. The abbey is as a cold as a witches' tit in winter and far too remote for my liking.'

'The estate and village provided a very good income for your father.'

'And also, a large amount of time and trouble in upkeep. I could sell and invest the money elsewhere to gain a return without the bother of caretaking all of this.' Wayland flicked his fingers towards the cottages. 'Why should I concern myself with all of it?'

'Because it is your family legacy. Listen, Wayland, you must not sell any of it. I will run it all for you. It will be my time, my efforts. You do not need to do anything but spend the money it generates.'

'But for how long will it do that? If there is another agriculture slump, that income will shrink.'

'Please do not do anything hasty.'

Wayland shrugged. 'I cannot promise that selling the estate is worth considerable thought.'

Max gazed about the high street trying to see it from Wayland's fresh eyes and really studied the stone buildings, the little cottages, the few shops, the blacksmith beside the inn and across from them, the church with its square tower and surrounding graveyard. Yes, the cottages were old, but he spoke to the villagers weekly, always listening to their concerns and mending broken roof slates or unhinged doors and so on. He was happy to have a pot of black tea with them and listen to what they had to say and make changes when needed.

Max sipped his ale and could just make out the labourers working at the end of the high street where it dipped to go down the hill towards Larkson's Pit. At the beginning of spring, he'd employed men to start laying cobbles over the dirt to lessen the mud ruts when it rained. There was still a long way to go before all the street was cobbled, but he'd made a start. One day the whole of the high street would be complete, and the improvement would aid everyone in the village. A neglected village would not benefit the estate. Too many times he'd seen the result of villagers leaving in droves to work in the factories of the cities, and whole villages become abandoned and left to rot.

Everything he did in his role of estate steward, or land agent as the title was becoming to be called, was in the spirit of making this village and the estate better because he cared about it all. He took pride in his efforts and enjoyed having good relationships with the locals, especially when he wasn't born here and they eyed strangers warily.

He never wanted to leave. Where would he go? How could he leave Caroline? The thought of Wayland selling up alarmed and appalled him.

Wayland emptied his glass with a last swallow. 'Are there any loose women of the night in this village? I could do with visiting one.'

'No, not that I am aware of.' Max suddenly felt protective of the village women, many he knew well from either buying something from their market day stalls or who were related to a member of staff from the estate. 'You shall have to wait until you return south.'

'How inconvenient.' Wayland grinned. 'Surely there is a lonely widow who is a penny or two short for her rent?'

'I have absolutely no idea.' The word *widow* had Max thinking of Caroline, and of Trixie, now he knew her past, but it was a past that Trixie had put behind her and his cousin would never know about it.

'No doubt there is a maid at the abbey only too willing to earn a few shillings for a night in my bed.'

Max made a mental note to speak with Mrs Hoskins, the housekeeper, to have the maids kept out of his cousin's presence and all bedroom doors locked. 'Shall we go and speak to the vicar?'

'If we must.' Wayland pushed himself up from the bench he sat on by the inn's front door. 'But I do not want to be kept long with some blustering old fool full of his own importance.'

'Tomorrow is market day. That would be the ideal time to speak with the local people and inform them about Uncle Richard.'

'Yes, very well.' Wayland paused as they walked up the path to the vicarage beyond the church. 'What is this fellow's name?'

'Mr Paul Porter. He is a decent enough reverend. His sermons are short, thankfully.' Max knocked on the door and it was soon opened by an older woman. 'Good day to you, Mrs Porter.' Max removed his hat. 'Would we be able to speak to your son, please?'

'I'm sorry, Mr Cavendish, but my son is attending a sick child down at the pit cottages.'

'Ah. Then we shall call another time.' Max turned to go but Wayland took a step towards the door and glared at Max.

Sighing, Max smiled at Mrs Porter. 'May I introduce to you, my cousin? Lord Stockton-Lee. Sadly, my uncle has recently died in India.'

Wayland bowed. 'Mrs Porter.'

'I'm very sorry to hear such unhappy news, my lord. I only met your dear father a few times in church, but he gave my son this placement five years ago and we've been very grateful for it.'

'Will you ask your son to call on me at the abbey? I would request a reading for my father this Sunday.'

'Absolutely, my lord. The moment he's home I'll tell him.' She bowed her head to Wayland and then to Max.

'Right, what shall we do now?' Wayland rubbed his chin.

'I can show you the improvements to the road. We are cobbling it. The men have started at the bottom of the hill and have just reached the top.'

His lips curling in disdain, Wayland shook his head. 'I think not, cousin. I would be bored within a blink of an eye.'

'We could visit a few of the shops?'

'As you say, I will see the townsfolk tomorrow at the market that will be as much as I can stomach. No, another gallop is in order.'

'We can visit Thomas.'

'Thomas? Thomas is here? Where is he?'

'He is at Springwood Farm, learning the trade of being a farmer before he returns to Oxford in the autumn.'

'Poor fellow. Why is he living at a farm when he could be at the abbey learning from you?'

'He does learn from me, but he needs to be able to make decisions for himself. Springwood was abandoned, and it was the perfect solution to make the farm valuable again and for Thomas to get his hands dirty.'

'What kind of brother are you to force Thomas to live in a cottage when he could be at the abbey?'

'I live in a cottage on the abbey grounds, Wayland, very comfortably I might add.'

'Well, yes, the abbey is a frozen mausoleum in winter. I do not blame you for finding alternative accommodation. Come, let us visit poor Thomas and rescue him from the mind-numbing endeavours of farming.' Wayland strode ahead and soon they were riding through the village and then dashing out onto the narrow dirt roads spreading through the countryside.

Wayland rode Lucifer too hard, jumping hedges and streams, scattering sheep and cattle and startling farming families.

Thomas greeted their cousin with open arms, excited by the unexpected arrival. The three of them supped ale at Springwood before they rode the lanes for a while, visiting other village inns.

Max was pleased, and tired, when they were finally trotting back into the abbey's stables and Lucifer hadn't been injured.

'I shall see you this evening at dinner, cousin.' Wayland threw the reins to a groom. 'No more dining alone in your cottage while I am in residence.'

Deep in thought, Max walked back to the estate office. Wayland's thoughts of selling the estate filled his mind. He would compile future figures and exciting ideas to show Wayland. He had to prove to him that keeping the estate was a worthwhile endeavour. Max had to convince his cousin that selling would be foolish. He just prayed that the plan would work.

CHAPTER 4

*I*n the hot midday sun, Caroline packed away the empty trays from the stall's table. The high street heaved with villagers and farmers from surrounding areas. Market day always drew a large crowd of people from the area. It was the one day local folk could buy what they needed without having the expense and time of travelling hours into York or any of the other bigger towns.

'What a morning.' Trixie collected the baskets which had been filled with pats of butter, rounds of cheese, loaves bread and a few currant cakes. 'It still excites me when people spend their hard-earned pennies on bread that I've made.'

'You're getting a name for yourself,' Caroline commented. 'Your bread is very good. It's all the practice you've been putting in.'

'Thanks to Annie and yourself for teaching me.'

'Here's Annie now.' Caroline smiled to the older woman who carried her own empty baskets from her stall where she sold handmade candles. Annie Aspall had become a dear friend and who helped them when Caroline arrived on

Howard's doorstep one winter's night with a badly injured Trixie.

'How was your morning?' Annie asked, eyeing the cleared table. 'Sold up everything?'

'We did, yes, and early, too.' Caroline shook out the table-cloth and folded it. 'How did you go?'

'Not bad.' Annie tapped one of the baskets over her arm. 'Only a few sticks left. Where are the girls?'

Trixie tutted. 'Not here helping us pack away, that's for certain!'

Annie smiled for she loved Elsie and Bertha like they were her own grandchildren. 'Bless. Leave them be.'

'They were walking Prince and Duke around earlier.' Caroline took one end of the trestle tabletop and Trixie took the other. 'They are teaching the puppies to walk on a lead and be around other people.'

'Prince and Duke are more sensible than my sisters at times, so I don't see how that will work out.' Trixie chuckled.

'Ladies, please let me help.' Thomas Cavendish appeared from the crowd and took the tabletop from them. He hoisted it over his head as easily as he lifted a bag of flour. 'Where's your cart, Caroline?'

'Over by the blacksmith's.' Caroline and Trixie gathered their things and followed him. 'We'll come back for the legs.'

'I'll stay here and watch them,' Annie told them, standing guard over the table's wooden support legs.

At the cart, Caroline helped Thomas secure the tabletop. 'I thought we'd have seen you before now, Thomas.'

'Yes, well, you can blame my cousin on that.'

'Your cousin?' Trixie glanced at him.

'Wayland, now the new Lord Stockton-Lee.' Thomas looked tired. 'My uncle has died in India. Wayland has come to give us the news and is staying a while. We have been visiting a few of the local families who knew our uncle well.'

Caroline thought of Max. 'How very sad. You and your brother have our condolences.'

'Max is sensing the loss keenly. He was closer to our uncle than I was.' Thomas ran a hand over his face. 'Forgive me, ladies, I feel a little rough today. We dined with Wayland last night and our cousin insisted we stayed and drank with him until the dawn. Max left us at some point, and I wish I had done the same. My head is banging like a drummer boy.'

They fell into step and headed back to the market stalls. Thomas carried the table legs back to the cart and then said he was going to the inn for some refreshments. 'Will you be attending the fair this afternoon?' His question was for Trixie.

'Yes, we promised Elsie and Bertha we'd take them. They've never been to a country fair before,' Trixie replied, blushing slightly.

'I shall see you there then. Ladies.' Thomas tipped his hat and sauntered off.

'Where are the girls, Annie?' Trixie scanned the street, which now the stalls were packing up, was thinning of people.

'They're about here somewhere. I'll head off home, lass,' Annie said to Caroline. 'If I see the girls, I'll send them to you.'

'Thank you.' Caroline gave the other woman an affectionate pat on the arm. 'We'll see you this afternoon?'

'No, lass. My fair days are over. I'll see you all on Sunday at church.'

Trixie gathered Annie's baskets for her. 'You'll come for Sunday tea afterwards as normal?'

'Aye, lass, I will.'

'Where could they have got to?' Trixie said when Annie had walked away.

Before Caroline could reply, she spotted Mussy coming out of the general store and waved him over. 'Have you seen the girls?'

'Yes. They're sitting in the graveyard with some other children and the puppies.' Mussy tucked several newspapers under his arm. 'My delivery has arrived.' He tapped the newspapers. 'You are all packed away. I would have helped.'

'Thomas helped us,' Trixie said. 'I'll go and find the girls and meet you back at the cart.'

'Are you ready to go?' Caroline looked at Mussy, who had dark circles under his eyes. She'd heard him coughing most of the night.

'I am indeed.' He gave her a soft smile that did little to remove the haunting look from his eyes. 'An early night for me, I think.'

'You'll give the fair a miss?'

'Indeed.'

She slid her hand through his arm. 'Some honey in your tea will ease your cough.'

He didn't reply, for they both knew honey wouldn't heal him.

Caroline's step faltered ever so slightly as Max walked through the lingering people towards them. With him was a tall, lanky man looking proud and important. The man could only be his cousin and he was by far the best attired gentleman in the whole crowd.

'Ah, Mrs Lawson.' Max's warm smile gave Caroline a familiar tingle of awareness. 'I am glad to have seen you.' He turned to the man standing beside him. 'Cousin, may I introduce you to Mrs Caroline Lawson, one of your tenants, and her friend, Mr Septimus Casey. Mrs Lawson, Mr Casey, this is my cousin, Lord Stockton-Lee.'

Caroline held out her hand. 'It is a pleasure to meet you, your lordship.'

Wayland's eyes widened in surprise at Caroline's cultured tones and manners. 'Indeed, it is refreshing to meet a personable young woman such as yourself, Mrs Lawson, especially in this village of dolts and fools.'

Max rolled his eyes. 'Forgive my cousin, he has just been bumped into and eggs were dropped onto his boots.'

Mussy held out his hand. 'I am delighted to make your acquaintance, your lordship.'

Again, Wayland stared in shock at Mussy's refined voice and his suit of dove grey with a bright yellow cravat and pink waistcoat. He shook Mussy's hand as if in relief to be in the company of a gentleman.

'I just met with Thomas,' Caroline spoke to Max. 'He told us of your uncle's passing. What a terrible time for you all.' She looked from Max and then to Wayland. 'My condolences to you both.'

'It has been a great ordeal, Mrs Lawson. One is never quite ready for the death of a parent.' Wayland's tone was grave, his eyes downcast. Then he glanced at Max. 'Perhaps Mrs Lawson, her husband and Mr Casey would care to join us for dinner tonight?'

Caroline blanched. 'Oh, no, I think not, my lord.'

'Nonsense!' Wayland clapped, his apparent grief quickly diminished. 'But I insist!'

'Mrs Lawson is a tenant, Wayland,' Max murmured. 'Tenants do not dine at the abbey,' he whispered to cover Caroline's embarrassment.

'That may be a rule we can break just this once?' Wayland's eyes narrowed.

'You are in mourning,' Max grounded out between

clenched teeth as though speaking to a troublesome child. 'You do not entertain while in mourning.'

'What a bore you are Max!' Wayland snapped. He turned to Mussy. 'Mr Casey, do you have an establishment close by? Perhaps I could call on you?'

Mussy gave him a lazy look. 'Alas, your lordship, my situation is dire. I live by the kindness of my lovely Caro and share her home at Hopewood Farm.'

Wayland's eyebrows rose. 'Is that so? Where is your family from?'

'Manchester.'

'Not London?'

'Indeed not. Father is not fond of London.' Mussy smiled mischievously.

'How could one not be fond of London?' Wayland was incredulous.

'I concur. I adore London.' Mussy gave Caroline a little playful nudge. 'One day I hope to show its delights to Caro.'

She stared at Mussy for it was the first she'd heard him mention it, then she realised Mussy was playing Wayland.

'If you come south, you must leave your card,' Wayland suggested. 'I would be delighted to escort Mrs Lawson around to see London's attractions.' He peered at Caroline, eyeing her up and down. 'I shall visit you instead, Mrs Lawson, and meet your husband?'

'My husband is dead, your lordship.' She didn't like the way he looked at her.

'Is he indeed?' Wayland tilted his head, his narrowed eyes focused on her.

Caroline shivered despite the heat of the sun and stepped back. 'If you would excuse us, my lord, Mr Cavendish, we must be getting home.'

'Will you be attending the fair, Mrs Lawson?' Max asked.

'Yes. We are all going.'

'I shall see you there.'

Wayland chuckled. 'I had not thought to attend but now I just might. Until later, Mrs Lawson, Mr Casey.'

Caroline bowed her head and with Mussy beside her marched away.

'What a strange fellow,' Mussy murmured.

'I don't like him and what was that nonsense about London!' Caroline hissed.

Mussy laughed and then coughed. 'It is a bit of fun, Caro. That conceited fool did not expect to see a gentleman at a village market and thought himself to be a prince amongst idiots.'

'Agreed. He doesn't seem a likeable fellow. Nothing like his Cavendish cousins.'

'That is because Stockton-Lee is the one with all the money and title. It breeds arrogance.' Mussy shrugged as though it was the way of things. 'And the truth is my father enjoys his time in London a great deal.' He winked.

Caroline tutted with a laugh. 'Oh, Mussy!'

When they reached the farm, Elsie and Bertha scrambled down from the back of the cart ready to run off with the puppies.

'Oh, no you two don't.' Trixie took the puppies' rope leads. 'You've work to do before we go to the fair. We unload the cart, then there is the washing to sort and soak.'

Elsie groaned. 'But it's a lovely day.'

'Aye, it is,' Trixie agreed, passing the leads to Caroline. 'And you've had all morning to do as you please. Now it's time to work or you won't be going anywhere this afternoon.'

Inside the house, Caroline sent Prince and Duke to their

bed in the corner of the kitchen, where exhausted, they curled up into balls and fell asleep instantly. She unpinned her hat and pulled off her gloves, before building up the fire in the range to boil the kettle.

Jacob came in, taking off his boots at the door. 'How was the market?'

'We had a good morning. Sold everything.'

'Grand.' He took off his hat and wiped his brown hair out of his eyes.

'Tea?'

'Thanks.' Jacob hovered by the table.

Caroline paused in scooping tea leaves into the teapot. 'Is something wrong?'

'I want to go and see our Sarah,' Jacob blurted out.

'Is that wise?' Caroline frowned.

Jacob hung his hat on the hook behind the door. 'I'll be careful, but I need to know if my sister and the kiddies are doing all right in Walmgate.'

'You're taking a risk. What if Dolan or his men see you?'

'I have to chance it. I can't settle here properly not knowing if me sister is well or in need of help. You understand, don't you?'

'Understand what?' Trixie asked coming through the door carrying baskets.

'I'm off to see our Sarah,' Jacob stated quietly.

Trixie stared at him. 'Are you mad? You can't go back. Dolan knows you too well. His men will recognise you. Do you want another beating?'

'I've taken my punishment. Dolan has no reason to lay into me again.'

'Of course he does, especially if he thinks you know where

we are.' Trixie slammed the baskets on the table. 'He hates all of us.'

'Dolan doesn't have any idea where I've been for the last six months. He has no idea I've been with you.' Jacob shrugged. 'Let's face it. I don't think we are at the top of his list to worry about. He's dealt with us and that's an end to it.'

Caroline mashed the tea. 'You truly think that?'

Jacob held up his hands. 'As I see it, yes. We aren't important to Dolan.'

'You're a fool to believe that.' Trixie took the baskets into the scullery and strode back into the kitchen, her movements jerky. 'His men nearly killed you, nearly killed *me*.'

'You will come back?' Caroline asked calmly, seeing that Jacob wouldn't be dissuaded.

'Yes.'

Trixie glared at Caroline. 'Don't encourage him!'

Sighing, Caroline poured out the tea into four cups just as Mussy entered. 'He needs to see Sarah. We have no right to try to stop him.'

'What's all this?'

'Madness, that's what it is!' Trixie stormed into the narrow hallway, and they heard her footsteps going upstairs.

'She's just worried about you, that's all,' Caroline murmured.

'Aye.' Jacob sipped his tea. 'But I must go.'

'To York?' Mussy sat at the table.

'Aye.'

'Then I'll go with you.' Mussy gave him a nod before looking at Caroline. 'We can take the gig. I can drive him into Walmgate and help him search for his sister and drive him back. It'll be quicker and safer than being on foot.'

'I agree.' Caroline took two teacups and went upstairs to Trixie's bedroom that she shared with her sisters.

She found Trixie sitting on the window seat looking out over the barns. The blue sprigged summer dress Trixie wore showed off her slight figure, her dainty bones. Her brown curls had grown shoulder length and farm life had given her rosy cheeks. She appeared to be a healthy young woman in her prime, but those who knew Trixie could see the haunting in her eyes from a past where she had to sell her body to survive, to give her sisters food and shelter.

Caroline loved her like a sister and never wanted to see her unhappy. Only, Trixie felt she didn't deserve happiness, and that was a hard barrier for Caroline to break down. 'Here. Drink this. You must be thirsty after selling all morning.'

Trixie took the teacup, her pretty small face mutinous. 'You know it's foolish of him, don't you? Jacob's safe here. Dolan and his pack of wolves can't hurt him here.'

'Maybe Jacob is right, and Dolan has sought his revenge and is done with us? He must have more to concentrate on than wondering about me and you.'

'Don't be silly, Caroline,' Trixie snapped. 'You've scarred Dolan for life. He will never forget us.'

'But the price has been paid, by you and Jacob being beaten and left for dead. What more could he want?'

'For you to pay, of course!'

Silence stretched between them, each deep in their own thoughts. Caroline wished she'd never set eyes on Dolan. Her guilt about Trixie and Jacob paying dearly for her escape weighed heavy on her shoulders. 'Let Jacob go and find Sarah, then he'll rest easy, or he won't. Either way, he'll know what's happening in York.'

'I'll be sick with worry the whole time he's gone.'

'We both will be.'

'And what if he doesn't come back?' Trixie gazed into the distance.

'That's his choice.' Caroline took Trixie's hand. 'I think he'll come back though.' She smiled. 'His heart is tied to this farm, to you.'

Trixie reared back nearly spilling her tea. 'Don't say that, Caroline. Jacob doesn't see me that way, as I don't see him. At best, Jacob might think of me as a sister, at worst someone to pitied. He knows my past, what I was. No man would want me knowing that and who could blame them? I'll remain a spinster and I'm fine with that.' Trixie gave the tea back to Caroline and stood. 'I'll go and check on the girls.'

Caroline remained on the window seat and drank her tea, wishing that life wasn't so cruel at times. Yet, she knew better than anyone that she was wasting her wishes on that.

That evening as the sun lowered, Caroline and Trixie, with Jacob and the girls, attended the fair set up on the edge of the village. Elsie and Bertha were in awe of everything they saw.

'Look at the lion in the cage,' Bertha breathed as they stopped to stare at a lion sitting in a red cage half asleep.

Glowing lanterns on poles were stuck in the ground between the stalls of amusements. Jugglers walked through the crowds throwing balls and knives. Colourful tents enticed people inside to watch magic tricks, games of boxing, or to view the fattest woman, the smallest man and so many other curiosities.

Caroline gave Elsie and Bertha some pennies to buy toffee apples, while Jacob and Trixie watched a monkey wearing a gold waistcoat dance for the crowd.

Caroline wandered on, wanting to give Trixie and Jacob some time alone. She smiled at some of the folk from the village, but kept strolling not wanting to stop and chat. A band played, drowning out the preacher who stood on a box and shouted at them all that their souls needed to be saved. In a grassed area, wrestlers battled each other, cheered on by roaring young men glassy eyed from too much ale.

A stage had been set up for gymnasts to perform and Caroline stopped to watch them twist their bodies and hurl themselves in the air with such ease and suppleness.

'They are amazing.' Mr Cavendish came to stand beside her.

'Incredible,' she agreed aware of him in every way.

'How is your aim?' he asked.

She frowned. 'My aim?'

'Want to try your hand at the coconut shy?' He grinned, pointing to a covered stall where children were trying to hit the mound of coconuts.

Caroline smiled. 'Oh, well, there's only one way to find out.'

The stall owner encouraged them to line up and gave them three balls each. Caroline really wanted to beat Mr Cavendish and concentrated on her first throw which took down two coconuts.

'Well done.' Cavendish applauded. His throw took down four.

Determined to do better, Caroline focused on the mound of coconuts and successfully knocked off two more.

'One throw left,' Cavendish murmured close to her ear.

A shiver ran down her back and she dared to turn to him slightly. His handsome face was only inches from hers. His blue eyes widened and that flare of desire sparked in her again. Her next throw was off and only hit one coconut.

Cavendish managed to clear all of his coconuts and was

given a small flower posy for his lady. Cavendish didn't explain to the stall owner that Caroline wasn't his lady and instead he bowed and presented the posy like a gallant knight. 'Flowers for the beautiful lady.'

Caroline smiled and, playing along, curtsied. 'Thank you, kind sir.'

She unpinned her straw hat and tucked the posy into the white lace band on the crown. She wore her best outfit of sky blue with white lace at the neckline and cuffs and as she pinned on her hat, she saw Cavendish's admiring look.

'Some refreshments?' he asked, gesturing to another tent where cordials and ale were sold.

'That would be nice.' She walked with him to the serving table and asked for a raspberry cordial and while Cavendish bought the two drinks, she glanced around for her family. Elsie and Bertha were watching a Punch and Judy show, and further away Trixie and Jacob were talking to some of the village folk.

'Shall we go and listen to the band?' He gave her one of the cups of cordial. 'There will be dancing later.'

'Dancing? I can't remember the last time I danced.'

'At your wedding?'

'No,' she said wistfully. 'It rained the evening of our wedding, and everyone left for home early. Not that there was a lot of guests just Hugh's family and some people from the village.'

'Would you dance with me?' His expression was one of hope and expectation.

Her silly heart drummed faster as though she was a silly young girl. 'If you'd like.'

'I would like nothing more right now than to dance with you,' his voice was soft, full of hidden meanings and promises.

Caroline wanted to reach out and touch his face, to trace his lips with her fingers.

'Max!'

Caroline jerked a step back and Cavendish swore under his breath. They both turned to greet Thomas and his lordship.

Wayland stood before her, his eyes narrowed, his head held high. 'My, Mrs Lawson, are you not just a beautiful rose amongst a field of cowslip?'

'Beauty is everywhere, my lord, if you're willing to search for it,' Caroline replied tightly.

'What shall we do first?' Thomas rubbed his hands together in excitement.

'If you'll excuse me, I need to find my family.' Caroline gave the cup back to Cavendish. 'Thank you for your company.'

'No, no,' Wayland interrupted. 'You must honour us with your presence a while longer, Mrs Lawson. There is much to see and do.'

'Forgive me, but I am here with my family and I promised the girls I would show them the prancing horses.'

'I heard they are excellent,' Thomas added. 'There's a small arena over the back there, all lit up. The horses jump through hoops on fire.'

'Then we should all go and watch this spectacle,' Wayland insisted, taking Caroline's arm.

Trying not to squirm out of his hold, Caroline allowed herself to be walked over to the arena where a crowd was gathering. Tall lanterns were placed around the fences to create a sense of magic and flare as shadows flickered.

'Do you want me to find Miss Wilkes and her sisters?' Cavendish asked Caroline.

'Yes, go,' Wayland ordered. 'I would like to spend some time with Mrs Lawson and get to know her better.' His smile was overbearing, like his manners.

Caroline pulled her arm from his grasp. 'I think it is best that I find my family. Good night.'

Wayland stepped in front of her, blocking her way. 'A few minutes with your lord is surely more important than being with your family who are enjoying themselves without you? Come, stay with me. Let us talk.'

Stiffening at his warning tone, Caroline's annoyance grew. 'Nothing is more important than my family, my lord. If you'll excuse me?' She waited for him to move aside.

'Wayland, allow Mrs Lawson to join her family,' Cavendish demanded.

'Of course.' Wayland waved her away, but as she passed him, he bent close to her ear. 'We shall meet again.'

In the darkness of predawn, Caroline hitched the gig to Dossy by lamplight and led her out into the yard. Dossy's hooves sounded loud on the cobbles in the quietness. Golden light spilled from the kitchen window and open doorway as Trixie stood on the step and said goodbye to Jacob and Mussy.

'We might be away overnight,' Mussy said to Caroline as the three of them joined her. 'If it gets too late to travel back, I shall get a couple of rooms at Bob Warburton's inn. We shan't risk being on the streets at night.'

'Very well. Give my regards to Mr Warburton if you do.' She spoke of their mutual friend who had a public house in York. 'Stay close to Jacob. Walmgate can be trouble on a good day.'

Mussy kissed her cheek. 'We will both come back safely. Try not to worry.'

Caroline stepped back with Trixie as the two men climbed onto the gig and with a click of his tongue, Mussy urged Dossy out of the yard.

'I feel today is going to be a bad day, Caro,' Trixie whispered.

'Don't! Be positive, for heaven's sake. Jacob and Mussy will be fine. We have to have faith in that. They'll be home before we know it.' Caroline strode towards the dairy. She would scrub the dairy buckets again before milking even though they were spotless, but she'd rather do that than sit at the kitchen table and be witness to Trixie's fidgeting.

Caroline worked in the dairy until midday. After milking the cows, she churned butter, turned the rounds of cheese, scrubbed the churner, skimmed the milk setting for cream and then she swilled the stone floor with soapy water and swept it out. Although one of the cooler barns, the August sun blazed outside, and she had worked up a sweat.

'Are you staying out here all day?' Elsie stood in the doorway.

'No, I'm finished now.' Caroline hung up the broom by the door.

'Can we go for a walk?' Elsie asked as they made their way back to the house.

'Have you done all your jobs?'

'*I* have,' Elsie said with emphasis. 'Our Bertha is still tidying away her slate and chalk. Our Trixie had us writing our letters just now, but it's too hot. Our Trixie's been cooking, and the kitchen is like an oven. Could we go and paddle in the stream with the puppies?'

'Yes, I think that is a fine idea. Let me change first. My skirt is dirty.'

Entering the kitchen, Caroline hid her surprise to see the table a mess of vegetable peelings and the results of Trixie's morning labour. A pot of stew simmered on the range, while a loaf of bread and a tray of scones cooled on the table.

Trixie had her hands in a large earthenware bowl mixing suet dumplings. She blew hair out of her eyes and gave Caroline a half grin of apology. 'I've made a lot of food.'

'Shall we go to the stream and cool off?' Caroline suggested, taking off her apron, knowing that Trixie was just as concerned about Mussy and Jacob as she was and needed to be busy to stop worrying.

'Sounds good to me. I'll just finish this.'

Within a short time, they were strolling the edge of the hay field and down the hill towards the stream at the bottom. Caroline gazed at the acres of planted crops, thrilled to see them growing under the summer sun.

'You're already thinking of the harvest, aren't you?' Trixie asked.

'Mr Cavendish said he'll bring men over from the estate farm to help with the harvest. We start on Monday if the weather holds.' Caroline clicked her fingers to Prince and Duke, trying to control them when Elsie and Bertha were dashing about sending them mad with giddiness. 'Girls! Walk! We need to teach Prince and Duke to behave. How can they work with animals if they are running about like wild things?'

Chastened, Elsie and Bertha walked sedately beside the dogs.

Trixie plucked a long strand of grass. 'I need to let Elsie's hem down again. She's growing like a willow, as Annie would say.'

'Bertha's not far behind.' Caroline stepped her way between the hawthorn bushes separating the fields from the stream, and beyond the stream was a thick hedge alongside the dirt road leading to the village.

Several trees grew along the stream casting welcome shade. Within moments the girls had their boots and stockings off and were wading into the shallow stream, the puppies eager to jump in after them. Caroline and Trixie soon followed suit and for a little while only laughter could be heard as they held up their skirts and kicked the cool water at each other.

'This looks like tremendous fun!' a voice rang out from the road.

Caroline jumped up onto the bank and dropped her skirts to cover her ankles, Trixie did the same and they faced the mischievous grin of Thomas and behind him, mounted on his black horse, Wayland, who watched them intently.

Thomas pushed his way through a gap in the hedge with a grunt and a curse to reveal himself at the stream's edge. 'Can anyone join in?'

'Yes, Mr Thomas, join us!' Elsie clapped.

'You caught us out, Thomas.' Caroline wiped her wet feet on the grass and looked for her stockings, while Trixie quickly slipped on her stockings and boots, her face red with embarrassment.

'Why should you not be having some fun on such a fine day?' Thomas jumped across the narrowest part of the stream to join them. 'Do not let us stop you,' he spoke to Trixie.

'The girls were hot,' Trixie explained not meeting his eyes.

Caroline frowned at her. They didn't have to explain themselves. There were on their own farm, playing in their own stream.

Wayland rode around to the drive and then along the bottom of the field to dismount under the tree. 'How delightful this is. One should always enjoy the summer days for they are too few, especially in this part of the country.' His narrowed gaze was becoming familiar.

Caroline dipped her head to him. 'Good day to you, my lord.'

'It is a pleasure to see you again, Mrs Lawson.' Wayland stood very close.

She could smell the alcohol on him and quickly looked at Thomas. 'Your brother is not with you?'

'No, some problem at the estate. The wall of the lime store collapsed or something, so he is conversing with the stone masons.' Thomas shrugged, swaying slightly. 'I am certain they could have managed without him, but he would not be persuaded to join us. So, Wayland and I decided to go for a ride to the village for an ale or two.'

'Or four or was it five...' Wayland sniggered. From his waistcoat pocket he drew out a hip flask and slugged from it before passing it to Thomas who drank a mouthful.

'Definitely five, or was it six?' Thomas laughed like a loon. He caught Trixie's hand. 'How delightful you look today, Miss Wilkes.'

Caroline's breath shortened. She'd never seen Thomas in this state before. She could tell by the redness of their cheeks, their loose way of moving that they had been drinking in the hot sun and looked worse for wear because of it.

Caroline glanced at Trixie who stared wide-eyed at her and with a slight nod, they turned together to the girls and called them from the water.

'Are you to invite us up to the house, Mrs Lawson?'

Wayland asked, sipping again from the flask. 'We could do with some more refreshments.'

She didn't want the man anywhere near her home or become more drunk, but he was her landlord, and she couldn't refuse him. 'Certainly, your lordship.' She clicked her fingers to Prince and Duke, who clambered out of the water and raced to her side where they shook their wet coats. Splashes of water flew over Wayland's boots and trousers.

'You damn curs!' He kicked out at the nearest dog, Duke, making him yelp in fright more than pain.

'Do *not* kick my dog!' Caroline bent down and grabbed Duke, glaring up at Wayland. 'He did nothing wrong!'

'The blasted dog wet my boots and trousers!' Wayland sneered.

'You're behaving like a spoilt child! And they will dry,' she ground out.

'*Your lordship,*' Wayland snapped.

Caroline stared him down, refusing to acknowledge his title.

'Your lordship!' he repeated.

Still she glared at him in furious silence.

Wayland advanced on her with his arm raised, riding crop in hand. '*Your lordship. Say it!*'

Standing tall, Caroline's anger grew as he made to humiliate her. 'Perhaps you might require refreshments elsewhere, *your lordship?* I doubt the contents of my cupboards would be to your liking.'

'You are *refusing* to give me refreshments?' He looked astounded and lowered his arm.

Trixie stepped forward. 'No, no, not at all, your lordship,' she whined submissively. 'Come up to the house, please,' Trixie cajoled. 'Thomas, yes?'

Thomas nodded. 'I shall fetch my horse.'

'Girls, come now.' Trixie hurried the frightened girls along.

'No. We shall not go up to the house.' Wayland's tone cut through the air. He turned to Thomas. 'I have had enough of sitting in damp filthy cottages being offered inferior refreshments. For weeks I have endured the fools of this parish. You go home, Thomas. I will return to the abbey.'

Chastised, and looking a bit green, Thomas bowed to them and waded back through the stream and into the hedge, within a moment he was trotting his horse down the road.

Caroline turned to follow Trixie and the girls, but Wayland grabbed her arm. 'Not so fast.'

Surprised, she raised her eyebrows at his hold.

'You and I need to have a little chat.' He lifted his head to Trixie. 'Your friend will be along shortly. Off you go.'

'I can wait.' Trixie held the girls' hands, her face white, but stubbornly determined. 'Or we could have some tea? We have scones. Caroline, let us give his lordship some tea and scones.'

'His lordship wouldn't want our *inferior* offerings!' Caroline pulled her arm out of his grasp and hurried to Trixie's side.

Wayland watched them march up the hill, but he didn't follow them, and Caroline let out a breath as they made it into the kitchen.

'Go upstairs and change out of those wet clothes,' Trixie barked at the girls.

'Will he come?' Caroline murmured, watching the door.

'I don't think so.' Trixie poked at the range fire. 'But make tea just in case. He needs to sober up.'

Hands shaking, Caroline set out the tea things. 'I thought he was going to hit me.'

'I thought so too. Why else do you think I spoke up?' Trixie glared at Caroline. 'You can't prod people like that, Caroline. He is a lord, and the law around here. He owns this farm and everything for miles. You can't speak to him as though he is your equal!'

Caroline knelt and patted Prince and Duke as if to make up for Wayland's harsh treatment. 'He deserved to be spoken to like that. He was cruel to Duke for no reason.'

Trixie gripped the poker. 'Men like him don't need a reason!'

Caroline stood by the window, but the yard was bare and quiet, just the chickens pecking. No sign of the odious man. 'Gracious, what if he evicts us?' She felt sick.

'I wish Jacob and Mussy were here,' Trixie whispered.

'I'll get about my work. I can't stay in the kitchen all afternoon. I don't think he'll come now.' Caroline stepped into the scullery and took her apron down from the hook. 'I'll be in the barn.'

'Do you want something to eat?' Trixie stirred the stew.

'No. My stomach is in knots. Maybe later.' Grabbing her hat, Caroline crossed the yard and into the barns. With Dossy out of her stall, now was a good time to clean it out.

She placed the wheelbarrow near the stall opening and began to fork out the old straw. Usually, the girls helped Jacob to do this job, but she needed to be alone with her thoughts. How foolish was she to goad her landlord? After all her hard work to keep the farm, she had to open her mouth and put it all at risk. She prayed Wayland wouldn't speak with Max and tell him to evict them.

Lifting a fork full of straw, she twisted to throw it in the barrow when she jerked in shock at Wayland standing there.

They eyed each other in silence for several seconds as though to weigh up the other's thoughts. Then, before she could make a noise, Wayland pounced, throwing her to the floor, pinning her with his body, his hand over her mouth and nose.

'You, madam, will be taught a lesson,' he whispered in her ear.

She mumbled against his hand, fear churning her gut.

'I will not be spoken to as you just did. Who do you think you are, hey?' He pulled up her skirts, his fingers strong and powerful as they tore at her clothing.

Caroline bucked and squirmed under him, screaming in her throat for help but his hand blocked her shouts, making them nothing more than grunts.

'You will respect *me*. I am your *lord*!' His weight crushed her chest, pushing the air out of her lungs. She couldn't breathe in or out and panic gripped her more for the lack of air than what he was doing with his other hand.

She twisted and struggled, trying to get free. Her skirts were pushed up around her waist, the straw sticking into her buttocks as he pulled away her undergarments in a ripping sound.

Caroline screamed in her throat, her mind, her heart, desperate to get him off her, to stop him from doing what he was going to do to her. No matter how hard she tried, the lack of air was weakening her. She felt faint, her eyesight blurred.

He whipped her over onto her stomach, pushing her face into the straw, his body heavy on her. She gasped, straw and dirt in her mouth. She couldn't find any air. Then she felt the jab of pain between her legs, as he thrust into her. She tried to shout but his hand slammed her head further into the bed of filthy straw, blocking out the light, blocking out the world. There was no air. She couldn't breathe. Blackness surrounded her, and she was happy to surrender to the fate of death and even welcomed it…

When she came around, she was alone in the stable. The dank smell of old straw filled her nose. He must have rolled her over onto her back before he left. Did he think she was dead? Staring up at the barn's roof beams, she slowly pushed down her skirts.

'Caro, I've brought you a drink,' Elsie's voice rang out as she came into the barn.

Before Caroline could tell her to go away, the child came into the stall, holding a glass. 'Trixie said you might want a drink… Why are you sitting on the ground? Have you fallen?' Elsie picked up Caroline's hat where it had landed.

'No!' Caroline fought hard to act normally. Elsie could never know what had happened to her. 'I… I…'

Trixie appeared at the stall opening. 'I thought we could invite Annie to share our meal? I'll send our Elsie over to fetch her.'

Caroline gaped at Trixie unable to speak, but her eyes silently begged for help.

Trixie frowned at Caroline sitting rumpled on the dirty straw, then paled. She blinked rapidly for a moment. 'Right, er… Elsie, love, go back inside and stir the stew.'

Once the child had gone, Trixie fell to the straw beside Caroline. 'He came back.'

Closing her eyes, Caroline relived the revolting attack in the mind. 'I tried to fight him.'

'The bastard!' Trixie swayed in anger. 'The dirty, filthy, horrible *bastard*.'

'He p-pushed me down. I couldn't breathe…' She started to shake.

'Let's get you up and inside, dearest.' Trixie helped ease Caroline up to her feet.

'We tell no one,' Caroline choked. '*No one.*'

'If you wish.' Trixie held her close. 'Did he hurt you anywhere else?' Trixie searched Caroline's face for marks.

'No.' Caroline sucked in a deep breath. 'There are other ways to hurt a woman without leaving visible marks, isn't there?'

'Aye, sweetness.' Trixie hugged Caroline tightly to her. 'But you'll be fine. You'll get through this. I know you will. I have in the past, many times. You just need to forget what happened. Don't give it another thought. He's not worth it. Don't let him beat you. He means nowt. Understand?'

Caroline nodded. She felt dazed but not a lot of physical pain, not yet. Humiliated, yes, and a simmering anger that coiled in her gut.

They stumbled from the barn and across the yard.

'I shouldn't have goaded him,' Caroline whispered. 'It's my fault.'

'No, you shouldn't have goaded him, but what he did to you wasn't your fault. He did it to punish you.' Trixie paused in the kitchen doorway. 'All we can hope for now is the bastard leaves for the south soon and never returns.'

Giving the excuse that Caroline had a headache, Trixie helped Caroline to wash and change and tucked her up in bed. 'Have a nap if you can.'

When the door opened a crack, Caroline turned her head and watched Prince and Duke nudge themselves inside her bedroom, a room they were never allowed in. They ran to her bedside and whined to be up with her.

Tears gathering in her eyes, Caroline lifted them both up and placed them on either side of her. She stroked their soft ears and looked into their brown eyes, which were full of trust, love and loyalty, exactly what she needed at that moment. 'Never again will either of you be away from me.' She hadn't wanted the dogs and up until now she'd been happy to let Elsie and Bertha have them as playmates, but not anymore. She needed protection. First Dolan tried to rape her, and look at the chain of events that started, and now Wayland had done the same and this time, he'd succeeded.

No more.

No more would she be alone and powerless.

A hard knot of pain and fury tightened in her chest.

She kissed Prince and Duke's heads. 'Let another man try to get the better of me and see what happens. Hey, my boys?'

CHAPTER 5

Trixie paced the kitchen, a blinding rage made her want to smash everything she saw. Two days. Two whole days since Jacob and Mussy had gone to York and Caroline was attacked and here she was having to deal with the sheer horror of it all by herself.

This morning after breakfast she'd sent the girls to Annie's house in the village for their constant bickering had driven her to distraction. She had enough to deal with without them carrying on under her feet. They complained because Caroline had taken Prince and Duke up onto the hills and banned the girls from following. Caroline had also banned the girls from playing silly games with the dogs, as well. Prince and Duke could be given a quick pat, and that was all. They had begun their training, and the dogs were no longer playthings for Elsie and Bertha.

Trixie understood Caroline's sudden harsh manner. Often, she'd been at the rough end of a man's hands when she worked on the streets, she knew what it was to be taken and used without thought or kindness shown. That had been her world, but it was never Caroline's. Her dear friend was suffering keenly, and Trixie didn't know how to help her. So, she let Caroline walk for miles each day with the dogs, training them to work with the sheep on the hills, training them to be her guards.

Hearing horse's hoofs on the cobbles, Trixie raced to fling open the door, hoping to see Mussy and Jacob but it was Thomas Cavendish. Her silly heart fluttered at his handsomeness, the soft way his overgrown brown hair fell over his eyes, his boyish smile. To her Thomas seemed clean, unspoilt by the harshness of life. He hadn't faced the filth of the wicked streets as she had. He was wholesome, genteel, a gentleman of decency. Yet, two days ago he'd turned up drunk and some of his shine had dulled in her eyes.

'Good day, Miss Wilkes.' Thomas bowed low, his eyes downcast, his usual happy manner subdued.

'Good day, Mr Cavendish.' She noted his fine clothes, his suit of dark grey, his polished boots. He may be learning the duties of being a land agent over at Springwood Farm, but he never looked as though he did any work.

'May I come in?'

Trixie glanced behind him. 'Is your cousin about?'

'No, no!' Thomas held up his hands as though in surrender. 'I come alone.'

She stepped aside so he could enter the kitchen.

Thomas took his hat off and held it, his fingers tight on the brim. 'I have come to apologise to you and Mrs Lawson.'

'Caroline is up on the hills with the sheep.' Trixie concentrated on the fire in the range and put the kettle on to heat. It saddened her that they were cool with each other, the tension palpable. They had become good friends she believed. He made her laugh and teased the girls to make them giggle.

Whenever he called in at the farm or when she saw him in the village, it brightened her day. She'd dreamt of him, of him holding her gently. Silly dreams that would never come true, not for someone like her.

'Miss Wilkes, Trixie…' Thomas stepped around the table, his face troubled. 'I am mortified by my behaviour. I should never have dismounted my horse and intruded on your little party at the stream. I am ashamed of myself for the state I was in.'

Trixie turned away. The elegant way he spoke was another example of why they could never be together, not that she thought for a moment that Thomas had deep feelings for her. 'I wish you and your cousin had never come here that day.'

'Understandably.'

She stared at him. 'Is your cousin sorry for his actions?'

Thomas flushed and dropped his gaze. 'I cannot speak for my cousin. His actions are for him to atone.'

Suddenly, she realised that Thomas was aware of what his cousin had done to Caroline. 'You know, don't you? You know he attacked Caroline.'

He nodded and rubbed a hand over his face and the eyes that met hers where full of regret. 'His lordship isn't an honourable man.'

'No, he isn't. What he did to Caroline…' Trixie's rage returned. She felt useless and upset that her dearest friend could be so hurt. 'Men like him should be castrated!'

'I am ashamed to call him my cousin.' Thomas bowed his head. 'When he told me, or hinted at what he'd done… I was horrified. Wayland thought it a good joke, that he'd put Mrs Lawson in her place for standing up to him. I am completely disgusted by him.'

'You should be!'

Anguish was written clearly on his face. 'How is she?'

'How would you expect her to be?'

'What can I do to help?'

Trixie shook her head. Thomas looked out of his depth, and he was. When had he ever had to face the consequences of something so vile? He was a boy in a man's body. Trixie's rage left as quickly as it arrived, leaving her deflated. 'Never mention it to anyone, but more importantly make sure *he* never comes here again.'

'Wayland will be gone soon.'

'How soon?'

'I do not know. He has no reason stay. He has full faith in Max controlling the estate.'

'I'm in no position to ask you for anything—'

'Please do!' he butted in.

'Make sure he leaves soon, please.'

Thomas reached out and took her hand. 'I will do everything in my power to entice Wayland back to the south.'

Trixie gazed at their joined hands, wishing circumstances were different, that she and Thomas could be equal, that she could be untainted.

Horse's hooves could be heard outside. Trixie snatched her hand away and raced to the window, praying it wouldn't be Wayland and hoping it was Jacob and Mussy. She sighed in relief and disappointment. 'It's your brother.'

'I must go.' Thomas slammed on his hat. 'It's too soon for me to see him after what Wayland has done. Max will see I am troubled. I cannot tell him the truth for there will be bloodshed. Max holds Mrs Lawson in great esteem.'

'So, your brother knows nothing?'

'Nothing at all. Wayland only told me last night because he was heavy in his cups and boasting about teaching Mrs

Lawson a lesson. I had no notion that when I left you by the stream that Wayland had other plans, or I would have persuaded him to return with me.'

'I should've seen it.' Trixie shrugged, hating herself for not reading the situation better, for not protecting Caroline from men like Wayland.

'How could you have known?'

'Because where I come from men like him are common as muck. All they do is take, destroy, want control and we women must bend to their wills or break.'

Thomas went to speak but the sound of boots being scraped stopped him. He opened the door as Max raised a hand to knock. 'I was just leaving, brother.' He headed outside and straight for his horse. 'I shall talk with you later. Tomorrow, perhaps…' Thomas mounted his horse and trotted out of the yard without a backward glance.

Frowning, Mr Cavendish stood in the doorway watching his brother leave. 'Is everything well, Miss Wilkes?'

'Yes, Mr Cavendish.' Trixie gave him a tentative smile. A young black and white dog sat on the doorstep, its tongue hanging out. It looked very much like Prince and Duke.

She invited him in. It was easy to like Max Cavendish. He had kept her secret and not told Thomas or anyone as far as she was aware about her tainted past. That only proved that he was a decent gentleman. Since the moment she met Max, she believed him to be one of the good men of this world, and they were thin on the ground in her experience. Instinctively, she knew he admired Caroline, even though her friend refused to admit it, but Trixie's instincts were finely tuned after years plying herself on the streets and she was certain Max Cavendish wanted Caroline to be more than just his friend. Only, had

Wayland spoilt that now? Would Caroline ever trust a man again?

'Is Mrs Lawson not here?' Cavendish looked at the empty dog crate.

'She's out with the sheep, training the dogs.'

'That was one of the reasons why I called. I thought to ask if she wanted to take the dogs to Mr Purcell's farm and have him teach us some more commands for the dogs. I have brought Princess.'

'Princess?'

'My dog.' He smiled self-consciously. 'If she is the sister to a Prince and a Duke, then she should be a Princess.'

'That makes sense. Your other reason?'

'I wanted Mrs Lawson to know the men are ready to start harvesting this week and will be here at dawn on Monday.'

'I'll let her know.'

Cavendish hesitated. 'The farm seems quiet. Where is everyone?'

'My sisters are visiting Annie Aspall and... Jacob and Mussy are in York.'

'York?' He scowled in slight confusion. 'I believed it was not safe for Jacob to return to York.'

'It isn't, but no one listens to me.' She threw her hands up. 'And now they've been gone longer than expected and I'm worried senseless! They travelled to York two days ago and should've returned by now.'

'And you are worried something has happened to them,' he stated with concern.

'Yes. You know the story about Dolan and why Caroline or me can't go back to York.'

'I do, and Jacob's beating for helping you both.' Cavendish placed his hat on the table and folded his arms. 'You believe something might have happened to Jacob in York by the hands of this Dolan fellow?'

'Honestly, I don't know, but why else would they've not come home?'

'What does Mrs Lawson think?'

'What do I think about what?' Caroline asked, coming in looking windswept and tired. 'Calm down, Prince! Duke, leave that dog alone.' She closed the door on the dog outside. Her eyes had widened slightly on seeing Max Cavendish but immediately her beautiful face closed down again. She clicked her fingers, and the dogs headed straight to their bed.

'We're talking about Jacob and Mussy not being back yet.' Trixie watched for Caroline's reaction, hoping it would spur her into some kind of emotion. Caroline needed something to break down the shell that she'd placed around her since Wayland's rape.

Caroline sighed and took off the cape she wore. Outside the wind brought drops of rain. Trixie was worried that Caroline wouldn't care if she caught her death up on those hills. Caroline had barely eaten or slept since Wayland's attack.

'I could go to York, if that would ease your minds?' Cavendish offered. 'I could ask around and maybe I can find them.'

'No!' Caroline snapped, then instantly looked contrite. 'Forgive me.'

'I want to help,' he soothed.

'We've got to do something, Caroline,' Trixie begged. 'It's been two days and not a word. If they were staying longer for some reason Mussy would've sent a note or something!'

'We don't wish to drag Mr Cavendish into our business.' Caroline fixed a hard stare on Trixie.

'I thought we were friends, Mrs Lawson, and friends help

each other in times of need.' Cavendish gave her a warm smile. 'Please let me be of assistance to you.'

Caroline raised her chin. 'Very well. But I'm going with you.'

'What!' Trixie's legs turned to jelly. 'No.'

'Either I go, or we both wait here, and no one goes. Which is it?' The stubborn set of Caroline's expression broke no argument.

Trixie knew her too well to suppose she would give ground on this. 'So, now I'll have another person to worry about.'

Cavendish held up his hand. 'I will never leave Mrs Lawson's side, Miss Wilkes. I promise you that.'

'Shall we go now?' Caroline collected her cloak.

'I need to inform my staff about what I am doing, and my cousin.'

Caroline jerked at the mention of his cousin. '*He* isn't coming!'

'No, no.' He looked confused.

'An hour then?'

'I will return in the carriage in an hour.'

When he'd gone, Caroline slumped into a chair. Trixie sat beside her and took her hand. 'I don't like any of this.'

'What choice do we have?' Caroline pulled her hand away. 'I'll go and change. Oh, and by the way, thank God and His mercies, there will be no child from that devil.'

Trixie stared, letting the words sink in. His lordship hadn't left a child in Caroline. She sagged in relief.

'I knew I was barren when married to Hugh, for we tried for a baby for two years and nothing. I cursed the fates because of it. Now, I'm thankful to be so.'

'Caro…'

'Don't say anything. I'm fine.' Caroline sucked in a deep breath. 'And don't worry yourself while I'm gone. Dolan dare not come anywhere near me...' Her face twisted in anger. 'I would happily kill him if he did.'

While Caroline was upstairs, Trixie tidied the clean kitchen, needing to do something. When the door opened and Elsie and Bertha came in with Annie following, Trixie embraced them.

'What's wrong, lass?' Annie asked. 'Are Jacob and Mussy still not back?'

'No, and Caroline is going to York to search for them.'

'Is that wise?' Annie frowned, lowering her voice so the girls wouldn't hear.

'No, but she's determined.'

'I'll go with her then.'

'Mr Cavendish is.'

Annie relaxed slightly. 'That's all right then, she'll have a man with her.'

Caroline came downstairs and raised her eyebrows at the girls sitting on the floor patting the dogs. 'I'm away to York, girls. Now, I trust you not to be silly with Prince and Duke. They need to behave.'

'We can train them while you're gone, Caro,' Elsie said, nudging Bertha. 'Won't we? We'll make them sit and heel just like you do.'

Trixie noticed Caroline wore her best dress of soft blue and white lace and winced. She looked lovely when she needed to be in the shadows. 'The dogs will be fine, Caro, but why are you wearing that? You'll stand out like a three-legged man wearing that in Walmgate.'

'Exactly!' Caroline pinned on her straw hat with white roses on the brim. 'I'm not hiding anymore, Trixie.'

'Not hiding?' Trixie felt light-headed. 'Are you mad?'

'Quite possibly.' The icy look in Caroline's green eyes turned them to the colour of wet moss.

'Nay, lass…' Annie wrung her hands. 'Might it be best if you just let Mr Cavendish go alone?'

'No, Annie, it wouldn't be for the best. Mr Cavendish isn't familiar with that part of York.' Caroline kissed them all on the cheek and rubbed the dogs' ears. 'I'll be back as quickly as I can.'

Trixie believed Caroline said those last words for the dogs.

CHAPTER 6

*I*n the enclosed carriage, Caroline stared out of the window at the passing houses of Blossom Street. Her thoughts lingered on the short time she'd worked as a scullery maid at Greenleigh House. It seemed an age ago since she'd been there.

She'd not spoken to Cavendish the entire journey to York except to answer his question was she comfortable, which she replied yes. How could she not be when travelling in a sprung carriage sitting on padded leather seats? Normally she rode in the gig or the farm cart. It stuck in her throat that it was the estate's carriage, which meant it belonged to him, Wayland, but she couldn't help that and to have refused would have appeared odd to Cavendish. The last thing she needed was him wondering why she refused a perfectly good carriage.

It saddened her that before Wayland did what he did, she would have enjoyed spending the day with Max Cavendish, they had always got along so well, but now she couldn't relax with him. He needed to be kept at arm's length. She couldn't soften, couldn't be caught off guard again. Not that she believed Cavendish was a horrible person, not like his cousin, but she couldn't trust him. She couldn't trust anyone ever again.

The carriage needed to be left behind once they reached Walmgate. She glanced at Cavendish, his handsome profile, as he looked the other way. 'We must walk into Walmgate. The carriage will draw attention. If people living in the yards and tenements think we are gentry, they'll not tell us anything.'

'If that is your wish.' He nodded.

She waited until they had crossed Ouse Bridge over the river. 'We should stop along The Pavement and walk the rest of the way.'

Cavendish banged on the carriage to get the driver's attention to slow down. Once on foot, Caroline walked purposefully even though she had no idea where Jacob's sister lived in the warren of poverty-stricken streets and mean yards of Walmgate.

Along Fossgate, Caroline paused slightly at Overton's Lodging House, remembering Mrs Overton's rudeness, of the humiliating experience of the landlady throwing her out on the street. That action had led Caroline to seek a room at Dolan's lodging house, or what she thought was a lodging house but was actually a brothel run by Dolan. She shivered, hating that man more than words could say. Dolan and Wayland, men who took, who controlled, who ruined lives.

'Should we ask someone?' Cavendish broke into her thoughts.

'Um… yes.' Caroline looked around and stopped outside of The Black Horse, a public house.

'Shall I go in?'

'We both will.' Caroline refused to be seen as a delicate woman, letting a man do everything for her. She pushed open the narrow door and entered the dimly lit taproom. The smell of stale beer and smoke hit her like an invisible force. Eyes adjusting to the gloom, she proceeded to the bar where an unkempt woman was refilling lamps with oil.

'We don't serve women in the front bar, madam,' the woman grunted. 'If you're wanting owt you need to go to the snug to be served.'

'I only want to ask a question,' Caroline replied. 'I'm looking for a woman, Sarah Adams or Sarah Clarke is her married name. She's a midwife and recently moved from the Water Lanes.'

The woman's expression showed her lack of interest. 'Never heard of her. Unless a body drinks in me pub, then I don't know 'em.'

'Thank you for your time.' Leaving the pub, Caroline glanced down the road. 'I don't think Sarah frequents pubs.'

'Perhaps some of the shops?' Cavendish took Caroline's elbow, making her jump.

She stared at him, but he kept his gaze ahead, searching the shop facings for a likely place to ask. He was being a gentleman, and his light hold was considerate, but his touch started a stream of emotions running through her and now wasn't the time for her to be weak and think about anything other than finding Sarah, which might lead to Jacob and Mussy.

Caroline quickly entered a general store and headed straight to the counter. Again, she explained who she was looking for.

The shopkeeper, wearing a white apron tied around his waist, tapped his chin. 'Adams... No, nothing rings a bell but Clarke. I did have a Mrs Clarke on my credit books last month. New to us as well, and I wasn't keen to give her credit, but she returned the next week and paid what she owed. I've not seen her since. It may not be the same Mrs Clarke you're looking for.'

'Do you know where she lives?'

'Give me a minute and I'll check my book.' The shopkeeper turned to the counter behind him and opened up a drawer, pulling out a leather-bound ledger. He turned a few pages, flipped back one, and then forward a few more pages, running his finger down the columns.

Cavendish smiled at Caroline. 'This looks promising.'

'Are we that lucky to find her so soon?' Caroline was doubtful. She gazed about the tidy shop, its shelves lined with all manner of things from sweeping brooms to caustic soda, bars of soap, scrubbing brushes, tin buckets, balls of twine, wicker baskets and on the other side of the shop were sacks of tea, flour and salt. Fleetingly, Caroline wished their local village had such a shop. The one benefit from living in a city was the availability of anything you wanted, if you had the money for it, which she and Trixie never had.

'Here we go.' The shopkeeper brought the ledger over to them. 'Mrs Sarah Clarke, Melrose's Yard.'

'It is worth a try,' Cavendish murmured.

'Thank you, sir.' Caroline nodded to the shopkeeper.

The shopkeeper seemed uncertain, his eyes roaming over Caroline's pretty dress. 'Madam, Melrose's Yard isn't for the faint-hearted. It's… well… rough, if you get my meaning. Be careful.'

Cavendish shook the man's hand. 'That is good of you to warn us.'

Outside on the street, Caroline adjusted her gloves. 'The shopkeeper wouldn't have said that to me if he knew I once lived in the Water Lanes,' she murmured and walked up the road. She searched between the buildings, reading the signs of the alleyways and cut-throughs that more often led to yards of condensed poor housing.

Within ninety yards they passed six more pubs lining the road before St Dennis' Church loomed on the corner of St Dennis Street. Opposite the church was Foundry Yard.

Glancing further down, Caroline saw the sign to Melrose's Yard above a walkway. 'There.' She pointed it out.

'Stay close.' Cavendish had been watching a group of youths loitering about the church's gravestones.

The dreariness of the buildings became more pronounced once they entered through the narrow entrance covered by the low roof from the building above. Inside the muddy yard where the sun didn't penetrate, two storey dilapidated timber houses lined both sides. The noise of the iron foundry further down the yard rang in Caroline's ears. The stink of sewerage and rot filled her nose.

Children played at the bottom of the outside staircases or sat at the top of stone steps leading down into cellars, all dressed in rags, faces gaunt and dirty. Not one of the dozen children who stared at them wore shoes.

A woman heavy with child stood holding a bucket, talking to an older man. They both turned and scowled at Caroline and Cavendish. 'What thee be wantin' around 'ere?' The woman took a step towards them. 'Are thee lost or summat?'

'I'm… we are, looking for a friend, Mrs Sarah Clarke or Sarah Adams, a midwife.'

'Aye, an' what thee wantin' 'er for?'

'So, Sarah is here?' Caroline asked hopefully.

'I ain't sayin'.' The woman shrugged. 'Who are thee, anyway?'

Movement on the steps coming up from a cellar caused Caroline to turn.

'*Caroline?*' Jacob hurried to her, his expression a mixture of surprise and relief. 'I'm so glad to see you.'

'Why haven't you come home?' Caroline took his hands.

'It's been an ordeal. Come with me.' He nodded to Max. 'Mr Cavendish.'

'Mrs Lawson and Miss Wilkes have been deeply concerned,' Cavendish said, following them down the wet steps.

At the bottom, Jacob stopped. 'We couldn't make the journey home. Mussy is ill.'

'Ill?' Caroline's heart sank. 'How bad? You've been gone two days.'

'His coughing became worse as we drove to York that morning. I ended up taking the reins to allow Mussy to rest, but he found it difficult to breathe the closer we got to York. He passed out a few times from coughing so hard and not catching his breath. I drove here to Walmgate and asked around for Sarah, it took me hours before I found her, and I only did by chance when I spotted our Pete running down the street. By then Mussy was feeling a little better, but that night he grew worse again and collapsed. Our Sarah's been caring for him.' Jacob opened the weather-damaged wooden door and led them inside.

'Couldn't you have found a way to let Mrs Lawson know?' Cavendish asked.

Jacob raised his eyebrows in surprise. 'No, sir. I can't read or write and Mussy wasn't well enough to be able to hold a pen, even if we did have one or the money to send it.'

'Ah, yes, of course,' Cavendish murmured, contrite.

The darkness of the cellar made it difficult to see anything at first, but slowly Caroline made out the dank brick walls, the small glowing fire in the hearth. A table stood in the middle and, at the far end, several mattresses were spread on the floor. On one of them lay Mussy. She raced to his side, ignoring the two children on the other mattress. 'Mussy! It's me, Caroline.'

Mussy groaned and squinted up at her. His grey face looked like death. He'd never recovered his good health since his imprisonment, but now he looked skeletal. 'Caro,' he wheezed.

'It's me.' She held his thin hand. 'We'll get you home.'

'Yes, home... Feel the sun...' Harsh coughing convulsed him. Mussy put a piece of rag to his mouth. Caroline held him up, not knowing what to do to ease his breathing. When Mussy lowered the rag from his face, Caroline gasped at the blood sprayed on it. Mussy gazed at it and then at her, his eyes full of pain, but also of recognition of the future ahead.

'Are you strong enough for a carriage ride?' she said quietly.

He shook his head and closed his eyes.

She left him to sleep and stepped to Jacob and Cavendish who stood by the table. 'He needs a doctor,' she whispered.

'Aye,' Jacob agreed. 'But there's not many of those around these parts. Sarah has taken on a lot since she moved to this yard, being a midwife, and it's helped her to be accepted by the folk living here. Our Sarah's out delivering a baby now. Her husband, Wilf, he's done a runner, left her high and dry when they moved out of the Water Lanes, the slimy coward. I never liked him.'

'We have to get Mussy home.' She glanced back at him sleeping on the stained mattress, a thin blanket his only covering.

Moisture beaded and ran down the grubby walls. The fusty stink of the gloomy cellar, which was chilly despite the warm day outside, and the feeble light filtered by a narrow window by the door gave the place a dungeon feel. Mussy would be reminded of his prison cell.

'I shall go and fetch the carriage.' Cavendish moved towards the door. 'The sooner we get Mr Casey out of here and into fresh air the better he will be.'

Caroline looked at Jacob. 'Are you coming home?'

'Aye. Our Sarah doesn't need me. She was happy but surprised I came to find her, but I know she's all right.' He gestured towards the two children. 'The kiddies are well. I've given her all the money I have, though she didn't want to take it. She's earning enough to feed them and keep a roof over their heads, such as it is.' He grimaced, his face miserable. 'I'll come once a month and give her any wages that you give me. I don't need much money. I've got a warm bed and good food at the farm.'

'You're a good brother, Jacob, and I'm glad you're returning home with us. We'd be lost without you.'

He blushed and turned away. 'I'll go and get Dossy and the gig.'

'Where are they?'

'Next door at the foundry. The foreman there let me keep Dossy in a shed, and the gig is outside of it. Our Pete and Mary have been feeding Dossy grass from the churchyard.' He gathered the harness. 'I've checked on her twice a day as she wasn't liking the noise from the foundry.'

'And Dolan?' She didn't want to say his name, but it had to be done.

'I've asked a few people, but Dolan doesn't come around here, stays more in the centre of town. Our Sarah heard that Dolan has been playing the big man. Somehow, he's got some money behind him now and a few important people are in his pocket. He has a club. Imagine that?'

'He should be in prison.'

'Aye, but slimy people like him get away with things when money is involved.'

'Do you think we could visit York again without the worry of him caring about us?' she asked.

'Is it worth the risk?'

'I've stock to sell at the market in a few weeks. Mussy might not be well enough to do it.'

'Well, we have a bit of time to sort that out.' He stepped to the door. 'Come on, our Pete, Mary, come and help me harness Dossy.'

Alone with Mussy, Caroline sat with him, perched on the end of the mattress. He wheezed with every breath, his face pale and bloodless. When the door opened, she expected Cavendish, but Sarah came in and Caroline got to her feet. 'Sarah.'

'It's grand to see you again, Caroline.' Sarah looked like Jacob, but an older and more tired version. Her brown hair was tied up haphazardly, her black skirt mud-stained at the bottom. She knelt beside Mussy. 'You've come to take him home,' she stated.

'Yes. We were so worried when Jacob and Mussy didn't return.'

Sarah's eyes were shadowed. 'When they got here, I thought Mr Casey wouldn't see the next morning. He was in a terrible state, still is. You know he has TB, don't you?'

Caroline sighed, the heavy weight of the illness bowing her shoulders. 'Yes.'

'He's nowt but skin and bones,' Sarah whispered. 'He'll need a lot of caring, but…'

'But what?' Caroline whispered back.

'I doubt he'll make it through the winter. I've seen it so many times before.'

Caroline refused to accept the shattering diagnosis. 'He will. I'll make sure of it.'

No more was said as Cavendish and Jacob returned. They both lifted Mussy up between them and carried him through the mud with many onlookers gaping at the scene. Caroline shuddered at the filth of the yard and the wretched poverty. How had she managed to stand living in such conditions in the Water Lanes? If she hadn't returned to Howard's farm and he hadn't taken her in, then maybe her and Trixie and the girls' fate would have been to end up in a similar yard as this. They'd had a lucky escape, and she'd fight hard to never be in a situation again where they might have to live like this.

The carriage waited on Walmgate and behind it stood Dossy and the gig.

'Thank you for caring for Mussy.' Caroline squeezed Sarah's hands in gratefulness. 'And if you're ever in need, come to the farm.'

'Thanks, and good luck to you,' Sarah said and then embraced her brother. 'Come visit when you can.'

'Aye.' He tousled the children's hair and climbed into the gig.

Cavendish handed Caroline up into the carriage and she settled herself next to Mussy who leant against her shoulder barely awake. Producing a blanket from under the seat, Cavendish helped Caroline place it around Mussy despite the warmth of the day. She caught Cavendish's gaze and gave him a tender smile in thanks before she concentrated on Mussy. In the brightness of the late afternoon sun, Mussy appeared greyer and more drawn.

Caroline held him close. She'd never let him die.

CHAPTER 7

Max poured two whiskies and passed one to Wayland who lounged on the sofa, his eyes half closed.

Settling himself in a chair by the fire, Max watched the flames. His thoughts drifted to Caroline, her delicate features, the flash of a tight smile she gave him in thanks when he left her last night after they'd returned from York. For some reason that he couldn't understand, there was an awkwardness from her towards him that there had never been before. Had he offended her in some way?

'Where were you all day yesterday and today, Max?' Wayland asked, crossing his legs at the ankles. 'I tried to find you.'

'Today I have been organising men in the fields for the harvesting. Yesterday I was in York.'

'Why York? You never mentioned it to me.'

'It was a last-minute decision.' Max sipped his drink, preoccupied with Caroline.

'I might have come with you.' Wayland watched him closely. 'Why did you need to go to York?'

'I was helping Mrs Lawson.'

Wayland's hand jerked a little. 'Mrs Lawson?'

'Yes. She needed to go to York to search for her friend, Mr Casey, and her labourer, who had not returned as planned. She was quite worried for their safety.'

Sitting up straight, Wayland gave Max his full attention. 'Why was she worried about two grown men?'

Max rubbed the back of his neck tiredly. It'd been a long day. 'In York there is a scoundrel and his band of thugs who have a vendetta against Mrs Lawson and her friends.'

Eyes narrowed, Wayland leaned forward. 'A vendetta? That sounds extremely dramatic.'

'The man, Victor Dolan, is a madman. He kept Mrs Lawson hostage in an attic, had his men beat up Jacob and Miss Wilkes for helping Mrs Lawson to escape him. The blackguard should be in prison.' Max would enjoy meeting the fellow one day and knocking his teeth down his throat.

'Fascinating…' Wayland rested back on the sofa. 'Why does he hate Mrs Lawson so much?'

'He wanted her as an attraction for one of his high-class brothels.'

Wayland nearly choked on his whiskey. 'Good God. There is more to this Mrs Lawson than one realises. A nefarious past it seems.'

'She is innocent in all of this,' Max defended.

'There is never smoke without fire, Cousin.' Wayland smirked.

Max didn't want to retaliate for Wayland loved a good argument and Max just wanted his bed. He drank the last of his drink and put the glass on the table beside him. 'I shall retire. It has been a long day.'

'Indeed,' Wayland murmured.

The following morning, Max left his cottage and walked the pebbled path to the abbey through the extensive formal gardens which glistened in the morning light from the dew. Dressed in a black suit, he noticed many of the estate staff still wore black armbands and were waiting to board the carts that would take them to the village church for the Sunday service.

The carriage stood on the drive and Max reached the bottom of the front steps as Wayland descended, pulling on his gloves. 'Good morning.'

'Let us hope Reverend Porter does not drone on this week as he has done previously,' Wayland said, climbing into the carriage. 'Is Thomas not joining us? Though who could blame him? Porter likes to hear the sound of his own voice. His sermon at Father's memorial service was a prime example of how to bore a congregation.'

'I suspect Thomas will meet us at the church.' Max climbed in and sat opposite Wayland for the short ride to the village. He was looking forward to seeing Caroline, and hoped she'd attend the service and not stay home to care for Mr Casey for he wanted to see her lovely face and speak with her, if only for a few minutes.

At the church, the villagers and tenant farmers were packed in, filling all the pews, save the Stockton-Lee pew set at a right angle to the pulpit. He smiled sadly at the stone plaque erected on the wall denoting his uncle Richard's achievements. Many parishioners bowed their heads as they passed it in a mark of respect. It delighted Max that his uncle was so well revered.

He searched for Caroline and found her seated midway down the aisle. She kept her head down and didn't look up as he passed.

'Where is Thomas?' Wayland asked as they sat in the family front pew.

Max frowned. He'd not seen his brother for days. 'He should be here by now.'

'We shan't wait for him.' Wayland nodded to the reverend to begin.

Reverend Porter raised his hands and welcomed the congregation, they sang hymns and prayed for departed souls.

Max glanced around and found Caroline as everyone resumed their seats, but she kept her head bowed.

When the service finished, Wayland and Max were the first down the aisle to shake the reverend's hand at the doorway. While Wayland chatted to Porter, Max edged his way through the throng to find Caroline.

'Mrs Lawson.' He waved her down as she exited the church.

'Mr Cavendish.' She bowed her head in acknowledgement.

'How is Mr Casey faring?'

Standing stiff and straight, Caroline glanced at the gate as though desperate to escape. 'He is much the same as when we found him. Doctor Pike visited last night and will return this afternoon, but there is little he can do for Mussy. We simply have to build up his strength again and get him well.' She took a step back, her gaze going over Max's shoulder. 'Excuse me, I must go.'

'Mrs Lawson,' Wayland drawled, coming alongside Max. 'I hear you have been keeping my cousin occupied when he should be about estate business.'

Max watched the colour drain from Caroline's face and he

became furious. 'No, Mrs Lawson is not at fault, Wayland. I offered.'

Wayland lifted his head regally. 'Ah, our dear Max cannot resist helping a damsel in distress.'

Caroline's top lip curled, disgust written all over her face. 'That's because he is a *true* gentleman, unlike some.'

Max stared in shock at her obvious dislike of his cousin.

'Come now, Mrs Lawson,' Wayland waved his hand dismissively, 'such blatant generalisation can lead you into trouble.'

'There is no generalisation about it. Some men have the trappings of status, education and wealth, yet they abuse their position simply because they can, because they have the power to. Those men are not gentlemen.' Her eyes raked him up and down with utter loathing before flicking to Max. 'Good day, Mr Cavendish.' She turned to go but spun back to curtsy deeply, mockingly. '*Your lordship*,' she spat with distaste before marching away.

Lost for words, Max tried to comprehend what had just happened.

'That bitch needs putting in her place *again*,' Wayland growled. 'Who does she think she is?'

'Don't call her that!' Max snapped. 'Have you upset Mrs Lawson in some way?' He kept his voice low as other people were mingling close by obviously wanting to speak with their lord.

'Upset her?' Wayland snarled. 'I am Lord Stockton-Lee! I shall treat people any way I wish, and that high and mighty bitch is no exception.'

'Keep your voice down, for pity's sake!' Max hissed, looking around. He was getting close to wanting to punch his cousin's filthy mouth to shut him up.

Wayland sneered at him. 'Do not ever tell me what to do, Max. Neither you nor she can talk to me with such disrespect and get away with it.'

'Calm down. People are looking.'

'As if I care. I am their *Lord!*' Wayland glanced around at the gathering with a look of contempt and stomped towards the carriage.

Max walked with him, nodding to those he passed. He didn't understand any of what just happened. 'Let me talk to Mrs Lawson. She is upset about her friend, Mr Casey. I am certain she did not mean any disrespect.' But even as he spoke, Max knew differently. Caroline hated his cousin, and he wanted to know why.

In the carriage, Wayland tapped his leg in anger. 'Where was Thomas? How dare he not attend church as a member of this family, out of respect for me! It is the one time we show a united front to the whole parish.'

'I shall ride to speak to Thomas the minute we reach the abbey.' Max had no idea what had kept his brother from the service, but it had better be a good excuse. The whole morning had been a disaster.

'I will not be leaving for London tomorrow as I planned.' Wayland's tapping became faster. 'I wish to stay a few days more.'

'Of course,' Max murmured, a little deflated.

He wanted Wayland gone so he could be left alone to run the estate without his interference. Already Wayland had dismissed two housemaids and a groom in fits of temper. He'd upset Mrs Hoskins by breaking a vase when he stumbled to bed drunk and knocked over a hall table and, which was worse, for trying to compromise some of the upper chamber maids into his bedroom. His cousin was rude to the staff and demanding. Wayland stayed up late drinking and rose just as late disrupting the normal order of the servants' routine. And now Wayland seemed to have greatly offended Caroline and that annoyed Max more than anything else.

* * *

TRIXIE WATERED the vegetables from the bucket, the sun hot on her back as she worked. When she got to the end of the row, movement caught her eye. Thomas stood by the gate. Her chest tightened at the sight of him, and she took a deep breath to calm herself before walking towards him. 'Good afternoon.'

'Good afternoon. I did not mean to interrupt you.' Thomas opened the gate for her.

'I was nearly finished and needed a break.' She wiped the sweat from her face with the back of her hand. 'Would you like some tea or cordial?'

'No, thank you.'

She studied him, he seemed ill at ease. There was no laughter in his blue eyes anymore. 'Is something wrong?'

'Can we walk for a moment, away from the house?'

'Aye.' She placed her bucket by the gate and fell into step with him as he headed towards the open fields.

Thomas pulled at a long stem of grass. 'Wayland is remaining at the abbey for another week or more, apparently. I thought you should know so you can warn Mrs Lawson. Max told me that Wayland is angry at the way she spoke to him at church this morning.' Thomas halted beneath a large tree and gazed at crops in the fields. A gentle breeze swayed the tops of the hay crop. 'She needs to stay away from him.'

'Caroline has no plans to speak to him ever again.' Trixie

was afraid of her friend's anger which simmered day and night. When she learned of Caroline's confrontation with Wayland, Trixie worried if anything would come of it. Although Caroline had every right to hate the man, he was their lord and a man of power, and Caroline needed to remember that.

'Warn Mrs Lawson to be careful, to hold her tongue if she is in his presence. Wayland won't stand for another show of disrespect.'

'He deserves it!' Trixie snapped, angry that Wayland was able to do as he pleased and get away with it. 'He could've left Caroline with child!'

Thomas paled. 'Has he?'

'No, thankfully, but he might have done,' Trixie argued. 'Caroline's life would've been ruined. How is any of that fair?'

'It is not fair at all.' His shoulders slumped. 'I detest him for what he has done. I am finding it difficult to be in his company, but I dare not tell Max why. Max bought the lie that I was too ill to attend church this morning. The truth is being in Wayland's company galls me.'

'I wish he'd leave and never come back.'

'Mrs Lawson needs to try to put it behind her.'

'She was taken against her will, Thomas!' Trixie flared. 'It's changed her.'

He bowed his head in shame. 'Of course.'

'When I first met Caroline, and she came to live with me, she was gentle and quiet. Frightened and sad. She couldn't handle the way we lived, the filth of the Water Lanes, the lack of comforts, the stink, the wretched people, the ugliness of it all. She was brought up differently to that. All she wanted to do was escape it and take us with her. Caroline struggled to cope living in York, but it made her stronger. The reserved woman I met became fierce, she had to or die. Mussy calls her a warrior.' Trixie shrugged, not having the clever words that Mussy used to describe Caroline. 'She won't back down when she sees something is wrong.'

'She has to with Wayland, or he will destroy her.' Thomas looked at Trixie, his gaze tender. 'I would call you a warrior, too.'

Trixie smiled. 'No, I'm simply a survivor. That's all we can do, just survive each day as it comes.'

Thomas reached out and took her hand. 'I admire you greatly, Trixie.'

Thrilled at his touch, at the sincerity of his words, Trixie's chest swelled with emotion. 'And I you, Thomas.'

He gently pulled her closer to the tree to shield them from the house. 'Can I kiss you?'

For an answer, Trixie wrapped her arms about his neck and welcomed his mouth to hers. For the first time in her life, she kissed a man willingly and the sensations of it made her legs wobbly.

'My darling girl,' he breathed against her lips. 'I have longed to do this since the first moment I laid eyes on you.'

She shivered under his touch, his arms around her holding her against him. They kissed again, and she gloried in it. Her first proper kiss given by someone she craved. So many times, in the past, she had to ward off men from kissing her as they used her body. Kissing never something she allowed, kissing made the act personal, and it was never personal to her just a way to earn money. Yet this kiss, Thomas's kisses, were a beautiful thing, tender, passionate, full of yearning. He saw her as desirable, a person, not a piece of flesh.

'You are so precious,' Thomas whispered. 'I know we should not be doing this, but I do honour you.'

'No one can see us. It'll be our secret.'

'I shan't give you up, no matter what my brother says.'

Jerking back, Trixie's heart hammered. 'Your brother? What did he say?'

'That I should not think of finding a wife, not yet.'

'Is that all?' She dropped her arms. Had Max told Thomas about her past?

Thomas grinned, some of his old self returning. 'What else can he say? He knows how highly I think of you, but Max is practical and believes I cannot support a wife, at least not at the moment. I will in time though, trust me.'

The joy seeped out of her. How foolish was she to think that someone like Thomas, an educated man, the cousin of a lord, could possibly marry her, a former prostitute? Max, as kind as he was, would tell Thomas everything to protect him.

'Would you wait for me, Trixie? Until I have finished university? As much as I do not want to return to Oxford, I must. My uncle paid for my tuition, and I must honour that, but will you wait for me?' he asked eagerly. 'I would obtain a position as a land agent somewhere, on a grand estate.'

She turned away, flinching at every word he spoke. He made it sound so easy, only Thomas had no idea of who she was, or had been, and when he did, he'd never think of her in the same way again. She couldn't bear to see the disappointment in his eyes when he became aware of her past. Better that they remained friends, because then it wouldn't come out, but if Max knew of Thomas's serious wish to wed her, he'd tell Thomas the truth and everything would be destroyed. No, she had to be sensible, had to be the one to dash his dreams before they took hold of him.

'Trixie?' Thomas frowned. 'Have I spoken out of turn?'

She nearly cried at the uncertainty in his eyes. How she

wished she could make him happy. 'I'll never be your wife, Thomas.'

'Why so?'

'Because I'm poor. I can't read or write hardly at all. My sisters are more educated than me.'

'We can solve that problem. I will teach you, or we can hire a tutor…' His words drifted away as she shook her head.

'I'm not of your class.'

'I care nothing about that.'

'You should. You'd be a laughing stock marrying someone like me.' She kept her voice controlled, not daring to give into the miserable emotions tearing at her. 'You need to marry someone of better birth than me. It's what you deserve.'

'You are the one I want.'

She shook her head. 'No. No, I'm not.' She walked away, head held high with her heart breaking.

Near the house, Jacob came out of the barn pushing the wheelbarrow. He smiled on seeing her. 'Where are the girls? They were supposed to help me clean out the hens' boxes, the cheeky beggars are hiding from me.'

'I'll go find them,' she said bleakly.

'Trixie?' Jacob lifted his head, and they both watched Thomas trot down the drive on his horse. 'Did Thomas Cavendish upset you?'

'No, why would he?'

'Gentlemen don't need reasons to upset folk,' Jacob murmured, watching her closely. 'Caroline is not herself after having words with his lordship, and now you look ready to cry.'

'I'm fine, Jacob.'

'You'd tell me if anything were amiss, wouldn't you? You can trust me. I'll always look after you.'

His words made her want to cry even more. 'You're a good friend, Jacob.'

'Trixie—'

'I'd best get on.' She hurried away not wanting to hear what else he had to say.

CHAPTER 8

Caroline whistled Prince and Duke to come around. Prince dropped to the ground, his nose in the grass, focused on the sheep huddled by an outcrop of rock. They were high on the hills behind the farm, on the edge of the boundary. From here was a great view of the house and outbuildings, the cattle grazing in the front field, the dairy cows near the back of the barn.

Men, women and children were in the fields harvesting, local people she'd hired, and some from the estate Max had sent to her. She should be down there helping but she couldn't cope with being amongst people, listening to the innocent chatter about everyday things, joking and laughing. She didn't want to join in or try to find the will to laugh. She had nothing to laugh about. Jacob was in charge and thrived on it, while she had escaped up on the hills to be alone with her dogs.

Duke crawled low, eager to get the flock under his control. Both dogs were so intelligent it surprised Caroline. She had no training herself on how to direct dogs around sheep, but the instinct bred into the dogs made it easier for them to learn that she could guide them with whistles, commands and hand movements. The dogs were growing fast, leggy and building muscle from the long days roaming the hills and the huge quantities of food she fed them.

So intent was she on watching the dogs move the flock to the next rise, she didn't hear or see the rider ascend the hill until Prince growled and came to her side. Caroline whipped around at the sound of creaking leather and stiffened in fear as Wayland sat upon his horse. 'What do you want?' she snapped.

'Is that any way to greet your lord?' He lounged in the saddle, one hand resting on his thigh. 'Maybe I should dismount and teach you a lesson again?'

Caroline's heart banged, her mouth went dry. She clicked her fingers, and both dogs stood by her skirts on alert. 'Touch me and my dogs will tear you apart.'

He laughed. 'They are not even fully grown. Besides, one snarl and I will shoot them dead.'

Utter hatred for him curled in her stomach. They had a rifle in the barn, Jacob used it to shoot rabbits and vermin. From now on, she'd carry it with her. A warning shot over his head might deter him from attacking her.

'Well, I shall continue my way back to the abbey.' He lifted the reins. 'Oh, before I forget, your quarterly rent has been raised. Max will give you the details.'

'You've raised the rent?' She stared in shock.

'I have. It is now double what you pay.'

She gasped. 'You can't do that! I have an agreement with Mr Cavendish.'

'An agreement he arranged on behalf of my father. I am the lord now. All tenants shall be awarded new contracts.'

'In your favour,' she sneered. 'Farmers won't be able to pay it. They'll walk away from their farms.'

'Then I will sell the land to the railways. A track line from York to Ripon might easily come straight through this farm.' His grin was evil. 'I have no use for this estate and selling the land to the railways would make me a very rich man.'

Caroline started to shake. 'You can't do this.'

He laughed. 'I can.'

'Why do you want to ruin people's lives?' she said desperately.

Wayland shrugged, then smiled evilly. 'We could always come to some agreement between us?'

She understood his debauched meaning. 'I'd rather hang myself from a tree.'

He laughed again, but there was no humour in it. He nudged his horse closer to her making her step back and the dogs' growl. Wayland's eyes were slits in his face as he peered at her. 'There may come a time quite soon when you may actually beg for that option.' He jerked the horse's head around and galloped away.

What did he mean? She watched him until he was a speck riding on the village road, her mind frozen. Prince licked her hand bringing her back to the present and Duke sat by her skirts. Wayland's words echoed in her brain. Double the rent... Double the rent...

Trudging back down the hill, she pushed away her fears of leaving the farm as Elsie and Bertha came running up to join her.

'There's a tinker in the yard,' Elsie said breathlessly. 'Trixie's getting him to sharpen the kitchen knives.'

'And Mussy's shaving razor,' Bertha added. 'Do you want anything sharpened?'

'No, I don't think so.'

In the yard, Caroline noticed the travelling tinker had set up his wares on a blanket. He sat on a three-legged stool and was smoothing the edge of the bread knife, while Trixie and some of the labourer's younger children watched on.

The man looked up as Caroline approached, his smile revealed blackened teeth. His clothes were ragged, but he seemed healthy enough. 'Good day, missus.'

'Good day.' Caroline jerked her head in the direction of the house to Trixie. While Elsie, Bertha and some of the other children plied the tinker with questions as he worked, Caroline poured water into the dogs' bowl for them to drink.

'What is it?' Trixie asked, coming inside.

'Wayland found me on the hill.'

Trixie's eyes widened. 'He didn't—'

'No, but the threat was there.' Caroline made tea, her movements jerky. 'He's doubling the rent.'

'Dear God!' Trixie gripped the back of a chair. 'How will we pay it?'

'Pay what?' Mussy stepped into the kitchen from the hallway. Weak but determined to be out of bed, he spent most days reading either outside in the sun or by the fire in the sitting room.

'His lordship has doubled the rent,' Trixie informed him.

'Why would he do that?' Mussy frowned, lowering himself onto a chair by the table. Painfully thin, his skin a pale grey colour, he did everything slowly so as not to aggravate his cough.

'Because he can. Because he cares nothing for people.' Caroline poured a cup of tea for the three of them. 'Because he is the very devil.'

'Will the sale of the beasts at the market cover it?'

Caroline took her cup and leant against the dresser. 'It might but it would leave us destitute. We need the profits of the animals to buy the crop seeds for next year, and ideally, we'd need to buy more stock to replace the ewes or cows that didn't breed this year, or who are too old. Besides, Mr Bent must have some return on his investment. Then there's the cost of repairs on the farm, food, clothes and Jacob should have a wage…' Her words ran out at the enormity of the bleak future ahead.

'And we were just finding our feet here, too,' Trixie whispered.

'We cannot leave,' Mussy said on a sigh. 'We have no place to go.'

'Maybe we should talk to Mr Cavendish,' Trixie said. 'He's a good friend and he might be able to change his lordship's mind.'

'It is worth a try,' Mussy agreed.

'And what if Mr Cavendish can't change his mind?' Caroline snapped. 'You know we'll have to leave, don't you? We'll be homeless.' Fear drove her anger. 'Our lives will be ruined.'

Mussy started coughing, harsh wracking coughs that bent him double. Trixie rushed to his side while Caroline poured him a cup of water. Mussy took Caroline's hand. 'We will sort this out,' he panted.

When Mussy's breathing was under control, Caroline left Trixie to watch over him and she went out to milk the cows. The tinker was packing away his tools and chatting with Jacob, though he watched her as she walked across the yard. Caroline turned away from them both, knowing that Trixie would pay the travelling man from the money tin on the mantel. She heard the girls and children playing about in the barn, their laughter floating in the air and for a moment

Caroline paused and listened. Such innocent laughter. She could have cried at the sound of it. But instead, she straightened her shoulders and headed for the milking shed. Somehow, she'd have to find the money for the rent, the alternative would be unthinkable.

* * *

WITH A SMILE, Trixie gave the customer their change and the loaf of bread they'd bought from her stall. It still surprised her that folk bought the food she'd made. Living in the slums of York, she'd never been able to cook well. Their squalid room had no cooking facilities, just a pot over a smoking fire. Scraps of food was bought with what pennies she had to feed her sisters and herself. Caroline coming into her life showed her another way to live. Moving to the farm, meeting Annie had also altered her way of thinking about food, about cooking. Under their teachings Trixie had found skills she never knew she had. She could cook, and cook well, and what is more, she enjoyed doing it. Now within the farmhouse kitchen and with fresh ingredients grown in her own garden she cheerfully fed her family on good wholesome food.

'We're down to the last loaf,' Caroline said, rearranging the stall table. 'Two pies and the pound cake.'

'I'll give one of the pies to Annie if they don't sell by the time we pack away.' Trixie scanned the thinning crowd. Market day brought out everyone early and when the weather was fine, people would linger and chat to neighbours or farmers from further afield. However, today the storms clouds brewed overhead, obscuring the sun and folk began to head home.

'We might get caught in the rain on the way home,' Caroline muttered, stacking the empty baskets. The dogs were sleeping under the table and the girls were somewhere in the village playing with their Sunday school friends.

'There's Mr Cavendish,' Trixie said to Caroline. 'You should go speak with him before we leave.'

Caroline nodded, her face tightly controlled. It'd been four days since Wayland had accosted Caroline on the hill and Trixie knew her friend hadn't been sleeping well for she'd heard her pacing the bedroom during the night.

Before Caroline could leave the stall Jacob hurried up to them. 'Have you seen the girls?'

'They're around here playing somewhere,' Trixie told him as she sold a rabbit and potato pie to a late customer.

'They were near the well earlier,' Caroline said.

'I've looked all around the village for them.' Jacob rubbed his chin. 'They wanted me to fix their skipping rope, but when I spoke to their little friend, Florrie, she said the girls got into a cart.'

Max Cavendish joined them, smiling. 'Good day, Mrs Lawson, Miss Wilkes, Jacob.'

'Good day, Mr Cavendish.' Trixie smiled at him before frowning at Jacob. 'Who's cart? Was it Farmer Purcell? Has he got another litter of puppies to sell?'

Mr Cavendish tilted his head in thought. 'Purcell has no more puppies, but I do know he's gone to a village near Ripon to attend a horse fair today. He asked me if I was going, too.'

'Have you seen our Elsie and Bertha, Mr Cavendish?' Trixie asked him.

'No, I have not.'

'Apparently, they've climbed into some farmer's cart.'

'To be taken home?' Mr Cavendish asked.

Trixie marched around to the front of the stall scanning

the thinning crowd. 'They know not to leave the market square after last time!'

'Last time?' Mr Cavendish enquired to Caroline.

Caroline continued to pack away. 'A few months ago, the girls and their friends went off down to the stream down behind the blacksmith's. They wandered further away, running about and squealing as young girls do, but they scared Mrs Blanchard's mare and young foal. We heard Mrs Blanchard shouting before we saw the girls who were running back to us. We gave Mrs Blanchard a loaf of bread to calm her. Anyway, Elsie and Bertha have been warned to stay in the village.'

'I'm going to look for them.' Trixie untied her apron and threw it on the table. 'I'll tan their backsides if they've gone off again.'

'I'll look by the church,' Jacob said.

'And I shall ask at the inn,' Mr Cavendish added.

Annoyed at her sisters' antics, Trixie strode across the market square, searching the stalls. She asked a few stall-holders if they'd seen her sisters, but each shook their head. She peered down the little laneways between houses and the few shops, even entering the small general store and having a look, but it was empty.

Growing worried, Trixie headed back to Caroline. 'Any word?'

Caroline had cleared the stall. 'No. Annie is helping as well. She's gone to her cottage to see if the girls are there.'

'They'll be punished for this!' Trixie fumed. 'I mean it, Caro. They've had it too soft. They do as they like every day.'

'They have jobs to do about the farm.'

'But not enough!' Trixie snapped. 'They idle away each day

doing as they please. If we were in York, they'd be working twelve-hour shifts by now.'

'Yes, in some filthy, dangerous factory, half-starved.' Caroline grabbed the baskets and headed for the cart. 'You don't want that for them.'

'No, of course not. I'm just worried.' Trixie gathered the rest of their things and followed. 'We spoke to them about wandering off.'

'Then they will be punished.' Caroline placed the baskets in the back of the cart. 'Where have you looked?'

'The whole of the high street.' Trixie turned as Jacob and Mr Cavendish joined them.

'Nothing.' Jacob took off his hat and brushed his fingers through his hair.

'We need to ask people to help search,' said Mr Cavendish.

'I'll go home and see if they've wandered back there.' Caroline clicked for the dogs to jump up into the back of the cart and gathering her skirts hoisted herself into the seat. 'If they aren't at home, I'll return here.'

Trixie watched her go, praying that the girls had gone home. She was torn between anger and worry. At the moment, anger was winning. 'I'll walk around behind the church and down to the cattle yards,' she told the men.

'I'll walk the stream.' Jacob jogged off.

Mr Cavendish gave her a small smile. 'I will ride down the hill towards the pit cottages. They might be playing with some children there.'

'Thank you. I need to speak to their friend, Florrie. I doubt the girls would have gone in some stranger's cart.'

'The other girl might be mistaken? We will find them, try not to worry.'

She nodded and set off, embarrassed that her sisters were

causing all this fuss. They would be cleaning out the pigsty, Dossy's stall and doing every other awful job on the farm for embarrassing her.

Trixie wasn't sure which cottage Florrie lived in but saw Reverend Porter leaving the churchyard and crossing the market square. 'Reverend Porter!'

'Good afternoon. It's Miss Wilkes, isn't it?' He seemed in a hurry and barely stopped walking as Trixie stepped alongside of him.

'Yes, I am. I'm looking for my two sisters, Elsie and Bertha.'

'Elsie and Bertha? They are missing?' he repeated in surprise.

'We've been searching for them for a while now. Florrie told our Jacob they got into someone's cart, but I want to ask her myself. Only I don't know where she lives.'

'Florrie…? Florrie Winthrop? She attends Sunday school with your sisters.'

'Yes.'

'Florrie lives with her grandparents at the bottom of the hill. The cottage with roses over the front fence. The gate is broken, so be careful.' He patted her arm. 'I really must go. I'm to visit a dying man.' He rushed off along the lane leading out of the village between the cobbler's house and another old cottage.

Taking the high street, Trixie nearly ran down the hill to the cottage with the rambling roses over its front fence. She fumbled with the gate latch and finally knocked on the door of the rundown house.

'Aye?' A little girl no more than three years old answered, jam smeared around her mouth.

'Is Florrie here?'

An older man came to stand behind the small child. 'Aye, our Florrie's here. What ye be wanting with her?'

'She's friends with my sisters, Elsie and Bertha. I can't find them.'

'They ain't here, lass,' the old man said kindly, missing most of his teeth in a face full of a grey shaggy beard. He shouted over his shoulder. 'Florrie!'

Florrie, older than the other child by a good five years, appeared wiping her hands on a cloth. 'Aye, Grandpa?'

'This 'ere lass is lookin' for her sisters.' Grandpa motioned towards Trixie.

'Elsie an' Bertha ain't here, Miss Wilkes,' Florrie said.

'Where did they go?' Trixie asked, trying to keep the urgency out of her voice and remain calm.

'They climbed into a cart.'

'Whose cart?' Trixie wanted to shake the girl for giving her drops of information.

'I dunno. I've never seen the men before.'

'Men?' Trixie's blood iced in her veins. 'Men?'

'What men, lass?' her grandpa asked, his hand on her thin shoulder.

'I dunno, Grandpa.' Florrie looked ready to cry. 'I didn't hear what they said to them.'

'Which way did they go?' asked the old man.

'The York Road.'

Trixie stared in horror. The York Road... York... Dolan... Had Dolan found them? 'Oh God!' She fled the cottage, lifting her skirts high, she ran up the hill. 'Jacob! Jacob!' She kept calling for him as she raced into the market square.

Mr Cavendish found her first. 'What has happened?'

'They've been taken!' She bent over, panting. 'Two men, in a cart, York Road.'

Jacob hurried over to them and she repeated the painful words. 'We must hurry, but Caroline has the cart.'

'I'll run to the farm and get the cart.' Jacob sprinted away.

'Miss Wilkes, can you ride a horse?' Mr Cavendish asked.

'No.' She brushed away the tears gathering in her eyes.

'Will you ride behind me on my horse? We can meet Jacob at the crossroad near the farm.'

Although she'd never ridden a horse in her life, Trixie nodded and quickly followed him to where his horse was stabled behind the inn.

'We will find the girls.' Mr Cavendish mounted his horse and then pulled Trixie up behind him. 'Hold on.'

CHAPTER 9

*C*aroline drove Dossy away from the village and along the dirt road towards the farm. The afternoon sun was dipping low, the sky streaked with dusky pink and orange. Her mind was occupied with the rent increase and how they would pay it. Mussy said they'd manage, but she didn't have his confidence. Wayland wanted to ruin her, she knew that. He wanted to punish her for speaking out to him, for defying his authority, for not bowing to his superiority. She should have kept quiet that day by the creek. When would she learn to act meek and subservient as Trixie did? Was there something wrong with her for not acting as other women did? Had her convent education opened her mind to thoughts that shouldn't be there? Had the time of living in her uncle's house given her too much freedom so she could never accept a man's control? But what of her carefree marriage to Hugh, a man who had never demanded anything from her, had that ruined her mind, given her ideas above her station as a working-class woman?

As a widow she had even more independence, more

authority over her life, was that proving wrong, making her assertive in her behaviour, her opinions? Women should be obedient, docile, and she used to be once. In the convent she'd listened to the nuns, said her prayers, worked hard at all the tasks set for her. However, somewhere, lying dormant was this other Caroline she'd become, one who had a mind, stubbornness and even ruthlessness. This new Caroline had grown stronger after Hugh's death, after the ordeal of living in York. The new Caroline had smothered the meek one… and now she was paying the consequences.

Ahead she saw a wagon stopped by the side of the road a mile or so from the farm. In amazement she saw Elsie and Bertha sitting on the seat beside the driver and a man crouching in the back.

Slowing Dossy down, Caroline's anger at the girls leaving the market rose. 'Elsie! Bertha!' She climbed down from the cart. 'What do you think you're doing? Get down at once.'

The crouching man jumped out of the wagon as Caroline approached. 'Are you Caroline Lawson?'

'Yes. Who are you?' She glanced at him, a stranger, before glaring at the girls. 'Get down. We've been looking for you two. You're both in so much trouble.'

'That man said you'd told him to take us home,' Elsie cried, pointing at the driver.

Suddenly, the innocence of the event dropped from Caroline like a stone. She stared at the brute of a man standing in front of her and at the seated driver. Her heart raced. They knew her name. She swallowed down her panic. 'Get down, girls.'

'They aren't going nowhere,' the ugly brute said, advancing on Caroline. 'They and you are coming with us.'

Fear crept up her spine like a trail of ants. She stepped

around the vile man, dressed in dirty working clothes, and quickly stormed over to the wagon. 'Girls, get down.'

'I don't think so.' The driver kept a grip on Bertha's arm and one hand on the reins.

Bertha tried to wrench her arm free as Elsie cried harder.

'Let them go.' Rage burned through Caroline. Prince and Duke leapt down from the cart, growling at the man nearest to her. 'Let those girls go or my dogs will tear you both into shreds.'

Standing in front of her, the ugly man's face twisted in evil humour, his bent and squashed nose had been broken in many a fight. Slowly he withdrew a knife from his boot. 'One move from those dogs and I'll gut them.'

Pure hatred clawed at Caroline. More men who used pain and torture to control her. 'Why do you want the girls?'

'We don't. They were bait,' the driver sniggered. 'For you.'

A gasp broke from her. 'Girls, run!'

Elsie screamed and half-fell, from the wagon's seat. She cried out when she landed on the ground, but scrambled to her feet, getting tangled in her petticoats. Bertha bit the driver's arm and he yanked his hand back with a loud howl. Bertha dashed to the edge of the seat and jumped, landing in the ditch by the side of the road.

'Go!' Caroline yelled, needing to get the girls to safety. She spun around to her dogs. 'Prince. Duke. Home! Take the girls home!' The two dogs seemed confused for a moment, wanting to protect her but also do as she bid.

The man on the road lunged for Caroline. She fought him, trying to see if the girls had got away. Prince and Duke were confused, not knowing who to protect. The driver climbed down and kicked at Prince who yelped.

'Home, Prince. Home, Duke!' Caroline screamed, watching

the girls stumble across the fields. The dogs hesitated as she fought both men. 'Home!' She yelled, desperate to be free, but needing to make sure the girls would be safe. 'Away home!' she commanded the dogs. Finally, they raced away to the girls.

Abruptly, the cold edge of a steel blade was at her throat, and she stilled.

'Now, enough of all the nonsense,' the brute with the knife whispered in her ear. 'Get the ties, Herb,' he instructed the driver. 'We'll tie this wildcat up.'

Caroline panted, her heart thumping in her chest. 'You'll not get away with this.'

'We'll see about that, my beauty.' He chuckled and lowered the knife so he could hold her with both hands.

Sensing an opportunity to flee, Caroline twisted and pushed at his chest. She ran a few steps before the driver, Herb, younger and faster than the brute, caught her on the other side of the ditch.

'I got her, Buck,' he shouted, manhandling Caroline back to the wagon.

Buck, the brute, sneered at Caroline then punched her on the side of her head.

The world went black.

* * *

CAROLINE JERKED awake and instantly gagged at the rag in her mouth. Darkness consumed her. Something was over her face, a canvas sack she couldn't take off as her hands were tied. She panicked, mumbled, thrashing.

'Shut up back there!' a male voice reached her.

She lay still, listening, rocking with the motion of the wagon she was in. Pain throbbed in her temple where Buck had punched her, knocking her out. Taking slow breaths through her nose, Caroline had to keep calm. Her eyes adjusted to the bag over her face, and daylight filtered through little rips in the canvas. She was lying on her back and carefully rolled over onto her side. The gag tasted foul, and her mouth filled with saliva, for a moment she panicked again. She closed her eyes and counted to ten until her breathing calmed.

How long had she been unconscious? Had the girls reached the farm? Had Prince and Duke kept them safe? Tears filled her eyes, remembering the frightened faces of Elsie and Bertha. Were these two men acting alone? Were there other men waiting at the farm to take the girls and Trixie? Why did they want her?

Noise grew over the sound of the wagon wheels and the horse's hoofbeats. Caroline heard a bird squawk, vehicle traffic and a distant boat horn. They were near a river. York?

Her head cleared at the sound of boots on cobbles, of hawkers calling out, of factory whistles screeching.

York.

Victor Dolan. He'd found them. A sob caught in her throat.

The wagon halted. 'I'll throw that sheet of canvas over her,' Buck said. 'We can't risk anyone seeing our cargo.'

'I'll be glad to get rid of her. I'm ready for a drink and no mistake,' Herb replied.

The canvas sheet covered Caroline, blocking out the light. Her head banged against something hard as they jolted along. She vaguely remembered the wagon having some crates in the back. She kicked out a little, her boot connecting with something firm.

The noise of the city grew louder, the wagon stopped and

started, lurching her back and forwards until finally it stopped.

'Where are we to put her?'

'In the cellar.'

The canvas sheet was flung from her and hands grabbed her arms, hauling her out of the back of the wagon.

'Don't try anything, wildcat,' Buck growled in her ear.

'Please let me go,' she begged.

'Not likely.'

She stumbled blindly as they dragged her along, their grips like vices. She knocked into one of them, who cursed.

'Take her bloody hood off so she can walk,' Herb complained. 'We'll all be dead at the bottom of the stairs at this rate.'

Caroline listened intently. Stairs. A cellar.

Suddenly, the hood was whipped off her head, pulling some of her hair pins out as well. Her hair fell about her shoulders. She had no idea where her bonnet was.

They stood on a landing just inside a doorway leading straight off a narrow lane. She was roughly escorted down the dimly lit staircase and along a deep cellar that had arches at intervals. Wine racks and barrels filled most of the arched recesses. The smell of brandy and dampness was strong in her nose.

'In here.' Buck opened a door at the end of the cellar to a darkened room. Buck let her go but Herb still had her other arm. Buck struck a match and lit a lamp on a wooden table. Golden light circled the room, showing the brick walls, the wooden floor. A mattress was in the corner and a bucket. The table and a chair were the only other pieces of furniture.

Herb flung Caroline onto the mattress while Buck left the room. She landed with a thump on her bottom.

When Buck returned, he held a jug and a tin cup. 'Water.' He placed it on the table. 'We'll be back later. Don't start screaming. No one can hear you down here. Above is a pub and next to it an ironmonger who has a forge out the back. You'll not be heard over the racket he makes hammering all day.'

'What's going to happen to me?' she asked as Buck used his knife to cut the rope around her wrists.

'No idea. That's not for us to decide.'

'Then who?'

'Our boss.'

'Who is?' she asked, but she already knew.

'Victor Dolan.'

Confirmation of it only heightened Caroline's fear. 'Please, please, let me go. I'll tell no one. I'll move away, emigrate, anything, just let me go, please.'

Buck laughed without humour. 'If we let you go, we'd end up at the bottom of the Ouse.'

They walked out, and she flinched as the lock struck into place. She paced the cellar, looking up at the tiny slit of the only window in the room and wondered what to do. She had to get out of here. Could she reason with Dolan? In her heart she realised Dolan wouldn't have taken this risk only to let her go. She'd escaped him once, he wouldn't allow it a second time.

Dolan would show her no mercy. She would have to fight for her life.

* * *

MAX DREW BACK on Queenie's reins as they entered Hopewood Farm's yard. With one arm he carefully lowered Miss Wilkes to the ground just as the kitchen door opened and the girls came rushing out, crying. Relief poured out of Max as he dismounted. 'They have returned!'

Miss Wilkes hugged her sisters, crying with them. They were all talking at once.

When Mr Casey came to the door, looking like death Max went to him. 'I am pleased the girls are safe.'

Mr Casey grabbed Max's arm causing him to startle. 'Caro. The men took Caro.' He began coughing, holding a handkerchief to his mouth.

'What did you say?' Miss Wilkes gaped at him.

Elsie wailed. 'They've taken Caroline.'

Max's heart seemed to plummet to his boots. 'Mrs Lawson? They have taken her? Who has?' He couldn't comprehend what he was hearing.

'Oh, dear God.' Miss Wilkes covered her face with her hands.

'It'll be Do-Dolan,' Mr Casey choked out.

'We must go!' Max strode for Queenie, raging that his lovely Caroline had been abducted.

They turned as Jacob drove the cart into the yard. 'This was abandoned by the side of the road,' he said, smiling at the girls. 'You little minxes. Where have you been?'

Trixie rushed over to him. 'Jacob, Dolan's men have taken Caro.'

The smile dropped from his face to be replaced with a look of horror. 'Dolan has found us.'

'We can waste no more time.' Max mounted Queenie, turning her about.

'Wait, we'll come with you.' Miss Wilkes dithered for a moment, then ran to the girls. 'You're to stay with Mussy.' She gripped Elsie's arms. 'I'm trusting you to keep the farm going, do your work, help care for Mussy. Understand?'

Elsie nodded tearfully.

Mr Casey held up his hand. 'No one needs to care for me as I am going with you.'

'No, Mussy, you're too ill. Our cloaks.' She ran into the house and came out again just as quickly carrying two brown cloaks. 'Caroline will need a cloak, it'll be dark soon.'

'Miss Wilkes!' Max was eager to be gone. There was no time for any of this.

'Stop, all of you!' Mr Casey stood tall and straight not stooped over as he'd started to do. 'We simply cannot go charging into York without a plan. We must be clever. Cleverer than Dolan. Let us go into the kitchen and talk.' He turned and moved inside without waiting for an answer.

Max dismounted and strode into the kitchen and stood at the table, frustrated at the delay but knowing Mr Casey was correct. They needed a plan.

Miss Wilkes sent her sisters into the other room and the four of them faced each other.

'We must play this with a careful hand,' Mr Casey said.

'Informing the police is the first step,' Max stated.

Jacob shook his head. 'We don't know who we can trust. Dolan has some of them in his pocket.'

Miss Wilkes clasped her hands together, her face pale with worry. 'Dolan will want to sell Caroline to his gentlemen friends. That's what he wanted to do before. She's so pretty and like a lady, so he knew he'd get a good price for her.'

Max fought hard not to swear in rage.

'She might be at one of his brothels?' Jacob suggested.

'No, Dolan will keep Caroline away from those places. He'll command a high price and for that he'll need her somewhere nice, presentable...' Miss Wilkes frowned. 'A private residence.'

'His own place?' Jacob asked.

A cold shiver came over Max. 'No, probably private rooms in a gentleman's club.'

Mr Casey sighed deeply. 'Yes.'

'Right, well, our Sarah said he had a club, but didn't know where. There's a gentleman's club on Blake Street. I did a bit of building work on it a few years back. Dolan might have bought into it,' Jacob said, scratching his head in thought.

'Dunlop's.' Mr Casey nodded, breathing heavily. 'And Field and Watts at the end of Lord Mayor's Walk. There's a few lesser-known ones, too. I am a member of Dunlop's.'

'What if Dolan has his own club, one we're not aware of? One that isn't a part of the established ones?' Miss Wilkes spoke quietly.

'It is possible.' Mr Casey looked at Max. 'The thing is those clubs are gentlemen only. So, you and I will have to be the ones to go. I can introduce you as a potential member.'

'That is what we shall do.' Max's head throbbed. They had to hurry.

'You will need to wear more than tweeds, my good man.' Mr Casey gave Max a glimmer of a smile.

'I will return to the abbey and collect my dinner suit and the carriage. Mr Casey will fare better in the carriage than in an open cart.' Max headed for the door, but Mr Casey touched his arm.

'Please call me, Mussy. I think we are past the formalities, do you not agree?'

Max patted his back gently. 'And I am Max. I will return as soon as I can.'

'We need to take the girls to Annie's,' Miss Wilkes said.

Jacob stepped around the table. 'While you get ready, I'll see to the animals.'

Max cantered Queenie along the roads to the estate. He entered the stables at the abbey in a dash of flying pebbles. John, the groom took Queenie's reins from him as he dismounted. 'I will need the carriage, John, immediately. Tell Trivett, it will be an overnight stay in York.' He spoke of the carriage driver.

'Of course, sir.'

'Also, have a message taken up to the house that I shan't be joining his lordship for dinner and send my apologies.'

'Very good, sir. Your brother has also cancelled so I hear. We were prepared to stable his horse for the night.'

Max gave Thomas a few seconds of thought. Thomas was acting strangely of late, and he needed to find out what it was all about, but that was a problem for another day. He sprinted through the arch in the wall and across a spread of lawn to his cottage hidden from the house by a broad sweep of trees and gardens. It took him only minutes to locate all he needed to dress as a gentleman and pack into a leather case.

It was a crushed trip from the farm to Annie's cottage in the village. The girls sat on Miss Wilkes and Jacob's laps opposite Mussy and Max. Thankfully, Annie welcomed the girls without a fuss and wished them godspeed as they left.

Twilight descended over the land as the carriage rumbled through the countryside. Max's mind circled in many directions with no clear thought. Some bastard had taken the one woman he cared about. A villain he'd never met or even seen. Dolan was an unknown assailant to him. How was he to find the scoundrel? And if he did find him, how would he convince the blackguard to give him Caroline?

Max felt sick at the thought of her being harmed and

mistreated. She deserved to be given kindness and care. He knew she didn't share the same emotions about him as he did for her, and being patient wasn't a strong virtue for him, but he needed to wait for her to be ready to see him as a man she might come to love. At least he hoped she would come to that. Longing for someone who saw you only as a friend was difficult. Caroline had gone through enough in the last few years without him demanding affection before she had the time to feel it.

Yet, this mad dash to York felt as though things had to change. Caroline needed protecting. Yes, she was headstrong and independent and very capable, but Max sensed a vulnerability underneath. Lately she'd been distant with him, developed a hard shell. He didn't understand why when he'd helped her so much with the farm. Something wasn't right. However, now Caroline faced a great danger and who knew how she'd recover from it?

The city streets crept out to greet them as they left the countryside and entered the outskirts of York. Darkness was nearly complete with golden glows appearing in houses as they passed. A streetlamp lighter was walking on stilts to ignite each gas lamp.

They rattled over Ouse Bridge. He glanced at the city on the opposite side of the river and wondered where in its bowels did Caroline dwell. Boats plied the inky black river, their lights shimmering on the surface, or were moored to the wharfs and docks along the river. Singing rang out from one of the nearby public houses and the cobbles echoed with the noise of the footfall of hundreds of boots. Vehicles of many descriptions pulled by horses criss-crossed the bridge slowing them down as the streets became congested.

'I have told Trivett to stable the carriage and horses at the

Black Swan Hotel on Coney Street,' Max said as the carriage made its way up Low Ousegate, passing St Michael's Church. Max sent up a quick prayer that they would find Caroline tonight.

Turning left along Spurriergate, Max kept his gaze on the people walking past, searching their face for Caroline. Along Coney Street, Trivett drove the carriage through an arch and around to the back of the Black Swan Hotel. Max left him to arrange stabling for the two horses and the carriage.

In the hotel, they asked for rooms and were told there was only one.

'I don't need a room,' Jacob said. 'I'll walk the streets all night and try to find out what I can.'

'Me, too,' Miss Wilkes added.

'It's not safe,' Jacob warned Miss Wilkes. 'We don't need to be looking for two of you.'

'I'll stay with you,' Miss Wilkes argued. 'I'll not spend the night going mad in this room wondering what's happening.'

Max changed his clothes behind the screen. 'Where do we start?' Max asked when he emerged dressed in his finery. He wasn't as familiar with York as they were, especially the back-streets and the narrow lanes inhabited by thieves and vagabonds.

Miss Wilkes appeared pale and edgy. 'This is the first time I've been back since we escaped Dolan.'

'Nothing will happen to you. I won't let it,' Jacob told her before giving Max his attention. 'What I heard when I was visiting our Sarah was that Dolan had gone up in the world. He's got in with some monied gentlemen. He gets them what they want, and they keep him out of jail.'

Max took a deep breath and nodded. 'Then let us go and

enter the world of the dubious gentlemen that call Dolan, friend.'

THE SQUEAK of a rat woke Caroline from where she dozed sitting on the mattress, her head resting on her bent knees. In the dimly lit corners of the cellar, several rats scampered back and forth, lifting their pointy noses to sniff the air, scenting her.

She stood, shaking out her skirts, sending the rats bolting for the holes in the brickwork. No daylight showed outside the little window. Her stomach grumbled with hunger. She'd used the bucket to relieve herself and the smell of urine hung heavy in the air. Her skirt and bodice were dirty, her hair a tumbled mess about her head and welts appeared on her arms and legs from lice bites.

Voices drifted to her from the other side of the door. She watched in dread as the lock turned and the door opened. Buck entered first, carrying a bucket of water and a small basket of items. Behind him, Herb carried a tray of food, the smell of which made Caroline's stomach rumble again.

Then, before anyone spoke, Dolan strolled in. Caroline thought she'd faint as he grinned at her.

'Now isn't this lovely?' Dolan drawled. 'Mrs Lawson, we meet again.'

Caroline gripped her skirts in fear as she stared at his hideous face, a face she had scratched the first time he held her captive, a face that had become deformed with ugly raised scars, which zagged down his cheeks in shades of red, pink and white. The expensive black suit he wore, the woollen long coat, the black highly polished boots, the jaunty angle of his top hat did nothing to draw the attention away from his disfigured face. She had done that.

They weighed each other up in silence, with equal hate.

She knew he'd never let her escape this time. She faced a man who had wealth now, and position. Gone was the smelly, dirty brothel keeper she had met that fateful night. Dolan had transformed into a gentleman, or as close as he could come to being one. She wouldn't be amazed if outside he had a carriage and pair waiting for him as well.

'So, Mrs Lawson.' Dolan waved towards the tray of food. 'We have brought you something to eat.'

Caroline refused to speak.

'There is also water and soap to wash yourself.' Dolan gave Herb a nod, and the younger man sauntered out and returned with a gown of silk in the colour of burnt orange edged with ruffles of white lace and large orange material flowers. Herb held matching slippers.

'I wasn't certain what colour to choose for you. I want you to stand out in a crowd.' Dolan peered at the dress. 'It is pretty, yes?'

She thought the dress was awful, but she wouldn't say a word to him.

Undeterred by her silence, Dolan continued. 'You will eat and then wash yourself, arrange your hair. When I come back in an hour, I want you wearing that dress. Tonight is a special night.' He grinned. 'But more on that later.' Dolan walked to the door and paused. 'One thing. If you're not ready when I return, I will cut off one of your toes.'

Her heart thumped.

'You see, you're worth a great deal of money to me, so I can't destroy your face as you've destroyed mine, but I can hurt you in other ways. Missing toes…' He shrugged. 'They can be covered with stockings and not deter from your loveliness. So, that is what I'll start with. However, if you continue to disobey me after that, I'll return to your little farm and, one by one, hurt those you love, starting with those little girls. Understand?'

Caroline choked back a whimper but refused to take her eyes away from him.

Dolan chuckled. 'I've never met anyone as beautiful as you, or as spirited. This is going to be entertaining.'

The lock fell into place behind the three of them and Caroline fell to her knees. Although she trembled, her eyes were dry of tears. Crying would weaken her. She had to think.

A rat poked its head out of a hole, sniffing the air, smelling the food. Quickly she stepped to the table and lifted the cover from the plate of food. Potatoes and slices of roast meat, swimming in gravy. Caroline ate it all, washing it down with a cup of water. She needed food for energy to beat Dolan.

Once she'd finished eating, she untied her skirt, pulling it down over her petticoat and shift and unbuttoned her bodice. She scrubbed herself, irritating the lice bites on her skin making her itch. The orange silk was cold, slithering over her but the dress fitted her shape well. It was the ugliest and most expensive dress she'd ever worn. In the little basket she found a comb and hair pins. By the time her hair was brushed and rolled into some form of shape at the back of her head and she changed her boots for the slippers, she was exhausted with nervous tension.

Dolan had her dressed up for his clients, she had no doubt of that. This evening, she'd be very likely taken against her will, more than once, and she'd have to bear it the best she could. She'd survived Wayland's violation, she'd had no choice, but at least this time she'd be prepared. In no way would she give Dolan an excuse to hurt the girls or Trixie. She'd suffer anything rather than be responsible for them being tortured.

Dolan whistled low when he returned and saw her. 'My, you're a beautiful woman, Caroline.'

'You have no right to call me that. I'm Mrs Lawson to you.' She held her head high, back straight.

'I'll call you whatever I damn well like, madam.' He punched her hard in the stomach.

Caroline fell to her knees with the blow, her breath stuck in her lungs. Pain spread throughout her stomach, and she fought for air.

'That was very satisfying,' Dolan gloated. 'I've been wanting to do that to you since the day you escaped my lodging.'

He waited a moment, then pulled her up to her feet. 'We don't want that pretty dress getting spoiled now, do we?' He brushed down her skirts. 'Tidy yourself.'

Shaking, Caroline re-pinned her hair, her breathing shallow. Her corset felt too tight as she struggled to calm down. Tears pricked her eyes, but she blinked them away.

'This won't do!' Dolan grabbed her hand and tugged off her wedding ring.

'What are you doing!' She fought him, desperate to keep the wedding ring that Hugh had given her on that magical day.

'You're not wearing this!' Stronger than her, he easily held her arm and pulled the ring off her finger and placed it in his pocket.

'Give it back to me, please. I'll hide it. I won't wear it,' she begged, distraught. That ring was her most valuable possession. Even when she was starving and without hope, she'd never considered pawning her ring. It was all she had of her marriage to Hugh.

Dolan gripped her arm, his deformed face sneering inches from hers. 'You'll behave this evening or there'll be consequences. Understand? Losing a ring will be the least of your problems.'

Caroline stumbled against him up the steep stairs as he pulled her along in the dark. The dress was too long, and she had to keep lifting it to walk. Once in the narrow lane, he fished the ring out of his pocket and dropped it through a drain grate.

'No!' She dashed to the grate only for Dolan to jerk her back to his side.

'Your old life is over.' He smirked.

Fighting back the tears, she glanced around trying to get an idea where in York she was. She needed to run, to hide, to escape this beast. She had done it once before, surely it would be possible to do it again.

'Don't worry about trying to work out where you are, Caroline.' Dolan sniggered. 'You'll not be coming back here. After tonight you'll have a whole new life.'

Outwardly she showed him no reaction, but inside she quaked at the ordeal ahead. What would this night bring? Where was Dolan taking her? To some grimy brothel in the backstreets?

In the carriage he gripped her wrist, a jubilant grin on his disfigured face.

Caroline turned away and watched the shadowy city streets. She recognised Aldwark before they turned into Goodramgate, then Deangate and drove past The Minster. On High Petergate they had to wait for the road to clear of a spilt cart load of vegetables. Caroline wished she was able to jump out of the carriage, but Dolan kept his fingers tight around her wrist.

'How did you find me?' the words broke from her.

Dolan gave her a long look. 'A stroke of luck actually, or fate. Who knows? A stranger found me and told me where you were living. I sent a man disguised as a tinker to make sure he was telling the truth.'

The tinker who sharpened their knives. Caroline closed her eyes in despair.

'It seems you have made another enemy, Caroline. A gentleman who seems to hate you as much as I do.'

'A gentleman?'

'Yes, he was a stranger to me, but not to you. Lord Stockton-Lee.' Dolan grinned. 'I fear he doesn't like you very much, my dear.'

Astonished, Caroline clenched her fists in anger. Wayland! Hadn't he done enough to hurt and humiliate her? How did she deserve all of this? Simply because she had stood up to him, called him out on his conduct? She wished she'd never spoken to the man, never laid eyes on him.

When the carriage halted before a splendid stone building on Marygate near the ornate church of St Olave's, Caroline's breathing grew fast in fear.

Suddenly, Dolan gripped Caroline's chin, forcing her to stare into his ugly face. 'Remember, be on your best behaviour. You're not some slut off the street and these men inside are not dock workers. This is fine society you're entering, and I expect you to behave accordingly.'

Fine society? Caroline's mind raced as he escorted her up the steps and inside. A maid collected Dolan's coat, but he'd forgotten to bring a cape for Caroline and for a moment he'd looked annoyed at the mistake. He yanked her hand through his left arm and turned to the double doors on their right, which were opened by a footman.

'Behave, and you'll live,' he murmured.

Caroline's stomach churned as they walked into an elegant room filled with gentlemen. Their chatter ceased as they all turned to stare at her. Her knees wobbled. About twenty gentlemen of varying ages stood or sat in small groups, drinking, smoking and a few played cards at a table at the far end of the room. Two young footmen held trays of drinks while black-dressed maids attended a long table displaying platters of food.

Dolan shook hands with the three gentlemen standing nearest to them. 'This is Caroline,' he told them proudly as though speaking of a wife.

Caroline held her chin high, her expression tight. Her gaze was full of disdain.

The gentlemen murmured something but as the chatter in the room reignited, she found it difficult to hear the mumbles and didn't care. She was ignored as the men talked and she took the opportunity to scan the room. Doors led off where the footmen came and left. Was it possible to escape through one of those doors?

'Don't even think about trying to leave,' Dolan whispered in her ear.

She jumped slightly.

'You'll be continually watched all night. So, relax and enjoy.' He passed her a glass of champagne.

Caroline turned away from him, sipping the sparkling drink simply because she was thirsty. Surprisingly, she liked the taste, her first try of such an expensive drink. However, she wasn't stupid. She had to keep a clear head.

'Now, Dolan, an introduction if you please?' A weedy

gentleman with a riot of curly hair which, even though liberally coated in hair oil, had started to spring from his head, sidled up to Caroline.

'Perry, this is Caroline. The lady I was telling you about.'

'You did not exaggerate her beauty, Dolan.'

'I told you the truth, Perry, that she would be worth your money, but you must outbid every man here.' Dolan preened like a peacock. 'I make good on my promises.'

Caroline stiffened. She was being sold to the highest bidder.

'Madam, a pleasure to meet you.' Perry bowed low. 'You are a delight.'

She inclined her head slightly.

'Excuse us, Perry.' Dolan grinned. 'I need to show Caroline off to the room. You're not the only gentleman wanting to see the goods.'

For the next hour, Caroline was paraded about the room like prime horseflesh at a market. Lust glowed in the men's eyes as she passed. They whispered between each other, and her humiliation grew. Ridiculous figures were mentioned for her.

'Why would these men spend that much money for me, for one night?' she asked Dolan when he paused between two groups of card players.

'One night?' Dolan laughed, his cheeks flushed. 'They aren't buying you for a night, Caroline, but for life. You'll be the winning bidder's mistress.' He shrugged. 'For how long they keep you is up to them and what they do to you after they've finished with you is none of my concern. My wish is they throw you in the gutter where you belong, or the river, I don't care which. It's the least you deserve.'

Rage burned deep in her chest. 'I scratched your face

because you were attacking me. All this is *your* doing. Your disfigurement is because of *your* actions!'

'Keep your voice down,' he growled between his discoloured teeth. 'You destroyed my face and I'll destroy you in return.' He grasped her hand and hauled her along to a corner. 'Stay here while I conduct a bit of business.' He beckoned Perry. 'Ah, my good man, do me a favour and look after Caroline for me, will you? Don't let her out of your sight.'

'Absolutely, Dolan.' Perry lounged against the back of an armchair and gazed at Caroline through a haze of cigar smoke. 'How did someone as pretty as you end up in this position?'

'Dolan kidnapped me.'

Perry's eyes widened. 'Kidnapped? That is interesting. He told us all that he found you in distress because you were homeless and friendless. A governess who had lost her position.'

She chuckled at that. 'I was a married woman, to a farmer. My husband died, and I came to York to look for work. I knocked at Dolan's lodging not knowing it was one of his houses of ill repute. He attacked me and I scratched his face which became infected and scarred.' She gave him a look of pure loathing. 'This is his revenge.'

Perry stared at her. 'Fascinating.'

'Everything Dolan has told you is a lie,' she said. 'If I was you, I wouldn't trust a word he says. He grew up in the Water Lanes. He's not of your class or breeding. Why would you even entertain him in your society?'

Perry shrugged. 'We understand exactly who he is. However, he is wealthy, and he has something on each and every man in this room. His hold over us makes us his puppets.'

'But surely, if you all came together you could get rid of him?'

Perry finished the last mouthful of his champagne. 'No one is willing for if we were to fail, the consequences would be ruin for us all.' His expression was one of resignation. 'You should know better than anyone how Dolan never forgets, never forgives.'

Caroline glanced about the room, planning how she might escape. Was there anyone willing to help her? She needed another brave person like Trixie had been that day when she'd rescued her. Only Caroline was aware that you didn't meet two people like Trixie in one lifetime. Someone willing to risk everything for another…

* * *

MAX GLANCED at Mussy in the streetlight. Mussy was dressed splendidly in a dark blue and white pin-stripe suit with a gold silk waistcoat and a ruby red cravat. Max's black suit looked dull by comparison. His stomach churned with nervous anticipation of what was to come.

'While you two are at the club, me and Trixie will speak to Mr Bent to see if he's heard anything about Dolan,' Jacob said. 'After that, we'll visit some of the brothels.'

A man lurched out of a darkened doorway and Miss Wilkes jumped and screamed. Jacob pulled her against him as Max pushed the stumbling man away.

'A drunk,' Max reassured Miss Wilkes.

Miss Wilkes held onto Jacob. 'This is a nightmare I can't wake from. Dolan has Caroline and if he sees me, he'll want to kill me as well.'

'You're safe,' Jacob soothed.

'We need to find her, Jacob, and then move away.' Miss Wilkes looked anxiously about the street.

Max took a misstep. 'Move away?'

'If we snatch Caroline from Dolan again, he'll want to kill us all. We can't stay near York. Once we have Caroline back, we've got to go far away from here.' Miss Wilkes stopped walking, tears running down her cheeks. 'What if we don't find her in time?' she sobbed. 'Dolan has her tonight. I can imagine what he's putting her-her through.' Miss Wilkes shuddered. 'Caroline will never be the same again when we do find her, if we find her,' she cried. 'Even now it might be too late and the Caroline we love is gone.' She wept into Jacob's shoulder.

A deep burning fury engulfed Max. 'Then we can waste no more time. We will search every building in this city until we find where Caroline is.'

Miss Wilkes dried her eyes and turned a miserable face to him. 'Someone will die from all this.'

Max clenched his jaw, his shoulders stiffening. 'Then it will be Dolan.'

He and Mussy left them at the corner of New Street and headed for Gillygate. At the club, Mussy straightened his stooped back. He looked at Max. 'You are my friend from university.'

Max nodded. 'Recently moved here from Lincoln.'

'Nephew of the late Lord Stockton-Lee.' Mussy cleared his throat, fighting a coughing fit. 'Let us face the wolves.'

'Ah, Mr Casey. This is a pleasant surprise,' the doorman greeted him. 'We believed you had moved away.'

'And I have, dear Nelson, but I have returned for a few days with my friend, Mr Maxwell Cavendish, of Lincoln.' Mussy shook the doorman's hand. 'How have you been?'

'Well, sir, well.' Nelson ushered Mussy and Max further into the foyer where a youth dressed in green and gold livery took their coats. 'Is Mr Cavendish looking to become a member, Mr Casey?'

'He is, Nelson. Is Sir Lionel here this evening?'

'Yes, he's dining as we speak but, no doubt, he will join you both in the drawing room afterwards. I'll mention your arrival.'

Mussy slipped Nelson a few coins. 'Thank you, Nelson.'

Climbing the wide staircase, Max was reminded of the club his father attended in Lincoln, one neither he nor Thomas had the opportunity to join. How different would his life have been if his parents had lived and he'd not been whisked away to the abbey after their funeral? Although a young man when his parents died, he'd been busy at university and not had the chance to forge a path of his own. Instead, he'd returned to the abbey after finishing his studies to guide Thomas through their shared grief. How would his life have been if he'd stayed in Lincoln?

Mussy greeted many a gentleman in the drawing room, introducing Max to each one. Sitting in two armchairs by the window, a footman brought them their order of two glasses of whiskey. Mussy crossed his legs, sipping the amber liquid with relish. 'I have missed this.'

'Whiskey?'

'All of it,' Mussy murmured.

Max sat on the edge of his seat. 'Time is wasting, Mussy. We cannot sit here at our leisure.'

'I need to speak with Sir Lionel. He knows everything that's going on in this city. If Dolan is frequenting this, or any, club, Sir Lionel will know about it as he is the president.'

Mussy sipped again and lifted his head as the door opened. 'Here he is now.'

Max watched an older man, fat and sporting large white whiskers enter the room, greeting those closest to him. Max and Mussy stood.

'Mussy!' Sir Lionel yelled at Mussy from across the room. For a large man he was quick on his feet and was soon shaking Mussy's hand vigorously. 'Where have you been, dear fellow? Indeed, we all thought you'd dropped off the face of the earth. I was dumbfounded when you received your sentence. Awful business, awful. I did what I could, dear fellow, I really did, but that old judge was a barbarian indeed, sending a gentleman down. A fine would have been sufficient.'

'Thank you, Sir.' A haunting expression crossed Mussy's face before he shook it off. 'Sir, please let me introduce you to a friend of mine, Mr Maxwell Cavendish, nephew to the late Lord Stockton-Lee.'

'Is that so, indeed?' Sir Lionel pumped Max's hand generously. 'What a pleasure. Indeed, it is. Your late uncle was a fine man. Indeed, he was. A fine man. Was one of the first gentlemen to write a cheque to support this club. Indeed, a fine man. I was disheartened to hear of his death. A tragedy indeed.'

Max wondered how more times the old man would say the word, indeed.

'More drinks!' Sir Lionel waved his hand to a footman and sat down in Max's chair. 'Are you wanting to become a member, Mr Cavendish? With your connections, indeed you would be welcomed. The board meets next Wednesday. I can sponsor you, indeed I shall!'

'Thank you, Sir Lionel.' Max bowed his head. In truth he had no need of gaining membership of such a club. He was far too busy running the estate to spend his time travelling to York to sit around with a group of men who spent their time drinking, reading the newspapers, discussing the state of the world and making business decisions that he had no interest in. He wasn't a wealthy man and although brought up to be a gentleman, his father had lost all their money in bad investments and Max had relied on his uncle's generosity. He was proud to earn his money by being employed by the estate and what's more he enjoyed it.

'I was wondering, Sir Lionel,' Mussy said, sitting opposite. 'Have you heard of a man named Victor Dolan?'

'Dolan?' Sir Lionel grunted. 'That jumped up wastrel. Yes, I have heard of him. Indeed, I have.'

'Is he a member here?'

'Good God no! I refused him!' Sir Lionel's bushy eyebrows rose angrily. 'A cad of the highest order. A common thief. Indeed, a gutter rat. He has no place in this club or in polite society.'

'We need to find him,' Max said with urgency.

'Find him? That blackguard? Why? You do not want to be mixed up with that little weasel. Indeed, you do not!'

'We have no choice,' Mussy said quietly.

'He has taken a friend of ours,' Max told him.

Sir Lionel sat back in alarm. 'Taken?'

'A woman, a respectable woman who he wants to take revenge on. We fear for her life,' Max added. He was conscious of the time going by.

'We cannot go to the police. Dolan has most of them in his pocket,' Mussy said.

'Indeed, he does!' Sir Lionel fumed. 'The scoundrel has blackmailed more men in this city than I can count. Many a good man has found themselves involved in Dolan's schemes and come out of the ordeal coated in humiliation or, at worse, ruined. Something needs to be done about him. That rat goes to ground often.' Sir Lionel tapped his thigh. 'I have heard though that he has his own club on Marygate now because he was kicked out of the others. Imagine a man like that having his own club where he can crow the loudest and strut about like a cock of the walk.'

Max put his empty glass on a side table. 'We should go to Marygate, Mussy.'

'You won't be admitted.' Sir Lionel shook his head. 'Dolan has men on the door.'

Max looked at Sir Lionel. 'I have no intention of going through the front door.'

Sir Lionel blinked in shock, then smiled in shared conspiracy. 'Indeed, my good man, indeed. Wait here. I might be able to help.'

CHAPTER 10

Caroline was starting to tire. Constantly being on edge, watching, waiting, preparing for who knows what took its toll. A clock chimed twelve times. Midnight. One awful day was over and another just beginning. Where would she be by this time tomorrow night? She dreaded to think that far ahead.

As the night wore on, some prostitutes had been brought in. These few women were a higher class than those that walked the streets at night. Their hair was arranged extravagantly, their dresses fine and of good quality.

A jubilant Dolan circled the room, which had become full of drunken men, talking and laughing, his face flushed with good humour. He'd been steadily drinking, not as much as the other men, but several glasses.

'Do you care to sit, Caroline?' Perry asked, coming up from behind.

She turned to him, stiffening in response to his closeness, the fumes of alcohol on his breath. 'I prefer to stand.' In truth her legs ached, but she couldn't let her guard down.

'Come, I insist.' He gently took her elbow and sat her on a chair by the refreshments table.

Caroline perched at the edge, her gaze on Dolan who spoke with a man who fiddled with his gold fob watch hanging on his waistcoat.

'That will be your man,' Perry said regretfully. 'I tried to outbid him, but it was impossible. Fairfield has more money than I.'

'He… He is the successful bidder?' Caroline swallowed in fear. Fairfield was tall, solidly built, wore a dark-brown suit and a thick black beard making him look older than he was. His thick arms looked strong. How would she overpower someone like him? He was a bull of a man.

'Fairfield is not a bad man. I have had many a decent conversation with him,' Perry said as though that should reassure her. 'Made his money in iron. Has a foundry here in York and another in Hull.'

'How did he become associated with Dolan?'

'Both foundries also hold a great deal of imported goods that have come by ship under the nose of the import authorities. York and Hull are easily accessible by boat. Fairfield and Dolan have a business association… evading the tax authority.' Perry gulped from his glass. 'Damn shame though. I was excited to have you as my mistress.'

Caroline's lip curled in disgust 'You would take me against my will? Is that the kind of gentleman you are?'

Perry glanced away. 'I would treat you well.'

'Treating me well would be to let me go free. What would your mother think of her son behaving like this?'

Perry flinched. 'You know nothing about my mother.'

'No woman would want her little boy to grow up to be a

man who treats women like commodities to buy and sell,' Caroline argued.

Two spots of colour appeared on Perry's cheeks. 'There are worse men than me, Caroline.'

'Oh, I realise that.' She glared at Dolan who was laughing uproariously at something Fairfield said. She leant a little closer to Perry, her voice low. 'Will you do right by the boy your mother raised and help me get away from here?'

A glint of something entered his eyes, then quickly disappeared. 'Dolan would kill me. As lovely as you are, you aren't worth dying for. Good luck to you.' He walked away.

Despair filled her and for a moment she didn't care what happened to her. She was tired of being scared, of watching over her shoulder for Dolan's next move. Ever since she first met him on that fateful night last year, he'd been like a ghost haunting her. She'd had enough.

She stood and walked over to a door and opened it. It led to a hallway, and she stepped out into it. Emboldened, she walked along, opening doors. One led to a bedroom where two couples were fornicating, another door led to a back staircase, while another led to a narrow corridor. Caroline hurried down the corridor, hoping it would lead to outside.

'May I ask what you're doing?'

She stopped at the voice behind her and turned around. Fairfield stood at the end of the corridor, a lazy smile on his face.

They stood facing each other, neither taking a step. 'I need the lavatory. Where is it?' she asked in an even tone as though speaking about the weather.

'Most people just use a pot in the corner of the room. One can be provided for you.'

The idea of relieving herself in front of everyone was revolting. 'I want some privacy.'

'That I can provide for you,' he drawled. 'I have my own room.'

She didn't move. 'I hear you are the winning bidder for me.'

'That's true.' He leant against the doorjamb. 'Whether I have paid above the odds is something I'm keen to find out.'

'Trust me, I'm not worth a penny. Dolan is acting as though I'm a virgin sent straight from heaven.'

Fairfield laughed suddenly. 'Yes, he is.'

'I was a wife for two years. Hardly a virgin if that's what you're expecting.'

He grinned. 'I think virgins are overrated.'

Her hopes fell.

Fairfield closed the distance between them. He lifted her chin with a finger and kissed her, not hard or softly, just a kiss.

Caroline kept her eyes open as did he and he smiled. 'You have spirit.'

'I will put a knife through you the minute your back is turned,' she murmured.

He laughed again, a surprisingly cheery laugh. 'Oh, I think you're going to be worth the money I've paid to that pond-dwelling worm.'

She raised her eyebrows in astonishment. 'You don't like Dolan?'

'Nobody does.' Fairfield chuckled. 'No one likes a black-mailer.' He took her hand and led her out of the corridor and up the back staircase.

Caroline's legs began to shake for she knew what was coming. Down another hallway, Fairfield opened one of several doors on this floor and escorted her into a spacious room, dominated by a large, canopied bed. The curtains were drawn, and a small fire glowed in the fireplace. Lamps were positioned on a set of drawers and on a wall table.

'It had begun to rain when I docked on King's Staith,' Fairfield said, adding a short log to the fire.

She didn't care if it was a blizzard out there.

Fairfield searched the room and then stopped to laugh at her quizzical stare. 'I'm looking for knives.'

'I'll use anything I can find as a weapon,' she warned.

In two strides he was in front of her, jerking her hard against his chest. 'You're a spitting cat that needs taming, lass.'

'Tame me? Never!' she flared, hating him.

She twisted her head away when he bent to kiss her, and he swore violently. Panic made her lash out. She hit him on the side of the head, stunning him and herself.

He laughed again and pulled her closer.

Suddenly they heard a commotion within the house.

Fairfield marched to the door and flung it open. Shouts and screams echoed up from downstairs. 'What the hell?'

A shot rang out making them both jump.

'Stay here!' Fairfield commanded.

'I won't!' Caroline ran after him, catching him up at the top of the main staircase that curved down to the grand entrance. Below gentlemen ran about, maids were tripping over their skirts, crying, footmen fleeing.

'Get behind me,' shouted Fairfield, easing down the stairs.

The front door was open and a crude-looking, working-class man stood there brandishing an iron bar, forbidding anyone to leave.

Fairfield grabbed Caroline's wrist and once at the bottom of the stairs, dragged her along to the drawing room, where it

145

seemed an army of young working-class men were fighting with the gentlemen. Glass shattered, chairs were thrown, tables overturned, the noise was fearful.

In amazement, Caroline fell back as Dolan came running out, waving a pistol in each hand, his eyes wild.

'Dolan, what's happening?' Fairfield asked him.

'We're being done over!' Dolan held the pistol to Fairfield's chest. 'I want paying for her, understand? Don't think you can rob me. I'll find you!' Dolan turned and dashed for the corridor that ran down beside the staircase.

'The agreement is null and void, Dolan. A crying shame as she would have entertained me, but I think your blackmailing days may have caught up with you and I want no part of it.' With that Fairfield hurried down the corridor and out through a door.

Dolan swore and started after him.

'Not a good idea, Dolan. You are not going anywhere but prison,' a voice warned, a voice that Caroline recognised.

Coming up the corridor as calm as if they were here for a social gathering were Max and Mussy and half a dozen men behind them.

Caroline nearly fainted in relief, they'd found her. Her heart swelled with emotion at the sight of them, but she was also terrified of them getting hurt.

Dolan backed up, each of his pistols aimed on Max and Mussy. 'Who the hell do you think you are coming into my establishment and causing this ruckus?'

'We are collecting something that belongs to us,' Max said, his eyes not straying from Dolan's face.

'Who are you? I ain't got anything of yours.'

'We'll be the judge of that,' Mussy said, looking pale but determined.

'Just get out and nothing bad will happen to either of you,' Dolan told them, standing in the middle of the hall. 'You don't know who you're dealing with. I will ruin you both.'

'Try your best,' Mussy said gayly. 'I've nothing to lose. You're outnumbered. Put the pistols down.' As Mussy spoke the words, Max rushed to tackle Dolan.

Dolan fired, hitting Max, who staggered.

Caroline screamed.

Max faltered but lunged for Dolan as did Mussy. The three of them fell down.

Caroline stood, staring, her hands over her mouth as they fought.

Abruptly, Dolan gasped, yelled in pain and then went limp.

Max rolled off him, his jacket opening showing blood seeping through his white shirt.

Panting, Mussy knelt back on his heels, a knife in his hands covered in blood, his gaze on the hole he'd made in Dolan's chest.

Caroline didn't know what to do, who to go to first.

The entrance cleared except for a few men, one an older gentleman with huge white whiskers. 'Indeed, that has settled a few scores. Indeed, it has.'

Max put a hand to his bleeding side and got to his knees.

'Don't move!' Caroline rushed to him. 'Stay still. You need a doctor.'

'Are you hurt?' Max's gaze roamed over her looking for injuries.

'No. No, not at all.' She wanted to touch him, soothe him but something held her back.

'Dolan is dead.' The old gentleman nodded. 'Let us get out of here. Indeed, we do not want to be found.' He helped a wheezing Mussy to stand. 'Go to the carriage, my good man.'

Caroline dithered, lost in the events of the night until a smash jolted her. The old gentleman knocked over two of the ornate lamps on tables by the stairs that had somehow remained intact. He strode into the drawing room, and they heard him moving things about.

'What is Sir Lionel doing?' Max murmured, wincing in pain as they edged to the front door.

Sir Lionel came out holding a lighted rolled up newspaper, he lit the spilt lamp oil and in a golden flash, flames spread across the floor. He walked to the other broken lamp and threw the lit newspaper onto it for it to ignite. Satisfied, he raised his hands. 'Indeed, a drink is called for.'

Caroline helped Mussy up into the carriage, he was limp as a rag doll and panting.

Max groaned in pain and closed his eyes as the carriage pulled away.

Over her shoulder, Caroline stared at the building. Flames were shimmering in the windows, crawling up the curtains. Soon the whole building would be alight, burning the evidence, burning the body of the man who would never hurt her again.

CHAPTER 11

*R*aking the soil, searching for hidden potatoes left behind by the labourers digging ahead, Trixie wiped the sweat from her forehead. Her arms ached and so did her back. The physical work of farming was still a challenge for her. She'd grown up in a city, the heaviest lifting she'd done was a bucket of coal or a basket of wet washing. Living on a farm had introduced her to a whole new way of life, taught her a whole new set of skills, and she found she liked the country.

The end of August sun burned her back. September was only a few days away, and they were hurrying to harvest the last field before the weather turned for autumn. They were late to harvest because the crops had been sown late, but fortunately the weather had held and harvesting at this time, long after all the other farmers had done so, gave them more labourers to employ.

For a moment she stopped and stretched, scanning the overturned potato field. Elsie and Bertha were along another row, gathering the potatoes as young boys dug in the soil to reveal them. Many of the village children were paid to help to gather in the harvest. Some of the children's mothers also were helping, Caroline had employed them for their knowledge and expertise.

She spotted Caroline driving the cart back to the end of the row. In the week since the ordeal with Dolan, Caroline had plunged herself into working hard with the harvest. Caroline rose before dawn and stayed out on the farm until well after dark. She would eat and then go to bed with barely a word being spoken. Trixie understood Caroline felt guilty for Max being shot, for Mussy murdering Dolan. They'd spoken little of what happened, but Mussy had told Trixie most of it.

Trixie was glad Dolan was dead, that the whole ordeal was finished. Though it still affected Caroline. At the hands of Dolan and Wayland, Caroline had suffered, and it would take time for her to heal, but Trixie missed her friend. She missed Caro's laughter, her softness, which had vanished since the day Wayland attacked her in the barn.

Raking and finding the odd potato, Trixie's basket began to fill. At the top of the field, Annie banged a tin ladle against a pot lid, signalling them it was time for a break and food.

Grabbing her basket, Trixie plodded up the hill to the others who were lining up for bowls of stew and chunks of bread. Caroline poured out cups of tea or cool cider.

Mussy sat on a chair under the pear tree, reading a book when Trixie joined him with her stew and cider. 'Can I fetch you anything?'

'No, dear girl. I am content.' Mussy smiled, placing his book on his lap. 'You appear hot. I am exhausted just watching you.'

'It's hard work for certain.' She ate the beef stew hungrily. 'But today is the last day.'

'I wish I could help.'

'Did you take those loaves of bread out of the oven?'

'I did.'

'Then that's all the help I need,' Trixie told him, chuckling.

'That's all right then as it is about all I *can* do,' he quipped with a grin.

Although weak physically, Mussy kept his manner light, despite what he'd done. No one blamed him for killing Dolan. He'd done it to protect Caroline, Max and the whole family. In fact, Dolan's death was a relief. Sir Lionel's idea to set the building alight buried all evidence. The men Sir Lionel paid to attack the club were unknown workers living in the bowels of the city, who'd do anything for a few shillings. They didn't know Max or Mussy. No one had been caught, and the club had burnt to the ground taking Dolan's body with it.

Trixie and Jacob had returned to the inn that night to find Max with a wound to his side, where the bullet scraped past. Mussy was cleaning him up and Caroline was sitting in a chair wearing only her undergarments and Mussy's coat. The blackened ashes of an orange dress curled in the room's fire grate. Before dawn had broken, they drove home in the carriage.

'She cannot continue as she is doing.' Mussy nodded towards Caroline.

'We all know that, but will she listen to any of us?' Trixie sipped her cider.

'She's become even more withdrawn.' Mussy sighed heavily. 'I thought with Dolan no longer alive... Well, I thought she might recover her spirits.'

'It's not possible while ever his lordship is still at the abbey.'

'Why? I have explained to Caro that the rent increase can be sorted. I will give her more money. I hardly need my allowance while living here.'

'It's not just the rent.' Trixie watched Caroline pour another glass of cider for Jacob.

'What do you mean?'

Before she could answer the sound of a horse and rider reached them. Trixie's chest tightened as Thomas rode up the drive.

'Young Cavendish has return from Lincoln.' Mussy pushed himself to his feet.

'Is that where he's been?' Trixie had wondered where Thomas had disappeared two weeks ago, after their kiss. She kept her gaze lowered as Thomas dismounted and walked over to them.

'Good day, Mr Casey, Miss Wilkes.' Thomas bowed.

They answered him in kind.

'Fetch a chair from inside and sit with us,' Mussy suggested.

Trixie glanced at Thomas, her heart thumping at his carefree handsomeness.

'I am happy to sit on the grass as Miss Wilkes is doing,' Thomas said, looking at the workers standing or sitting around chatting and eating. 'It's a glorious day for harvesting,'

'Would you care for a drink, Mr Cavendish?' Trixie managed to say.

'I am fine for the moment, thank you.' Thomas squatted down, snipping off a long grass stem. 'Mrs Lawson will be pleased to have the harvest finished.'

Mussy closed his book. 'Yes. We are taking the surplus

potatoes to the market in York next week when we attend the cattle market.'

'How is your brother?' Trixie blurted out.

'Recovering well,' Thomas replied. 'Max is not one for staying in bed. He has been at his desk every day.'

'His lordship is still with us?' Mussy asked idly, swatting away a fly.

'For another week perhaps, who knows? He keeps saying he misses London. Wayland has stayed here longer than any of us expected. He has been called upon by other families in the area and been kept busy returning visits. Wayland does enjoy being the centre of attention.' Thomas gave Trixie a small apologetic smile as if the explanation was not enough reason for Wayland to be still at the abbey.

Trixie rose, gathering her bowl and cup. 'I'll get back to work.'

'Do you need another pair of hands?' Thomas asked, standing. 'My small harvest has already been brought in and I am a free man today.'

'Another pair of hands are always welcome.' Trixie walked with him towards the others.

'Trixie.' Thomas touched her arm to stop her. 'I have done nothing but think of you, think of the kiss we shared. Have you? Have you thought of me at all?'

'Of course I have, but I told you. We can never be together. I'm not of your society and I'll not make a fool of myself or of you.'

'You would not be thought a fool. My circle of friends is very small.'

'Stop, Thomas, just stop.' Trixie didn't need the heartache of what might have been. 'You're going back to university. You have no time for planning for a future you think you want with me. Besides, I've my sisters to think about.'

'I would look after you all.'

Trixie noticed Jacob walking across the yard, his gaze on her. Since the night in York when they had walked the streets looking for Dolan and Caroline, they'd grown closer. Jacob promised nothing would ever happen to her, and she believed him. He cared for her. Jacob was her own kind.

'Will you please just think about us? We could be happy together.'

Trixie sighed deeply, unhappily. 'There's nothing to think about, Thomas. I couldn't imagine sitting at your cousin's table as your wife, could you?'

'Then we shan't sit at his table. We'll sit at our own. I care nothing for my cousin.'

She shook her head. He wasn't thinking. 'You are still a member of that society, it would be expected. I don't belong there.' She turned away, grabbed an empty basket and strode down the field.

Sometime later, Jacob came to her with a jug of water and a cup and another empty basket. 'The sun is hot. You need to drink.' He was coated with a thin layer of dust on his sweaty skin. Sleeves rolled back and shirt undone at the top, Jacob's skin had tanned during the summer. He looked healthier than he did living in York. Good food and hard work had broadened his chest, created muscles on his arms.

Taking the cup from him, she drank thirstily.

'What did Cavendish want?' Jacob's head tilted to one side waiting for her answer.

'He wants to marry me.' As soon as she spoke, she regretted it.

'Marry you? He's a toff. Why would he want to marry you, he can have anyone?'

Angry and hurt by the slight, she thrust the cup at his chest. 'I know I'm not worthy, you don't need to say it!'

'No, I didn't mean it like that. I'm surprised that's all. You're lovely, any man would want to marry you, but—'

'But what?' Hands on hips, she glared at him.

'Nowt. He's not right for you.'

'I shouldn't have told you.'

'Yes, you should. This is important. This affects us all.'

'No, it doesn't because it's not happening. As you say, I'm not good enough for him.'

He looked offended. 'I never said those words.'

'I don't want to talk about it. Just go away, Jacob.' She grabbed the empty basket and continued working.

'I'm sorry.' He placed the jug and cup on top of the basket she'd filled with potatoes and heaved it up. 'Do you want to marry him?'

'Just go, Jacob!'

When he'd walked back up the field, Trixie stretched her back which ached from bending over. The children's laughter drifted on the warm breeze, and she couldn't help but smile hearing Elsie's giggling. She didn't know how much work was going on in that group. One of the mother's, Mrs Kendrik, gave them a quick talking to, and the children went back to work. Trixie watched Mrs Kendrik, a woman from the village, one she knew slightly from having the market stall and talking to the local folk. Mrs Kendrik had a small baby wrapped in a shawl around her back and had mentioned her husband was a labourer at the abbey's home farm. The woman looked happy enough, content with her lot as far as Trixie could see. A woman happy to chat and laugh, wipe the dirt off her child's face, or give them a clout around the ear if they misbehaved. A wife and mother.

Trixie wondered if she'd ever be one. It had never been something she thought was in her future, especially not in York, where being a prostitute placed her on the lowest rung of society.

Only here in the country, only a few people were aware of her past, and Thomas wasn't one of them. She scanned the field for him and found him working alongside the cart, lifting the heavy baskets up onto it. Like Jacob he had his jacket off, sleeves rolled up. Thomas didn't know her, not the real her, and once the truth was revealed his ideas of them marrying would disappear. She had to tell him, then he'd continue on with his life without believing she should be in it.

She smiled slightly as Caroline traversed the upturned field to join her, Prince and Duke close by her skirts. Her dear friend hadn't been seeking her company or anyone's for days. 'You look as sweaty and tired as me.'

'It's worth it though.' Caroline swept her hands wide. 'Look at what we've achieved. The harvest is done. We've a barn full of potatoes, turnips, wheat and hay.'

'You should be proud of yourself.'

'I'm proud of all of us. Against the odds, we managed to do it as a team.'

'As a family,' Trixie added.

Caroline's expression tightened. 'Speaking of families, I heard Thomas mention to one of the women that his cousin is thinking of leaving soon.'

'He told Mussy and me the same. Hopefully, he actually does leave. He mentions it often and never goes.'

'It can't come soon enough.'

'Caro, please, don't think of him.'

'It was *him* who told Dolan where to find us, to find me.'

Shocked, Trixie stared. 'No...'

'Yes. That *beast* purposely travelled to York to find Dolan and tell him.'

'How did his lordship know of our dealings with Dolan?'

'Either Max or Thomas told him, obviously.' Caroline's green eyes glittered like broken emeralds. 'No one can be trusted.'

'Max saved you. He would never betray you,' Trixie defended. 'He was distraught the whole time you were gone.'

'Then it must have been Thomas. Max must have told him, and he told Wayland.'

They both looked to where the younger Cavendish was pouring water over his hot head.

'Thomas wants to marry me.' For a second time that day, Trixie spilled her secret. 'I doubt he'd want me once the truth of what I was is revealed. That's why I don't think Max has told him of our past.'

Caroline stared at Trixie. 'Have you and Thomas been meeting?'

'No! No, I mean, Thomas came here some weeks ago, and we talked and we...'

'What? What else did you do?'

'We kissed...'

Caroline's eyes widened. 'You never said.'

'You've barely been seen, Caro. You're up at dawn and not in until dark and then straight to bed. When have you been willing to sit and talk to me or to anyone lately? The girls miss you, Mussy misses you and *I* miss *you*!'

'I've been trying to cope!' Caroline snapped.

'And you've pushed us aside,' Trixie replied heatedly. 'We tread carefully around so as not to upset you and the girls

157

have no idea why the person they love so much no longer spends any time with them.'

'Oh, forgive me for hurting, for trying to… for trying to…' Caroline clenched her fists, her expression hard. Prince whimpered while Duke made a small growl in his throat, confused at her distressed manner.

'We love you, Caro,' Trixie whispered sadly. 'We only want our Caro back.'

'I think she might be dead…' Caroline murmured.

Trixie gently took Caroline's gloved hand. 'I don't believe that.'

Caroline squeezed Trixie's hand in response. 'I'll try harder to be better.' Head down, Caroline walked back up the uneven field.

Trixie watched her go and then bent to search the soil for hidden potatoes. If his lordship knew enough about them to tell Dolan, then it wouldn't be long before Thomas found out. She had to tell him before anyone else did.

CHAPTER 12

*R*eplacing the teacup on its saucer, Max put aside the invoice he'd received from the farrier. A silver platter piled with mail waited for his attention. Yet, he wanted nothing more than to ride Queenie over to Hopewood Farm and see Caroline. It upset him that she'd not been to see him in the two weeks since that awful night. Yet, he had not been to visit her either. For reasons he didn't understand something in her manner confused him, and he stopped himself from calling on her when it was all he wanted to do.

Abruptly he stood, wincing at the movement, as his wound twitched, reminding him of the ache. Carefully, he stepped to the window in frustration. How could he approach Caroline with the notion of revealing his feelings for her, of his desire and wish for them to be married? She had given him no incentive to imagine she felt anything for him but a mild friendship, perhaps gratefulness for rescuing her from Dolan's hideous plans.

Rain pitted against the glass, grey clouds hung low and heavy. A strong wind flattened the last of the flowers and tossed the highest tree branches. The mid-September day was as miserable as he felt.

Annoyed at everything and nothing, he sat back to his desk and shifted through the pile of mail without care until he saw a letter in his aunt's hand. Quickly, he opened it with the letter knife.

MY DEAREST NEPHEW MAX,

FORGIVE me for my late correspondence. Letter writing has been difficult for me since I lost Richard.

I am assured by now Wayland has informed you of the passing of your dear uncle. My darling Richard is no longer with me, and the loss is challenging to accept. However, I have no choice but to acknowledge my loss and continue in this life for as long as the days which are left to me. I know you will join me in my grief for you and your uncle were great friends. He looked upon you and Thomas as sons, more so really, for his relationship with his own son was tenuous at best.

I trust Wayland has written to you and told you of the details regarding how your uncle died. I cannot bring myself to repeat it again in this letter, I know you will understand.

Naturally, your uncle's death has left me in a situation of despair not only privately but socially, and for that reason I have no wish to return to England and will remain in India at our tea plantation. Solicitors will handle any financial concerns in England, and they will instruct Wayland on how to manage everything that his father built.

Unfortunately, my husband did not consider Wayland to be competent in business matters and shared very little with him.

Wayland will no doubt need guidance, and I write to you to beg for your help in this matter. Wayland has no head for business, unlike you. As my nephew, and his cousin, I pray you will do all that you can to ease his path through the murky waters of commerce the best you can.

On that matter I must bring to your attention my own will, which is safe with the family solicitors. Residing in India one can never know when a disgusting disease will carry you off to the grave as it did with my darling husband. Therefore, I have put my own affairs into order should I be taken suddenly. There is little for me to leave, but there are some title deeds, namely a townhouse in Oxford which I bequeath to Thomas and for you, I wish you to have my farm, Grange Lea. Your dear uncle indulged me when we were first married, when I was homesick for Lincoln and my family. He bought the farm and put the title deeds in my name, which scandalised a few of our friends that I should own property, but your uncle was a clever man.

Grange Lea is north of Lincoln on that great straight road, Ermine Street, do you remember it? Of course, you do. A road apparently built by the Romans. Grange Lea is between Ermine Street and the village of South Carlton. I stayed at Grange Lea a few times many years ago, always meaning to visit more often than I did. The cottage is tidily presented, prettily situated by a little brook, and there are numerous out buildings. The farm was once owned by the Bishops of Lincoln many centuries ago. There are eighty acres, if my memory serves me correctly, but it will all be detailed in the paperwork at the solicitors, write to them for it. You and Thomas both will have a small stipend from my father's inheritance to add to the one you receive from your late mother.

The farm is currently managed, and I understand you are happy at the abbey, however, should you ever find the need or the wish to strike out on your own, then you have a farm that belongs to you -

unentailed, without a mortgage and has been put solely in your name. It is yours now to do with whatever you wish.

Like me, there are times when I know you miss our home of Lincoln. It delights me that I can give you this land and you have a home of your home, an income, if you are successful at managing it, which you absolutely would be for you are clever and eager to thrive in whatever environment you find yourself in. I admire that. Your parents would be so proud of you, Max, as I am.

My dearest nephew, I am growing tired, and the light has faded where I sit on the verandah. The unique sounds of the jungle that edges the plantation grow louder as night approaches and its time I ventured indoors. So, I shall finish this letter and let it begin its long journey to your hands. I send it with all my love.

Write to me soon, dear Max, for I long to hear from those who are in my heart. Wayland writes little and fleetingly, yet I cannot blame him for he is extremely busy, more so now than ever. Take care of him for me, will you? Perhaps encourage him to come and visit me? My greatest wishes would be to see Wayland, Thomas and your dear self again, but I am not in the best of health to travel so far. Voyages are for the young and brave, and I am no longer either.

With sincerest love,
Your Aunt Lucille,
Low Cloud Tea Plantation,
Himalayas, India
1853

MAX READ the letter three more times.

He held it in one hand and paced the room, his mind

whirling, his emotions mixed and melancholy. His poor aunt. How she must be suffering. He sensed her grief, her loneliness. He wished she wasn't so far away, that he could jump on Queenie and ride to her. He loved his aunt as a mother. When his own parents died, Aunt Lucille had replaced his mother in his affections. Her kindness and caring knew no bounds. Once more she was showing him just how much she thought of him by giving him a farm.

A farm north of Lincoln.

Lincoln was home.

He couldn't quite believe it and glanced at the letter again to make sure he hadn't misread his aunt's wishes. She had given him land. No more would he have to work for another man. As much as he enjoyed looking after the estate, the pleasure had seeped away somewhat at his uncle's death. Wayland wasn't half the man his father was and although Max had all control in handling the estate, he still had to report to Wayland, and it just didn't sit right with him.

His cousin's visit had been the longest Max had been in his company and it reaffirmed his initial thoughts that Wayland wasn't likeable. However, his aunt had begged him to guide Wayland, if such a thing was possible, through his grief and dealings of being the new lord. Did his aunt believe Wayland was still a boy at school? Wayland didn't need Max, and his cousin hadn't shown any grieving over his father.

Max sighed deeply, conflicted. To do as his aunt asked meant remaining in Wayland's company, corresponding frequently when he wasn't. Wayland would not appreciate his help in any way, Max had no doubt about that. But perhaps he could persuade his cousin to travel to India and visit his mother? That would bring his aunt much joy.

The door opened and Wayland stood there. 'Good Lord, Max, are you never out of this room?'

Max hid the letter behind his back. 'It is where I work.'

'Go and get changed for dinner. I have guests this evening, remember?'

'Guests? No, you never mentioned it.'

'I am certain I did mention it.'

'No, I would have remembered.' Max checked his diary. 'I have nothing written down for tonight.'

'I must have forgotten to tell you.' Wayland waved his hand as if it meant little to him. 'It was a last-minute thing, as a sort of thank you to those families who have invited me to visit their homes while I was here. You know how it is. One must return invitations. Unfortunately, not one of these families are in the slightest bit entertaining.'

'It has not stopped you from dining out at their homes most evenings,' Max said wryly.

'Heavens man, I need some diversions from this silent tomb, even if it is simply to drink another man's cellar dry.' Wayland sniggered.

'You have done well, for someone who was only going to stay here a short time.'

Wayland rolled his eyes in boredom. 'I did not want to be accused of neglecting my duty as Lord Stockton-Lee of Misterton Abbey. I have paid my respects to all those families who admired my father. You should be satisfied at that, surely?'

'Absolutely.' Max had no doubt Wayland only stayed for his own intentions and nothing to do with honouring his position or his father. Wayland sought only to please himself.

'No doubt there will be a few daughters dragged along this

evening by desperate mamas wanting to marry them off. I have sent for Thomas as well. Safety in numbers and all that. Anyway, by tomorrow I shall be gone from here and all their efforts will be wasted.' Wayland abruptly went out without closing the door.

Folding the letter, Max slipped it into his waistcoat pocket. He wasn't sure why he hadn't mentioned it to Wayland, but some instinct held him back. Checking his desk was in order, Max left the room and strode out of the house. He nodded to a maid carrying a basket of washing to the laundry building as he made his way across the yard and along the path to his cottage.

In his bedroom, he undressed down to his trousers. A jug of hot water was brought over each evening from the kitchens and a fresh towel for him to use to wash. If he wasn't dining with Wayland, a maid brought over a tray of the evening meal the staff were having. As a member of the family, he could have stayed living within the abbey as he had done since moving here from Lincoln, but once his aunt and uncle left for India, the abbey seemed too quiet, too large and so he'd moved out to this little cottage, which was warmer in winter, and he was left to his own privacy.

Soap lathered over his face and neck, he swore slightly at the knock on the door. Likely it was one of the men bringing in a load of wood for his fire. Quickly washing off the soap, he towelled himself dry and opened the front door. His eyebrows rose on seeing Caroline standing there. She was the last person he expected to see. 'Mrs Lawson?'

'Forgive me for coming to your private residence. I was told you'd left your office for the day.'

'Come in, please.' Max stepped back to allow her to enter.

'I think not.' Her green eyes flickered to his bare chest and her cheeks flushed a little. Her gaze lingered on the bandage at his side.

'Allow me a moment to pull on my shirt.' He ran back into the bedroom and pulled on his shirt, tucking it in on his way back to the door.

'I won't take up much more of your time, Mr Cavendish.'

'Will you not call me Max?' He smiled at her loveliness. 'We have been through enough to allow ourselves less formalities.' He might have died for her if Dolan's bullet had lodged into his gut instead of skimming his side.

'Are you healing well?' she murmured.

'I am. Will you not come in?'

'No.' She took a step back. 'I simply wanted to ask you a question.'

'Ask away.' He smiled, desperately wanting to gather her into his arms and kiss her for the rest of their days.

'Did you tell your cousin about Dolan? About my past with Victor Dolan?'

Taken by surprise, Max stared at her. Had he told Wayland about Dolan? Then it came to him. 'Yes, I did. A few weeks ago. I had to explain why I needed the carriage that day when I took you to York to collect Mussy and Jacob.'

'So, it was you.' Her shoulders slumped like a kite without wind.

'I apologise sincerely for breaking your confidence.' He frowned, confused. 'I told Wayland because I do not lie when asked a question. It was simply a conversation, the bare details.' He thought quickly. 'I mentioned nothing to him of Miss Wilkes and her past, or of anything further than we journeyed to York to collect Mussy and Jacob and that you were worried for their safety because of that man Dolan. That is all.'

'It was enough.'

'What do you mean?'

'It doesn't matter now. Good evening, Mr Cavendish,' she said dejectedly.

'Wait!' Her disappointment in him affected him more than he cared to admit. 'Mrs Lawson, please, forgive me.'

'I'm not certain that I can.' She turned away.

Max stepped in front of her. 'Mrs Lawson, Caroline, do not leave. We can discuss the matter.'

'There is nothing to discuss. You are just another person I cannot trust.' The look she gave him was one of regret and something else, hurt.

'But you can,' he defended as he watched her walk away. That she could not trust him pained in a physical way. He wanted her to depend on him, to have faith in him, to love him even. Caroline was the only woman he wanted, needed.

He replayed the conversation again in his mind as he finished washing and dressing. Why would she ask if he had spoken to Wayland about Dolan? He didn't understand.

His mind on Caroline, Max entered one of the back entrances to the abbey. Footmen and maids bustled along the corridor and poking his head into the dining room, Max smiled at Mrs Hoskins. 'Everything in order, Mrs Hoskins?'

'Yes, sir,' the housekeeper said, her eyes on the maids who were closing the curtains on the evening light. A footman lit the candles placed down the centre of the highly polished table. Mrs Hoskins adjusted the position of a glass, not missing a thing. After a moment she stepped over to Max. 'Sir, is it true his lordship is leaving tomorrow?'

'I believe so.'

Relief flooded her face for a moment. 'Thank you, sir.'

Understanding her reaction, Max left them to it. His cousin had played havoc in the house with his demands and lecherous treatment of the maids. Max hoped he did leave in the morning and never came back.

He greeted Reeves in the hall. 'How many are coming tonight?'

'Twelve, sir, including yourself and Master Thomas.'

'Anyone I do not know?'

'All the guests are those you have dined with before, sir. The Collins, the Babbages, the Lovetts, and the Spaldings, including their two daughters.'

'Thank you, Reeves.' Max walked through the open double doors into the ornate drawing room. He always thought of his aunt when he was in this room, for she had decorated it and liked for them all to sit in here before dinner and talk about their day's activities.

Wayland stood by the fireplace, a drink in hand, staring into the small flames. Lamps and candelabras lit the room and the heavy curtains were drawn. 'Are you prepared for the banal chatter we will have to endure tonight?'

'That is a bit harsh, do you not think?' Max enjoyed the company of the families who his aunt and uncle entertained.

'The prices of sheep, wool or the increases of tax and so forth are dull and do not interest me.' Wayland shot down the last of his drink and refilled his glass from the drink trolley by the window.

'Then encourage different topics,' Max suggested.

'One can hardly ask them about the latest art gallery they have visited, can one? I doubt a gallery of any worth is within a hundred miles of here.'

Max sighed at his cousin's superior manner. 'There is much to talk about with your guests. The Russians have invaded the Danubian Principalities. The Turks will retaliate, and so Europe will erupt into another war and how will that affect this country? Emperor Napoleon the Third has married a Spanish Countess, there is religious trouble in the Netherlands, also Australia and New Zealand are arguing to stop the transportation of convicts. Did you know that a gentleman, Sir George Cayley, has created a glider which has travelled five hundred and sixty yards in the air? His coachman was convinced to be on board. Can you imagine such a thing?' Max was fascinated by all he read in the newspapers.

Wayland tutted disparagingly. 'These country families would not know about such things.'

'They would. If they read the newspapers as I do. We do not have to live in London to be educated about the world, Wayland. Treat them with more respect. Horatio Spalding is highly knowledgeable of world affairs and Mr Lovett served in India and has travelled widely. George Babbage was a member of York's council. You dismiss these men as simple country esquires at your peril. All three of those men are intelligent and worthy of friendship.'

'Yes, yes. You have made your point.' Wayland waved his hand at Max, ending the topic.

As the guests arrived, Max shook hands with the gentlemen and bowed over the gloved hands of the women. He knew them all well and was relaxed in their company, but his mind kept straying to Caroline. In the morning, he would call on her and make peace. He would not let her thrust him from her life. It was time to make his intentions clear.

'Max.' Thomas joined him, having just arrived.

'You are late.' Max frowned. His brother seemed perturbed. 'What is wrong?'

'I need to talk to you.'

'Now?' Max motioned towards Reeves who had come to his lordship to announce dinner was ready.

'Later.'

'What is it about?'

'My future,' Thomas said with determination.

It had gone midnight before all the guests had departed after what Max deemed a successful evening. He, Thomas and Wayland were in the library, drinking Scottish whisky made at the distillery originally owned by his uncle and now his cousin.

'Lovett is a bore,' Wayland announced with a slight slur. He'd been drinking heavily all night. 'His young wife, Mary, is too pretty to be landed with such an uninteresting man. Mary is his second wife.'

'Yes, I am aware.' Max murmured.

'I wager his first wife is happy to be dead just to escape his dull wittering.'

Max scowled at his cousin. 'I very much doubt that. No woman would want to leave her baby willingly. Lovett has had a difficult time of it. Left a widow with a tiny baby.'

'Well, he married quickly, not six months had gone by before he was wed again to a woman half his age yet again. Mary could have done better.'

'They seem a contented couple.' Max watched his cousin's sly expression. 'What is it to you, anyway?'

Wayland laughed, his cheeks flushed, his eyes bloodshot. 'Never you mind, dear Maxwell.'

'You are up to something.' Max sat straighter in the leather armchair.

'Let us simply say... Delightful Mary is after a bit of fun...' Wayland winked with exaggeration. 'And I am happy to oblige. I have invited them to London, as my guests.'

'No, Wayland.' Max rubbed a hand over his tired eyes. 'That is a terrible idea.'

'Lovett wants another child,' Wayland sniggered. 'Would it not be laughable if his wife carried another man's seed?'

The blood drained from Max's face. 'God no.'

Shrugging, Wayland swallowed more whisky. 'You are such a prude, Max. Mary could not get enough of me. Why do you think I have called at their estate so many times in the last couple of weeks? She is like a bitch on heat.'

Thomas abruptly stood. 'I must be away home.' He turned to Max. 'Will you come to Springwood tomorrow to see me?'

Max nodded, revolted by his cousin's behaviour. 'I shall head to bed myself.'

'Christ almighty!' Wayland threw his glass into the fireplace in a fit of temper. 'What is it with you two? Pathetic examples of men as I have ever seen! Stay and drink with me. Let us talk of women and wine and wild parties.' He laughed mockingly. 'No, I do not think you two have ever attended a wild party in your lives.' He waved his hand. 'Oh, go away, the pair of you. I am sick of the sight of you both.'

In the hall, Max put his hand on Thomas's shoulder. 'Do you want to stay at the cottage? The spare bed is made up. Dawn will be here before we know it.'

Thomas nodded and they quietly walked out of the abbey and into the gardens.

'I received a letter from Aunt Lucille,' Thomas told him. 'Did you?'

'I did.'

'She is so generous. The townhouse in Oxford.'

171

'And what will you do with the townhouse? Sell it, have tenants?'

'I have yet to decide.'

'There is no rush.' Max listened to the cry of a fox somewhere in the deer fields beyond the gardens.

'With the townhouse and my allowance from our uncle, I can provide for a wife and family.'

Max skidded to a halt on the pebbled path. 'A wife and family?'

The moon peeped out from behind the clouds, shadowing their faces.

'What is wrong with me wanting to have that?'

'You are too young.'

'I am twenty-one, Max. Old enough to know my own mind. I shan't be like you and be over thirty before I settle,' Thomas scoffed.

'You have more to consider than being married, Thomas. You have to finish your studies and graduate, obtain a position somewhere.'

'I am not returning to Oxford.'

'What!' Max shouted, causing one of the hunting dogs to bark. He marched into his cottage, annoyed. 'We agreed you would achieve your degree.'

'It is not what I want anymore.'

'How do you expect to advance in the world without it?'

'Advance? You mean be a gentleman like our cousin? If being like him means advancing than I would rather not.'

'I do not mean Wayland at all. Your allowance from our uncle is not enough, Thomas. You need to earn more to live a decent life, especially to support a wife and family.' Max stared at him. 'Do not throw away the opportunities you have been given.'

'I can gain employment. I can run an estate like this, you have taught me well.'

'You need to finish your time at Oxford,' Max implored.

'I want to marry.'

'You can, later, in a few years when you have established yourself. Thomas, we do not have the luxury of extreme wealth. Yes, we were brought up as gentlemen, but we do not have the money nor status behind us to fulfil those roles. Why do you think I became uncle's estate manager? I needed to earn more to supplement my allowance.'

'Then I will find a position as well,' Thomas said stubbornly.

Max strove for calmness. Getting angry wouldn't help the situation. 'Why the rush to do all this?'

'I am in love.' Thomas sat on the chair before the fire, his hands dangling between his knees.

'Are you going to tell me the lady's name?' Max untied his silk cravat. He was ready for his bed.

'Miss Trixie Wilkes.'

Max swore.

'Why do you have that reaction?' Thomas snapped. 'She is a good and decent person.'

'You can do better.'

'Go to hell, Max! What do you know of love, anyway? You have admired Mrs Lawson since the moment you met her, yet you are too much of a coward to declare your intentions. Not that she would have you.'

'Shut your mouth, Brother,' Max warned.

'I shan't! I will marry Trixie and you cannot stop me.'

'You do not have enough knowledge about her.'

'Nonsense.'

'Trust me in this.' Max huffed. 'I am away to my bed. We

shall talk more in the morning.' Mentally tired, Max closed the bedroom door. First, the surprising letter from his aunt, then Caroline standing on his doorstep with disappointment in her eyes, Wayland's immoral actions and now the argument with Thomas. He'd had enough for one day.

When he woke the next morning, Thomas was gone.

CHAPTER 13

*T*rixie fed the scraps to the squealing pigs as the sun rose above the horizon. Dew sprinkled the grass, coating the spiderwebs strung like bits of lace across the fields. Seeing the sunrise was still a surprise for her. In York she worked all night and slept in most mornings. At the farm it was the opposite. It was early to bed and early to rise as Caroline and Jacob did and she found she liked it.

'Enough of that noise, you lot,' she chastised the pigs.

The piglets had grown large and tomorrow would be taken on the back of the cart into York to Mr Bent's butchers. With Dolan dead, they were free to come and go from York now without fear. Trixie had hoped that Caroline would return to her old self now Dolan was gone from their lives, and, in some ways, she had, but there was still a hardness to Caroline that Trixie was determined to chip away at.

She stopped at the milking shed where Caroline was milking the cows. 'Do you need a hand?'

'No, I'm fine.' Caroline paused the gentle pulling of the teats. 'You can take that bucket to the dairy for me, if you don't mind?' She pointed to the full pail of milk. 'I brought the jug from the kitchen to be filled.'

'I'll do it now.' Trixie went into the dairy shed next door, carrying the full bucket and placed it in the stone sink. Later, Caroline would begin the process of churning the milk into butter or to make cheese. Filling the white porcelain jug with milk, Trixie covered it with a piece of linen and carried it across the yard. She smiled in surprise as Thomas rode in. She wished her heart didn't skip as much as it did whenever he was near.

'Good morning, Miss Wilkes.' Thomas dismounted. 'Forgive the early call.'

'Good morning. Would you care for some tea?' Trixie took a step to the back door.

'I wanted to talk to you, privately?'

'Come inside. Caroline is milking and Jacob has left to take a cartload of potatoes to a market in Ripon. Our Elsie and Bertha and Mussy are still abed.' She invited him in nervously. Why would he want to speak to her privately? 'Please, sit.' She placed the jug of milk inside the larder and when she came out Thomas crossed the distance between them and took her hands.

'I must speak with you.'

'Goodness,' she whispered, her breath tight at his touch, but seeing his anxious gaze she became worried. 'Is everything well, Thomas?'

'It will be if you agree to marry me.'

'What?' She froze.

'I have been gifted a townhouse, in Oxford, by my aunt. I will have an income to support us for I intend on leaving university and obtaining a decent position. We can live in the townhouse, or I will lease it and we can live elsewhere.

Anywhere you want.' His words all come out in a rush. 'I love you, Trixie.'

Joy leapt in her heart for a glorious fleeting moment, then withered and died as it had done so many times in her life. She pulled her hands free and stepped back.

'No, no, do not say anything yet,' Thomas begged. 'Let me explain again.'

'Stop!' Trixie spoke sharply, then remembered those who were asleep above their heads. 'I've told you before. We can never be married.'

'I will take care of you and your sisters. We can all live together as a family.'

'You don't listen!' she whispered harshly. 'It can never be.'

'Why? Do you not love me?'

She turned from him and gripped the edge of the table. 'You deserve more than me.'

'I am tired of hearing that.'

She spun to him. 'Who else has said it? Who else have you talked about this with?'

'Max.'

She shivered. 'And what did he say?'

'I care for none of his words.'

'What did he say!'

'That I am too young, that I do not know you well enough. I refuse to listen. I know my own heart.'

'Your brother is right,' she said sorrowfully.

'Then allow me to learn about you,' he said desperately. 'I will court you and we shall spend hours talking and learning about one another.'

She could have laughed in his face at the silliness of his request. He spoke of courting, as though she was a lady of high birth. A tragic mourning filled her. The time had come. 'Sit down.'

Slowly he took off his hat and sat at the table, his expression hopeful.

'I won't blame you if, when you've heard what I've got to say, you don't wish to have anything more to do with me.'

'I—'

She held up her hand. 'Hear me out.'

He folded his arms and nodded.

'I was born in the slums of the Water Lanes in York. My father died young, and my mother did what she could to keep me and my sisters alive, but when she died, I was the only one to provide for us. As a youngster I worked different jobs, trying to earn enough money to rent a disgusting little room and eat scraps. We were always cold, always hungry.'

'I can give you a better life and you can forget all of that.'

'I've a better life already, I have done since I met Caroline because she showed me I could be a better person than I thought I was. She gave me an escape from the life I lived. She brought me here.' Trixie stared out of the kitchen window as the growing light banished the shadows. 'From the age of fifteen, I earned money by selling my body.'

His gasp was the only sound in the room.

She closed her eyes at the pain of revealing her true self to him.

'A prostitute?'

'Yes. I earned more money doing that than working twelve hours every day in a mill or factory. I was good at it, sought after. I had regular clients. I could pay the rent on that horrid room. I was able to buy food for my sisters, coal for the fire.'

The scraping of the chair on the stone flags hurt her ears. 'Is this the truth?'

She turned to see the anguish, the hidden horror in his eyes. 'Yes. Why would I lie about something like that? I can't marry you. I was a woman of the night and not the pure virginal innocent girl you think I am.'

Thomas made a sound in his throat, tears filling his eyes. He grabbed his hat and dashed out of the door. Seconds later the sound of his horse cantering down the drive filled the early morning air.

The door to the stairs opened and Mussy, bent over and pale, embraced her. 'That would have been difficult, dear girl.'

'You heard?'

'I did not want to intrude, so stayed on the other side of the door, but I thought afterwards you might be in need of a comforting embrace.'

Trixie rested her head on his thin chest and held him tight. She could feel all his bones. He was a walking skeleton. 'Caroline says nothing beats a Mussy hug.' She gave him a gentle squeeze and then stepped to the range. 'I'll make us some breakfast.'

'Trixie.'

She glanced over her shoulder at him.

'Do not be ashamed. You did what you had to do to survive, to keep your sisters alive. If Thomas loves you, then he must be man enough to accept that.'

'Caroline said something similar.'

'Caro can be wise at times.' He grinned. 'Not always, mind.'

Trixie added more wood to the range. 'Thomas and me would never work. We're very different. I'd never be comfortable in his world.'

'A sensible thought.' Mussy nodded. 'And it is better you have realised that now and not listened to your heart which speaks only of passion and can lead you down a path of unhappiness,' he said softly, reflecting on his own experiences she didn't doubt.

Her sisters coming down the stairs stopped any more talk of Thomas and Trixie was glad. She needed to keep busy so as not to think about the man she had rejected. 'Here, our Elsie, get the frying pan hot for the ham and eggs. Our Bertha, set the table.' She set about making the breakfast, she'd work on mending her broken heart later.

* * *

CAROLINE PICKED a blackberry from the brambles that lined parts of the roadside near the farm. Further down, Trixie and the girls were doing the same, though Elsie and Bertha ate more than they put into their baskets. The girls had blackened lips and stained fingers. Prince and Duke were snuffling in the grass, searching for scents.

For a moment, Caroline stood and stared at the harvested fields. Grateful she had managed to sow and reap crops. They had money coming in with the sale of the potatoes and turnips that Jacob was taking to market each week. Tomorrow he would take the piglets, and any day now she was expecting the shepherd to arrive to take some of the sheep flock to market in York. The hard work she'd done since returning to the farm had paid off. There was still a lot more work to be done. The fields needed ploughing again and fertilising ready for the next sowing, but she wasn't able to do that while Jacob had Dossy. Ideally, she'd like to own another horse, but that was an expense she couldn't afford yet, and she wouldn't ask Max Cavendish to help as he'd done in the spring.

She wished Cavendish didn't come into her mind as often

as he did. Her thoughts about him were so confused. He'd risked his life to save her, yet by telling Wayland about Dolan, he'd been the one to put her in danger. She'd learnt the hard way that trusting people would lead to sorrow and hurt. Stupidly, she'd let her guard down when it came to Cavendish. She wouldn't do it again. Yet, it saddened her to cut him from her life. She had admired him, enjoyed his company, liked the way his handsome face lit up when he looked at her. No man since Hugh had come close again to affecting her heart and now it was ruined.

Elsie and Bertha teasing each other brought her out of her thoughts. Glancing at Trixie, Caroline wondered why her friend was so quiet. She'd hardly said a word all morning.

When the girls moved a little distance from Trixie, Caroline moved towards her. 'Has something happened?'

'Thomas was here this morning while you were milking.' Trixie selected a fat blackberry and put it in her basket. 'He asked me to marry him.'

'What did you say?'

'I told him of my past.'

'Oh.' Caroline understood Trixie's misery. 'How did he take it?'

'As you'd expect. He left the house in a mad rush, disgusted.'

She rubbed Trixie's arm in a gesture of comfort. 'He may come back.'

'He won't.' Trixie picked another blackberry. 'And it's for the best that he doesn't.'

Before Caroline said anything else the sound of a rider approaching along the road made them all look. She groaned on seeing it was Wayland. Cavendish said he was leaving. Would the monster ever be gone?

She prayed Wayland would continue riding past without stopping. Her prayers went unanswered as he pulled at the reins of the big black horse.

'What a delightful spectacle. Four sweet maids all industriously labouring in the sunshine,' Wayland crowed.

No one spoke. Trixie gestured for the girls to come closer to her while Caroline faced him with a glare of hatred.

'Come now, ladies, no greeting to your lord?'

Trixie and the girls bobbed their knees, but Caroline remained still, head held high in defiance.

'Trust you to show no respect,' he spat.

'Respect has to be earned.'

Suddenly Wayland lashed his riding crop at Caroline's face. The shock and the pain sent her reeling back, dropping her basket, spilling blackberries over the road and into the ditch.

Elsie and Bertha screamed and huddled closer to Trixie. Prince and Duke came running to Caroline, barking.

Wayland leaned down from the saddle, the leather creaking. 'You will acknowledge who I am!'

Her hands cupping her burning face, tears blurred her vision. The dogs growled menacingly.

'Who am I? *Say it!*' Wayland demanded from her, his arm raised, his horse side-stepping in alarm.

'Say it, Caro, please,' Trixie whispered.

Pain ricochetted around Caroline's head. 'You're scum!' she flung back at him.

The crop came down again, striking the other side of her face. Caroline cowered, gasping at the pain. Prince and Duke barked and snarled at the horse's legs, causing it to buck. Wayland whacked at the dogs. The girls' screams rose higher.

'Leave them alone!' Caroline darted forward, trying to

protect her dogs, who were barking and snapping at the horse unable to get to Wayland.

Wayland struck the top of Caroline's head. She cried out and stumbled. He hit her again and, as she dodged away, she lost her footing and tumbled into the ditch filled with brambles.

Wayland's laughter rang in her ears. 'That's where you belong, bitch, in a ditch. Start packing your things. I am evicting you! Be gone by sunset or I will have you thrown out onto the road with only the clothes on your backs!' He dug his heels in the frightened horse's flanks and cantered away.

'Caro!' Trixie flung her basket aside and scrambled into the ditch to help Caroline out.

The bramble thorns ripped Caroline's skirts as she untangled herself. With Trixie's help she gingerly freed herself from the thorns which scratched her skin and tore at her clothes.

'Do you think he meant it?' Trixie asked, shaken.

'The eviction?' Caroline pulled an embedded thorn out of her wrist and watched the blood bead. 'Yes, he meant it.'

'What will we do?'

She closed her eyes at the stinging of the welts on her face and the pricks on her skin. 'I have no idea.'

'You need to speak to Mr Cavendish.'

Hurt, anger and humiliation twisted together inside, curdling her stomach and clouding her mind. 'Cavendish doesn't own the farm. He has no say in what Wayland orders,' she said dully.

'But we can't leave here,' Trixie said in a panic. 'Where will we go? And what about the animals?'

Caroline raised her pain-filled gaze to Trixie. 'If we stay, murder will be done by either him or me.'

CHAPTER 14

*M*ax was in the abbey's library looking for a particular ledger on centuries of the abbey's sheep breeding, the descendants of which roamed the estate's fields. He'd had an urgent meeting with the head shepherd this morning, due to the sudden death of two of their prized rams. The shepherd had thought disease was the cause, and they had to move quickly to stop it spreading throughout the whole flock. The estate's rams were highly sought after for stud hiring and breeding and the death of two of their best rams had appalled him and the men who cared for the stock. The last thing they needed was an outbreak of disease. They had to act fast. He'd spent the morning helping to inspect the flock for any signs of disease, pushing all his other duties and his visit to Caroline to one side for the day. He needed to check the breeding ledgers to see if the rams they had left could be used with certain ewes. Interbreeding had to be avoided.

'Did you know!'

Max jumped at the shout. He turned, furious, to face his

brother. 'What in God's name are you shouting about? Calm yourself.'

'Did you know!' Thomas shouted again, his face was twisted in fury.

Max had never seen his mild-mannered brother so distraught. 'What? Tell me what has happened.'

'Trixie. Her past?' Thomas managed to get the words out, his fists balled in anger.

Max sighed, not wanting to deal with this right now. 'You have spoken to her?'

'Were you informed of her life in York? Tell me!'

'I was aware, yes,' Max said regrettably.

Thomas's fist landed on Max's jaw, jerking his head back. Pain shot along his face.

He hadn't expected Thomas to punch him in the face. He stepped back a pace or two, infuriated, rubbing his sore jaw. 'Hit me again and I will wipe the floor with you.'

'Come on then, do it,' Thomas jeered.

'Thomas, I understand you are angry.' Pain thudded along his jaw.

'You should have told me!'

'What is all this noise?' Wayland came in wearing his riding clothes, pulling off his leather gloves. 'Is this an inn or a library?'

'Shut up!' Thomas turned on him.

Wayland's face was a picture of amazement. 'I beg your *pardon!* Who the hell are you to speak to me in that way, you young pup!'

Max groaned. This was getting out of hand. He could throttle his brother at this moment. 'Thomas…'

'You can shut up as well.' Thomas spun back to Max. 'Keeping things from me, things I should have known. I have made a fool of myself, declaring myself to her. You might have saved me from that!'

'You have one chance to explain yourself,' Wayland uttered in irritation.

Thomas glared at his cousin. 'I shan't explain myself to you, *my lord*,' he taunted. 'You are the least deserving of anything, including your bloody title.'

'Thomas!' Max barked, stunned.

'Get out of my house!' Wayland snapped at Thomas. 'I have had enough of people disrespecting me today.' He looked at Max. 'Hopewood Farm, the tenants are to be evicted immediately.'

As if a bucket of ice water had been thrown over him, Max blinked in shock. Had the whole world gone mad suddenly? 'Hopewood Farm? Mrs Lawson? What do you mean?'

'I want her and the whole lot of them out by tonight. See to it,' Wayland demanded. He flicked a look at Thomas. 'And an apology from you within the hour before I leave this god-forsaken place.'

Thomas chuckled, but it was a horrible sound of anguish and hatred. 'Did Mrs Lawson stand up to you again, did she?'

'Say one more word and I will ruin you, Thomas,' Wayland ground out between clenched teeth.

Max stared at them both and had the creeping sensation that he was about to be involved in something that would change his life. 'What are you talking about Thomas?'

Thomas never took his gaze off their cousin, a contemplation of loathing. 'You tell him, Wayland. You tell dear Max here what you did.'

Uncertainty flickered in Wayland's narrowed stare. 'Not another word,' he warned.

'I was never one for orders, would have been terrible in

the army,' Thomas mocked. 'A bit like you, hey, Wayland? You break the rules, do you not? Take what is not yours, abuse your position, your power?'

'Get out!' Wayland took a step towards Thomas, but Max quickly jumped in front of his brother.

'Let us all calm down, shall we?' Max held up his hands between the two men.

'Tell my brother what you *did*,' Thomas said in a deadly tone.

'I am tired of this,' Max yelled, not wanting to hear anything because he felt it would devastate him. 'If you two want to act like children go ahead.' Max threw his hands up and walked away.

'Tell Max how you raped the woman he cares for,' Thomas murmured in an icy tone.

For a fleeting second, Max thought he'd misheard what Thomas said. Then an intense ache filled his heart as he stared at his brother and saw the sympathy in his eyes. The breath left his chest, the words dazed him, his brain wouldn't comprehend them. 'What did you say?'

Wayland strode to the drinks' trolley and poured himself a glass of brandy with a hand that shook slightly. 'I taught the bitch a lesson.'

Max wanted to beg Thomas to tell him it was all a mistake, that Wayland had not touched a hair on Caroline's head. 'Thomas?'

'I am sorry, Max.' Thomas held his hands up in appeal. 'If I had known what he planned I would never have left her that day…'

Slowly Max turned to his cousin in disbelief.

'She deserved it, Max,' Wayland defended himself. 'The mouth on her! No respect for her betters. Not that it matters anymore for I want her gone! I thought that Dolan fellow would do the job, but he was useless.'

'Dolan?' Max rocked back in shock at the admission. 'You told Dolan where Caroline was?'

'What if I did? She deserved it.'

A rage so consuming wiped out any other thought. Max hurdled a chair that was in his way and launched himself at his cousin. He grabbed hold of Wayland by the throat and pushed him up against the wall. 'You bastard!'

'Get your hands off me,' Wayland choked.

'Did you rape her?' Max tightened his grip around Wayland's neck. 'Answer me!'

Wayland, growing red in the face, gurgled a noise.

Max released the pressure enough for him to speak.

'I did not know you… cared for her,' Wayland gasped. 'The bitch is not worthy of you…'

Max punched him hard in the face. Sparks of pain shot up his hand and wrist, but he didn't care and punched him again. His third punch was in the stomach and as Wayland bent over with a grunt, Max brought his knee up to connected with Wayland's nose, the satisfying crack as it broke drove Max to pull him up and punch him on the jaw. Blood spurted from Wayland's nose. He groaned and Max punched him in the stomach again.

'Enough, Max!' Thomas pulled him away from their cousin, who fell to the floor in a sprawled heap like a forgotten rag doll.

But the rage that consumed Max couldn't be controlled. 'You filthy bastard! How dare you touch her!' He pulled Wayland up and punched him in the face again.

'Enough,' Thomas repeated, dragging him away. 'He's not worth it.'

Puffing, the red mist which had blurred his mind slowly dissipated. Max bent over, sucking in gulps of air.

The door was flung open, and Reeves stood there in amazement. 'Your lordship!'

'He fell off his horse, Reeves. On his morning ride he didn't take a jump clearly,' Thomas said dispassionately. 'Have some men carry him up to his room and his valet can put him to bed.'

'Shall I send for a doctor?'

Max shook himself as if coming out of a trance. 'That will not be necessary, Reeves. His lordship will only require a day in bed.'

'Very good, sir.' Reeves bowed and the stern look he gave his lord told Max that Reeves was no admirer of Wayland.

Thomas poured Max and himself a brandy. 'He will never forgive you for this.'

His knuckles throbbing, Max cradled his bruised right hand to his chest as he accepted the glass with his left. 'I do not want his forgiveness. I never want to see him again.'

'But you adore this estate.'

'Stay and be his land agent? No way. It was becoming a struggle to be in his company even before, but now...' Max swallowed the brandy in one gulp and wheezed as the fiery liquid trailed down his throat and hit his empty stomach. 'I must see Caroline.'

'Is that wise?' Thomas poured him another brandy.

'Why should I not?'

Thomas turned to stare out of the window. 'Was Caroline the same as Trixie?'

Max also gazed out of the window. Birds swooped low between the trees. 'No, she was not. Forgive me for not telling you about Miss Wilkes. I honestly did not know what to do for the best. I hoped you were not that infatuated with her and once you returned to Oxford, you would forget about her.'

'I could cope with the fact she cannot read or write. I could have taught her, educated her.' Tears glistened in Thomas's eyes. 'But for her to have sold her body... That many men had... had used her body. I thought her pure. Innocent. Low born, yes, but I cannot accept her having done that with men for money...'

'Yes...' Max said sadly, hating that his brother was hurting. 'But she did it for the right reasons, for her sisters.'

'Then she should have worked in a mill or as a maid or something!'

'Do not judge her harshly, Thomas. We have never been so poor or so desperate that we had to make such harsh decisions just to survive.'

'I will not see her again,' Thomas stated.

'That is your choice.'

'And I ask you not to court Mrs Lawson's company either.'

'Thomas—'

'No, Max. You are my brother, and I will do anything for you, anything. All I ask is that you forget about that family. For if you were to marry Mrs Lawson, then Miss Wilkes will be joined to us as well and I would have to face her time and again and I cannot do it.'

Max's hand throbbed and so did his head. 'You are asking me to choose between you and Caroline.'

'Is it a choice? I very much doubt Caroline Lawson will have you after everything Wayland has done to her and who can blame her?'

'I shan't give her up,' Max spoke with a broken heart. What

Wayland had done... She had suffered, and he had not been there to support her.

'She is not yours, Max, but I am your brother and I ask you to do this for me.' Thomas glanced at the door as footsteps passed. 'We should go. Wayland will probably bring charges against you, and if he does, I will testify alongside you that we found him in that state.'

'I cannot leave without seeing her.'

Thomas swore. 'Then I will meet you at the crossroads in an hour. We should head for Harrogate, not York.'

'I cannot just leave, Thomas,' Max said harshly. 'I have a life here. It will take more than an hour to sort out my leaving. This is our home, for God's sake!'

'You *had* a life here! Now it is over, and you must look to a new life. Forget this place, forget Wayland and everyone else. The abbey stopped being our home the minute Uncle Richard died.'

Max bowed his head knowing it was the truth.

'We have to go now, Max. It is the only option.'

'I am not running like a rat down a drain. I doubt Wayland will leave his bed for a couple of days. We have time to plan, at least tonight.' His thoughts surging, Max tried to settle his mind. 'Go home to Springwood Farm, pack properly, all of your belongings and inform your maid and your labourer, they are husband and wife, yes?'

'Yes.'

'Instruct them to look after the farm until they hear word from Wayland.' Max sipped the brandy, the ache in his hand, reminding him of what he'd done. 'I shall speak with Reeves. He will be in charge of it all until Wayland employs a new estate land agent. I need some hours to sort this out. I cannot leave without making arrangements for everyone else.'

'Max, they will cope. Let us go now. Leave it all behind.'

'They are good people, Thomas, and deserve me treating them well by informing them of the changes to come. I could not rest if I just ran away.' Max thought quickly. 'Give me tonight to settle my affairs and I will meet you in the village at seven o'clock in the morning. I shall ask John to take our luggage on one of the farm carts. Wayland will not even notice him, or the cart, is missing for a week or so. We shall go to York and decide from there.' He finished his drink.

'We can put our horses on the train and travel to Oxford to my townhouse.'

'You can, but I shall go to my farm near Lincoln.' Suddenly the idea of being his own man on his own land seemed like paradise.

'You have a farm?'

'A gift from Aunt Lucille, as you received. I was going to tell you all about it.'

'Thank the lord for dear Aunt Lucille.'

'I will call on Caroline before we leave.' Max put his hand up as Thomas went to speak. 'I will not be dissuaded on that. I must speak with her, explain what I am doing. Help her if I can for Wayland will want her off the farm as he threatened.'

Thomas nodded and walked to the door. 'I shall see you in the morning in the village.' As he opened the door Reeves came in and bowed.

'His lordship?' Max asked.

'Sleeping, sir,' Reeves said stiffly. 'His valet is attending to his… injuries.'

Thomas left the room, closing the door behind him.

Slumping into the armchair by the fire, Max rubbed his forehead in despair. Caroline, Wayland, Thomas and Miss Wilkes, it was all such a mess.

'Sir, if I may?'

Max looked up at Reeves. 'Yes?'

'Should anything come of his lordship's accident, if the police were to be involved... Well, I shall speak of what I saw. His lordship had tripped and fallen.'

Fondness for the old man filled him. 'Thank you, Reeves.'

'His lordship is not his father.' Reeves held his hands behind his back. 'His conduct since his arrival has not been that of a gentleman.'

'Sadly, I agree with you.'

'We have lost two maids. Gone because of what his lordship tried to do to them.'

'I am ashamed to call him my kin.' Max took a deep breath. 'Unfortunately, I can no longer live here, Reeves. I shall be gone in the morning. I regret to leave this burden on your shoulders, but you are now in charge of the abbey and the estate until my cousin is able to make different arrangements.'

Startled, Reeves nodded once. 'Understood, sir.'

'Sadly, you will have my cousin here for a little longer as he recovers.' Max stood. 'There is much I need to do. We shall speak again shortly. I will be either at my cottage or at my desk should you need me.'

Leaving the house, Max walked the familiar path to his cottage. It took him an hour to pack his trunks full of all his clothes, personal items, books and the miniature portraits of his parents and his uncle and aunt. He banked down the fire and placed the guard around it. By the door he dragged his trunk and a leather portmanteau. Princess watched him from her rug by the fire. He went to her and tussled her soft ears. 'Everything will be fine, girl,' he murmured, more to reassure himself than her.

Although tired, he knew there was much more to do.

Taking a lit lantern, he walked the paths to the stables. The yard was illuminated by several lamps as the grooms settled the horses for the night. He gestured to John, who walked out of one of the large doors carrying a bucket of water.

'Yes, sir?'

'At first light, I need you to have Queenie saddled. Also, load the luggage that is in my cottage on one of the farm carts and drive into the village to meet my brother. Take Princess with you. From there we shall travel to York.'

'Aye, sir.'

'Good man.' Max walked through the service areas, his heart heavy for he knew he'd not be returning to the house where he'd been so happy.

In his office he lit another lamp and a candelabra and placed them on his desk.

A slight knock on the door preceded Mrs Hoskins, who looked concerned. 'Forgive the interruption, sir, but I saw you enter.'

'What can I do for you, Mrs Hoskins?'

'Nothing for me, sir.' She stepped closer to his desk, clutching her hands. 'Mr Reeves has just given me the news that you are leaving.'

'I am.' The words were hard to say. He was letting his aunt and uncle down.

'We, all the staff, are dreadfully sorry to see you go. You're not one of us, but sometimes we felt that you were. You treated us so well and never once put on airs and graces as others did…' She tilted her head ever so slightly to mean Wayland.

He smiled with difficulty. 'We have all been in this house a long time, Mrs Hoskins.'

'Indeed, sir, and we have been blessed to serve you.'

'Thank you.' He cleared his throat that had suddenly tightened. 'Mr Reeves will be in charge of everything until his lordship makes other arrangements. I know you will support Mr Reeves unreservedly as he oversees a great deal more than his normal duties.'

'We will all support him,' replied Mrs Hoskins. 'We will manage, sir, don't worry about us. You look after yourself and Master Thomas.'

'I will, Mrs Hoskins, and well… thank you for everything.'

She closed the door softly behind her and Max began to sort out the onerous task of leaving behind his life.

Long into the night, he wrote letters until his sore hand ached even more. He absentmindedly ate the tray of food a maid brought in while he counted money for wages and wrote cheques to pay for bills and invoices. He updated accounting ledgers until his eyes blurred from tiredness. Still, he kept going as the hours ticked by. He did months' worth of work in one night…

A touch on the shoulder woke him with a start. He lifted his head from his folded arms on the desk and a pain shot up his shoulder from the awkward position he'd been sleeping in. Morning birdsong came from outside, and a grey light filtered into the office. The candles had gone out, and the lamps had run out of oil.

'Good morning, sir.' Reeves stood next to him. Reeves put a cup of tea on his desk and then started to collect all the envelopes Max had addressed to tenants, friends and businesses associated with the abbey.

'Good morning. Can you send those letters today? I have informed as many businesses as I can remember of my leaving. Any questions they have are to be directed to you.'

'Yes, sir.'

'Everything is in order for you. The wages are in the safe and there is a money tin to pay any outstanding bills I may have forgotten or which arrive after I leave. The safe number is written in the back of my diary.' Max gave the diary to Reeves.

'Very good, sir. John has collected your luggage and Princess. He's left for the village and your horse is saddled and waiting in the stable yard.'

'Thank you.' Max stood and pulled on his jacket. He took a quick sip of tea to wet his mouth, before grabbing his hat and coat. 'His lordship?'

'He apparently had an unsettled night.'

Max waited to feel guilty, but the emotion didn't arrive. What Wayland did to Caroline was far worse than the beating he received. 'Well, that is it then.'

Reeves walked with him out into the service yard where a number of servants were waiting in the dawn light. 'We all wish you the very best for the future, Mr Cavendish. It has been an honour to serve you.' Reeves shook Max's hand.

Touched by the words and their warm smiles, Max nodded, his throat tight with emotion. 'Thank you.'

He strode to the stables and mounted Queenie and with a final wave to the grooms, he trotted out through the arch in the wall and away from the abbey, his home. He couldn't think of that now though. It was too upsetting.

He set Queenie at a canter, wanting to reach Caroline quickly. He needed to speak with her, to apologise for mentioning Dolan to Wayland, for the anguish his folly had brought her.

The farm came into sight as the sun broke over the distant hills, streaking the fields in orange and gold.

Riding into the yard, he surprised Jacob who was carrying a crate. 'Good morning, Jacob,' he said dismounting.

'Good morning, Mr Cavendish.' Jacob lowered the crate to the ground.

'Is Mrs Lawson awake?' Max knew she would be because she milked the cows at dawn. 'Or in the dairy?'

'Neither, sir. She's gone.'

'Gone?'

'Aye. Caroline, Trixie, Mussy and the girls have left the farm.'

'To go where? The village?'

'Caroline wasn't sure as yet, just away from here.'

Max felt he was drowning. Caroline gone! 'Mrs Lawson should have come to me, I would have helped her.'

'That's unlikely, sir, isn't it?' Jacob folded his arms. 'Your cousin has evicted us.'

'But she did not have to leave immediately.'

'Sunset, he said yesterday as he whipped her with his riding crop.'

'He did what? He hit her?' Anger fired through Max. He should have killed that bastard!

'He attacked her while she and Trixie and the girls were blackberry picking along the hedgerow. Whipped the dogs, too. Caroline wasn't staying after that. They packed up their things and took the evening coach to York last night.'

'York?'

'Caroline's not wanting to stay in York, mind. This morning, they'll be getting a train.'

'Where will they be going?'

'Caroline didn't say. It'll depend on what train is first to leave the station this morning. She told me she'd write to me when they're settled. I'm going to our Sarah's for a bit once all the animals are gone from here, unless *his lordship* comes today and tells me to clear off!' Jacob said heatedly.

'He won't.' Max promised him.

'Well, I leave tomorrow when the shepherd comes to collect the flock for the market in York. I'll take the cattle herd to market myself and sell them. Caroline's going to need all the money I can get for her. The lot has to go now because we've nowhere to graze them. I'm taking the chickens and the milking cows to Annie's for her to have. I'm hoping Mr Purcell will buy the pigs from me, if not Annie will take them. Poor Annie, she's taken the news hard. She'll miss the girls.'

'I had nothing to do with any of this, Jacob,' Max told him, his mind racing. 'I must speak with Mrs Lawson. We can move the stock and run it on the estate until she is settled somewhere. She must not sell everything.'

'She has no choice. They'll end up in a city somewhere, that's what they were talking about last night. Caroline and Trixie can find work easier in a city.'

'No, she cannot just disappear into a city. How will I find her?' Max took his hat off and ran a hand through his hair in exasperation.

'You won't, sir. She doesn't want to be found and who can blame her? Caroline wants to forget about this place and all that's happened.'

Although he understood, it wounded Max terribly. He'd waited too long to tell Caroline how he felt and now he'd missed his chance. She was gone, and it broke him. 'I am leaving myself. Going to my farm in Lincoln. They can all come with me.'

'You are leaving?' Jacob's eyebrows shot up. 'That's surprising.'

'I can no longer be involved with my cousin.'

'He's a bad 'un, for sure. If you get to York in time, which I highly doubt, they're staying at the hotel near the station.' Jacob shook Max's hand. 'Good luck, Mr Cavendish.'

'If I miss them, would you get word to me that Mrs Lawson is well when she contacts you? My farm, Grange Lea, is north of Lincoln off Ermine Street, near South Carlton.'

'I don't know, sir, Caroline… well…'

'Yes, I understand she is eager to be rid of everything associated with this place. She has nothing but bad memories, but I love her, Jacob. I would marry her if she would have me.' There he'd said it out loud to another person, only not to the one it was meant for.

Jacob nodded.

Max pushed home his point. 'I just want to know she is safe and well, that is all.'

'I'll do my best, Mr Cavendish.'

Max mounted and urged Queenie down the drive. Shattered by the loss of Caroline and of his home, he wiped away the tears pricking his eyes.

CHAPTER 15

The early morning cold wind blew in Caroline's face as she walked down the shadowed Shambles in York. The sun had not yet reached high enough over the rooftops to banish the gloom of the narrow lane. Butchers were putting out their displays of meat, large hooks of pig carcasses, rabbits, braces of pheasants, and sides of beef. The smell of raw meat was strong and alley cats and stray dogs lingered about the cobbles, hoping to snatch a juicy morsel before being whacked with a broom.

She entered Mr Bent's butcher's shop and waited for two customers to leave before approaching the counter where Mrs Bent placed a slab of bacon onto the chopping block.

'It's you.' Mrs Bent took a large knife from a hook on the wall. 'Charles!' she hollered for her husband. 'We weren't expecting you.' She spoke coldly, as always.

'No, it was a sudden decision to come,' Caroline replied in the same tone. The two women stared at each other, both not liking the other.

Mr Bent, a large man with a larger smile, came out from

the back room and clapped his hands on seeing Caroline. 'Mrs Lawson! What a delight. Come through, come through,' he urged her around the counter, much to Mrs Bent's displeasure. 'How are you, dear lady?'

'Not so good, Mr Bent.' Caroline sat on the wooden chair he offered.

'I'm sorry to hear it. What happened to your face?'

She put a hand up to pull her hat a little lower, but her bruises and the cut on her cheek from Wayland's riding crop were difficult to hide. 'Trouble seems to find me wherever I go, Mr Bent.'

'Tell me what's going on?' He sat opposite her near his overcrowded desk.

'We've been evicted.'

His expression changed to shock. 'Lord, what a blow.'

'Jacob is still at the farm, he'll wait until the shepherd collects the flock tomorrow to bring them to market as we arranged. Then Jacob will bring the cattle to York for the beef auction, which is held on Tuesday?'

'Yes, it is. I'll be there.'

'We'll have to pay for the cattle to be held in the pens and fed until Tuesday but that can't be avoided. Once sold, all the money will go to you, to repay you for your investment. Our horse, Dossy, she'll be stabled and Jacob will tell you were when he gets here. Dossy is yours to either keep or sell.'

'Ah, lass.' He shook his head sadly. 'This was never the arrangement we had. We were to keep breeding on your farm for years to supply this shop, but also I could sell the surplus to the other butchers. Beef, pigs and sheep for years, that's what we were going to do.'

'I'm as devastated as you are, but nothing can be done.' Caroline gripped her reticule, distraught at the way her future had changed yet again. 'All the plans we made have come to nought. I have left a barn full of new hay, crates of potatoes and turnips, the animals, Annie…'

His big hands enveloped hers. 'Now, this is a setback, but not the end of the world, lass. We'll share the profits of the sales equally.'

'No, I can't, you invested money and—'

'Aye and you've invested time, blood, sweat and tears, too, no doubt.' He smiled. 'You've worked hard all year to build up that farm, you will receive an equal share of the profits.'

'Thank you.' She blinked away tears. 'Jacob will come to you after the sales. We aren't staying in York.' She shrugged slightly. 'We need to find somewhere new, a place that holds no memories on every corner.'

'I can understand that.' He patted her hand. 'But you'll let me know where you settle? We can write to each other as we have been doing. I'd like to know you're doing well.'

'I'll send a letter once we have a place.' She stood and impulsively embraced him. 'You've been the best of friends, Mr Bent.'

'Aww, lass, give over, you'll have me blubbering in a minute.' He held her tight for a second more and then stepped back. 'Take care, lass.'

Leaving the butcher's shop, Caroline headed back across the river to the hotel near the train station. Each step she took, she said a silent goodbye to the familiar buildings for she knew she'd not come back. She thought of Max and her heart twisted with a flash of longing. If things had been different, perhaps they could have explored something deeper than friendship, but Wayland ruined all that.

At the hotel, Caroline climbed the staircase to the rooms they stayed in last night. Elsie and Bertha were sitting by the window watching the trains and the people below and at their feet sat Prince and Duke. Caroline had paid extra to have the dogs in her room, but there was no way she was going to leave them tied up in the stables along the street where anyone might steal them.

'Where is Trixie?' Caroline asked Elsie, taking off her gloves.

'In Mussy's room. He's not well again,' Elsie replied, stroking Prince's ear.

Crossing the hall, Caroline quietly opened Mussy's door. Trixie sat on his bed, helping him to sip some water. Caroline stepped around to the other side of the bed. 'Mussy?' She held his hand.

'I am fine, Caro,' he croaked.

'A coughing fit,' Trixie explained. 'I've told him to rest until we board the train.'

'Are you well enough to travel?' Caroline asked him. 'We can wait until you are up to it.'

'Then we will never leave this hotel,' Mussy murmured. 'We must keep going, find a new home.'

'I shall go downstairs and look at the timetable.'

'No need,' Trixie said, standing. 'Mussy went downstairs to have a look. It was him standing in the draft by the door that started his coughing.' She took a piece of paper by the bedside and gave it to Caroline. 'The first London train leaves in half an hour. We'd have to change at Doncaster wherever that is.'

'London?' Caroline glanced at them both.

'South, it's warmer.' Mussy grinned, his face pale, his lips blue.

'Then that's where we'll go.' She nodded, decision made. 'London is a big place, so I've heard,' she joked to lighten the mood. 'We'll find work there.'

'Will Jacob come to London?' Trixie asked, looking unsure.

'He'll go wherever you are.' Caroline was certain of it. 'Once we have a place, I'll send a note to him and Mr Bent with our address.'

Trixie nodded. 'We'd best buy the tickets then.'

It took a while and a couple of porters to help get their belongings down to the station. Caroline paid for their tickets and also for Prince and Duke to be put in the luggage carriage. Another woman's dog was tied up near them and a cat in a basket was strapped to a shelf.

Caroline bent and fondled Prince and Duke's ears. 'Be good boys now.'

'They'll be fine, missus.' A youth wearing the railway's uniform came into the carriage carrying a trunk. 'I'll be travelling with them as far as Doncaster. I'll make sure they're looked after.' He put the trunk down and patted Duke's head. 'What a fine pair they are, missus.'

'They mean the world to me.' Caroline gave the boy a coin. 'Look after them and I'll give you another one at Doncaster.'

He tipped his hat to her, and she left the luggage carriage to walk up the platform to find the others.

'Calm down,' Trixie warned Bertha and Elsie who were giddy with excitement to be going on their first train ride.

Mussy, bent over slightly, coughing, gripped Caroline's hand. 'Let us board, I need to sit down.'

She helped him into the carriage, noticing how just the act of walking down the hotel staircase and through to the station had weakened him. He puffed and coughed as she eased him into a seat. 'Sleep if you can.'

'I shall be better soon,' he whispered.

'Of course, you will.'

'I hate being a burden.'

'You're family, never a burden.' She smiled tenderly. She stared out of the window, searching the faces on the platform, hoping to see Max, which was silly because he didn't even know she'd gone, but still a foolish part of her wanted to see him come after her.

Trixie settled the girls in the seat opposite and they squealed in part terror and part enjoyment as the train jolted forward. 'Shush now, or they might throw us off.'

Steam puffed across the window and the faces blurred and were gone as they chugged along the line leaving York behind.

Elsie gripped Bertha's hand. 'It's going so fast! Faster than a carriage.'

'We won't crash, will we?' Bertha whispered.

'No, we are very safe,' Mussy murmured. 'I have been on a train a dozen times and never had a problem.'

'We're going to be on the train for a long time,' Trixie warned them. 'Get yourself comfortable.'

The girls fought to be near the window until Trixie snapped at them that they'll take turns.

Eventually, silence descended on the little group and the rocking motion of the carriage soon lulled Mussy to sleep. After a while, tired of gazing at the passing countryside, Elsie quietly read a book to Bertha.

'London is going to be very different,' Trixie mused, watching a village pass by. 'Much bigger than York.'

'We'll be fine,' Caroline said with determination. 'We'll seek a house to rent and find jobs.'

'You make it sound so easy, it wasn't in York.'

'London will provide more opportunities than York. We have a bit of money this time, and Mr Bent will send us more with Jacob. That will tide us over until we find work. Mussy knows a little of the place, which will help.'

Trixie looked at Mussy. 'He's not good, Caro,' she whispered. 'Skin and bones.'

'Once we have a home, we'll build his strength up and he'll be fine. Imagine how many bookshops will be in the city, he'll be so happy.' Caroline refused to think of anything negative or she'd go mad. They'd left everything behind to start again. This move had to work for them all, she couldn't, *wouldn't,* contemplate anything else.

When they finally reached Doncaster, they were told they would have to change trains. The next train would be leaving in an hour.

'Let's stretch our legs,' Trixie said to her sisters, waking Mussy.

'I'll get Prince and Duke and make sure our luggage is taken off.' Caroline waited for other passengers to pass by before entering the corridor. 'I'll meet you on the platform. There might be a tea room.'

Prince and Duke were excited to see her. 'How were they?' she asked the youth.

'Brilliant, such good boys.' He pulled out one of her trunks. 'Are you getting on the London train on the other side of the platform?'

'Yes. We'll need all our trunks taken off.' Caroline took Prince and Duke's leads and led them down the ramp. 'Is it that train?' She pointed to the steam train puffing and hissing into the station and halting along the opposite platform.

'No, missus. Your train hasn't arrived. Doncaster is a busy station, trains come and go from all over the country. I think that one is for Lincoln.'

Caroline watched the train grind to a halt, wheels screeching. Lincoln was where Max was born. No, she didn't have the time to think about him. That part of her life was over.

The youth pulled out another trunk. 'I'll load your luggage on the platform and keep an eye on it until I leave. We'll be heading back to York in about twenty minutes, but the porters here are decent and will sort you out.'

'You're rather decent, too.' She thanked him and gave him another tip.

Outside the station was a little park with a square of green lawn. Caroline took the dogs to it and let them off lead to run about for a few minutes. The September weather had turned to grey skies and a cool wind caused the leaves to fall in showers of gold and red. Not many people were sitting in the park, the breezy autumn conditions discouraged anyone to linger. A train whistle blew, adding to the noise of the city streets.

Wishing for a cup of tea and hoping there was a refreshments room at the station, Caroline called the dogs to her side and walked back up the side ramp and onto the platform.

'Our train has been delayed,' Trixie told her.

'Why?'

'There's something wrong with the track a few miles away, so the porter told me.'

'Did he say for how long?'

'Another hour at least.'

'Is there a tea room?'

'No, just a gentleman's refreshment room. Mussy is in there. He's sitting by the fire.'

'Good, that'll keep him warm, but there's nothing at all for women?'

'We don't count it seems,' Trixie said testily.

Annoyed and frustrated, Caroline turned her face away from the wind that found its way into the station. 'Are we allowed on the train to wait?'

Trixie shrugged. 'Won't hurt to ask.'

'I was hoping for a cup of tea.'

'Why don't we walk into town and find an inn?' Trixie motioned for her sisters to join them. 'Our Elsie needs to relieve herself and our Bertha is hungry.'

'One day places like these might cater for women and children,' Caroline tutted.

'Aye, but that doesn't help us now, does it?'

Suddenly, a gentleman ran out of the refreshment room, hollering for a porter. 'Someone fetch a doctor. There's a gentleman in there who has collapsed.'

Caroline and Trixie stared at each other. Caroline threw the dogs' leads to Elsie and ran with Trixie along the platform and into the room. By the fire several men were helping Mussy into a chair.

'Mussy!' Caroline knelt beside him. He was limp and grey-faced.

'Is this your husband, madam?' one gentleman asked.

'No, my dear friend.'

'He's not well at all. Someone has sent for a doctor.'

'Thank you.'

'Some water.' A young serving maid came to them with a glass of water but although Caroline tried to get Mussy to sip it, most dribbled down his chin. Eyes closed, Mussy murmured something then coughed repeatedly until blood coated his lips.

'Here.' Trixie pulled out a handkerchief from Mussy's coat pocket.

Caroline dabbed his lips and offered him some more water. 'We'll get you a doctor,' she whispered, frightened by his paleness.

'We cannot… miss the train,' Mussy barely got the words out.

'There will be others.' She smiled to reassure him.

It took what seemed an age before a doctor came. Mussy dozed on and off, shaking with cold. Gentlemen came and went from the room, trains steamed in and out of the station and the sun lowered behind the rooftops before a young doctor came into the refreshment room.

'I am Doctor Gibb,' he said, shaking Caroline's hand. 'Tell me what has happened.'

Caroline told him about Mussy's health over the last few months as she woke Mussy with a gentle shake on his shoulder.

'Tuberculosis,' Doctor Gibb stated, having listened to Mussy's chest and back. 'That is what your doctor diagnosed?'

'Yes.'

'You know there is nothing I can do to cure that, don't you?' Doctor Gibb seemed about thirty years of age and his manner was kind, sympathetic.

Caroline nodded. 'We will nurse him back to health.'

He packed away his instruments. 'Your friend needs a warm bed immediately. St Thomas' Hospital is nearby. I can hire a hansom to transport him there.'

'He doesn't want to be in a hospital.' Caroline didn't want to tell this nice doctor that Mussy refused to be in a hospital because it would remind him too much of being in prison.

'A hospital is the most suitable place for him.'

'We will look after him.'

Doctor Gibb's eyebrows rose. 'That will be difficult whilst travelling.'

'We don't have a home,' Caroline said guiltily. If she'd not fought with Wayland, Mussy would be warm in his bed at the farm right now instead of sitting in a draughty room at a train station.

'Mr Casey needs rest, madam.' Doctor Gibb pulled Mussy's coat tight around him with gentle hands. 'I suggest you find an inn who can put you up at least for tonight. A warm bed and a good broth is very much the order for Mr Casey.'

Trixie, standing behind them, tapped Caroline's arm. 'I'll go into the town and call in at the first inn I see and get some rooms for us.'

The doctor put on his hat over thick wavy brown hair. 'There's the White Hare Inn on French Gate, opposite the Guild Hall. It's reputable. I'm friends with the landlord, I treated his wife.'

'Then we'll go there,' Caroline said to Trixie. 'I'll find a cart to take our luggage and the dogs.'

'I'll find a hansom cab,' Doctor Gibb said. 'I'll escort Mr Casey to the inn, and you can follow when you have sorted out your luggage.'

Caroline shook the doctor's hand. 'You have been most kind.'

He smiled. 'This is my last call for the day, so I have time to settle Mr Casey in a room.'

On the platform, Caroline hurried over to the station-master and explained the situation. Elsie and Bertha with the two dogs waited behind her, the girls nervously watching the doctor and Trixie assist Mussy to a hansom cab on the street.

'I'll personally see that your luggage is delivered to the White Hare Inn, madam.' The stationmaster clicked his fingers to two young porters standing by the ramp.

A gleaming black train, wheels squealing, steam hissing, pulled into the station as Caroline ushered Elsie and Bertha along the platform. 'We're to stay at an inn this evening and maybe tomorrow as well until Mussy is stronger,' she spoke loudly over the spurts of steam.

'Aren't we going to London now?' Elsie asked.

'Not yet. Now I need your help with Prince and Duke. I need you both to take them on walks for me while Trixie and I care for Mussy, can you do that?'

'Aye, we can,' Elsie answered.

'I'm hoping the landlord will allow the dogs in our rooms, but they might have to sleep in the stable if the inn has one.'

'They can't be without us, they'll be frightened,' Bertha cried.

'Mrs Lawson!'

Caroline turned at her name being called and gaped in shock at seeing Max and Thomas climbing down from the train. Her pulse raced at Max's handsome face though he looked concerned.

'Mr Cavendish, Thomas,' Caroline greeted them. She didn't expect ever to see them again.

'What a stroke of luck to find you here,' Max said, his gaze not leaving Caroline. 'I heard you had left the farm and was desperate to speak to you.'

'Your cousin evicted us.' The wind buffeted them, she held onto her hat.

'I had no knowledge of his intentions, I assure you.'

Trixie joined them. 'Doctor Gibb has taken Mussy in the hansom. French Gate is not far. We can walk,' she said quietly, after giving the two brothers a little nod of her head, her cheeks flushed.

Max frowned. 'A doctor has taken Mr Casey?'

'Yes, Mussy collapsed when we arrived. He's been taken to an inn to rest. We are going there now.' Caroline shielded

Bertha from the worst of the wind. 'We must go, good day to you both.'

'Wait!' Max held out his hand. 'Are you staying in Doncaster for long?'

'Only until Mussy is well enough to travel.' Caroline ushered Trixie and the girls a few steps.

'Then where are you going?'

She turned back to him, surprised at the interest. 'London.'

His eyes widened. 'Why London? Do you know anyone there?'

'No, but it's a city where we can find work and lodging.' Caroline took another step away.

'Which inn are you staying at this evening?' Max's coat flapped as the wind grew stronger.

'The White Hare on French Gate.'

'I will come and call on you in the morning, if I may?'

Thomas gestured to the other platform. 'Max, the Lincoln train leaves in ten minutes, it's the last one for the day and we have to get our luggage, the horses and Princess sorted onto it.'

'There is always tomorrow, Brother.'

'We are staying here?' Thomas said in surprise.

'Mrs Lawson may need our assistance.'

'We don't,' Caroline told him. 'Please don't change your plans on our account.'

'I would like to talk to you,' Max said, his tone full of hope. 'Please?'

'Forgive me, Mr Cavendish, but my priority is Mussy.'

'Then I will help you care for him,' Max said stubbornly. 'There are things we need to discuss. I shan't leave for Lincoln until we have talked properly.'

'We must go.' Caroline purposely kept walking, holding the dogs' leads. The light had dwindled to a deepening dusk.

Once out of the station she glanced at Trixie as the gusts blew leaves and papers down the street. 'I never expected we'd meet them again.'

'Me either.' Trixie sighed. 'It's embarrassing.'

'What could he possibly want to talk to me about?' Caroline mused, head down. 'He has nothing to say to me that I want to hear.'

'Don't be too harsh on him, Caro,' Trixie spoke against the gale. 'He's not his cousin.'

'No...'

'And he's not his brother either,' Trixie scoffed. 'Thomas could barely look at me.'

'It's Thomas's loss, Trix.' Caroline gave her a compassionate smile. 'Put him from your heart and mind. You don't need Thomas Cavendish.'

'No, but do you need Max Cavendish?' Trixie asked with raised eyebrows.

CHAPTER 16

$\mathcal{A}$t the knock on the door, Caroline rose stiffly from the chair beside Mussy's bed. In the double bed opposite, Trixie and the girls slept. Doctor Gibb had managed to secure them a room at the White Hare Inn, a good size one with a double and a single bed. Two rooms would have been more convenient, but he'd taken the only room left and Caroline had been grateful for his efforts.

Opening the door, Caroline smiled at the young woman holding a tea tray. 'Lizzy, isn't it?'

'Aye, miss. Me father is the landlord.' She stepped into the room and seeing everyone was asleep gently placed the tray on the small table in front of the fire. 'I'll bring ye up some coal,' she whispered. 'I thought ye'd like a cup of tea before breakfast.'

'That's very kind of you,' Caroline whispered back.

'Ye haven't slept in that chair all night, have ye?' The girl looked alarmed.

'Mussy stirred a lot. His coughing wakes him. I wanted to stay close to help him sip some water and stay warm.

Doctor Gibb gave him a sleeping draught, but it didn't last long.'

'Doctor Gibb is grand, isn't he?' Lizzy said with admiration. 'He was ever so good with our mam.'

'He is a rare man indeed,' Caroline agreed. 'How are my dogs?'

'Fine, miss. I've fed them some scraps this morning and took them out into the yard to pee.'

'I'm very grateful.'

'I'm sorry me father wouldn't let them be up here with ye, but they were warm by the kitchen fire. They both kept watching the door, waiting for ye.'

'We are never normally parted.'

Lizzy crept back to the door, wincing when one of the floorboards creaked. 'I'll be back shortly with the coal.'

'Thank you, Lizzy.' Caroline poured out a cup of tea, desperate to quench her thirst. It'd been a long night with small bouts of sleep. Trixie had stayed up with her until midnight, but then Caroline had told her to go to bed. It didn't make sense for them both to be awake.

Caroline opened the curtains a crack to peek out at the waking town. Horse and carts and loaded wagons passed by below, the rumbling wheels loud on the cobbles. Working men wearing flat caps went to their numerous jobs at foundries, factories, mills and malt kilns. Opposite the inn was the impressive Guild Hall with its four tall columns and arched windows. She'd never been to this town before and was curious.

Movement behind her made her close the curtain again. Trixie was climbing out of bed, wrapping a shawl around her shoulders.

'Morning,' Caroline whispered.

'Morning. How is he?' Trixie padded over to Caroline, rubbing the sleep from her eyes.

'Not a great night, but I feel there is some colour in his cheeks again.'

Trixie peered at Mussy. 'Yes, definitely. It's because this room is so warm.'

'It's what he needs.'

'I need the pot.' Trixie scowled. 'I can't do it near Mussy.'

'Use the pot on the other side of our bed. He's asleep, he won't see, and if he did, he wouldn't care.'

'I care,' Trixie snorted. 'Oh, tea.'

'I'll pour you a cup.' Caroline turned her back to pour the tea while Trixie relieved herself and got dressed. They stood sipping the tea watching the flames of the fire.

'Can I have one of those?' Mussy murmured, waking.

Caroline brought a cup over to him and helped him to sit up against the pillows. 'How do you feel?'

'Better.'

'You actually look it, too.'

'Back to my normal handsome self?' he croaked. He held the cup himself and sipped at it.

'You're always your handsome self.' She smiled.

'Flatterer.'

'Though you need a shave.'

He scratched at his moustache and the stubble on his jaw. 'I might grow a beard.'

'It would suit you.' Caroline straightened the blankets.

'This room is lovely and warm. Perhaps I could have an egg or something?'

'Of course. I'll go downstairs and ask.'

He grasped her hand. 'I need to build my strength up. I am not ready to leave you just yet.'

Her heart sank at the very idea of him dying. 'Absolutely. We're going to get you well.'

'Forgive me for delaying our journey.'

'A week or so will hardly matter. Your health is more important.' She squeezed his hand and went to the door as the girls woke. 'I'll see what can be done about breakfast.'

Downstairs, the inn was busy with early travellers heading out to catch a train or a coach. Caroline found Lizzy coming out of one of the back rooms carrying a bucket of coal.

'Oh, miss, I was just on my way up.'

'I'll take it, Lizzy, but I was wondering if we could have some breakfast here or do we need to go elsewhere for it?'

'No, ye can have it here, miss. We've a kitchen and a good cook. There's a table in the back room or ye can have it up in ye room.'

'In our room will be best, I think. Eggs and some porridge for the five of us?'

'Ham, too? We've got a nice leg of ham delivered only yesterday.'

'That'll be fine, thank you.' Caroline took the bucket from her and made for the stairs.

'Mrs Lawson.' Doctor Gibb came down the corridor from the taproom. 'How is the patient?'

'Better this morning, Doctor Gibb.'

'May I visit him?' Gibb took the bucket from her and they climbed the stairs together.

'My, this is an improvement,' Gibb declared, walking into the room and seeing Mussy sitting up, listening to Elsie and Bertha chatting to him. 'I am Doctor Gibb, if you don't remember.' He shook Mussy's hand.

'My saviour?' Mussy grinned, then coughed.

'I consider these wonderful ladies are your saviours, Mr Casey.' He looked at Caroline. 'I shall examine him.'

'Right, yes. We shall go downstairs and have breakfast, unless you need me?'

'No, not at all.'

'Mussy, your breakfast tray will be sent up,' Caroline said, ushering the girls out the door.

Doctor Gibb sat in the chair by the bed. 'Don't rush, Mrs Lawson. I can stay with Mr Casey for a while. I'm not due at the hospital for an hour yet.'

'He's nice,' Trixie said as they went downstairs.

'I hope we find a doctor as good as Gibb once we are in London,' Caroline said as Lizzy approached them. 'A change of plans, Lizzy.'

'Do you think we should write to Jacob and let him know we are to be staying here for a week or so?' Trixie asked as they were shown into a small room where one man was already seated at a table eating.

'It wouldn't hurt to inform Mr Bent where we are.' Caroline poured out glasses of water for them all from a jug on the table. 'I'll write to him after breakfast and ask if he'll visit Jacob at his sister's home and tell him of our situation.'

'I'll miss the farm, and all the animals and Dossy,' Bertha muttered sadly.

'Me, too.' Caroline patted her cheek. 'But we couldn't take Dossy to London.'

'Jacob will bring us the money from the sales of the stock, which is a relief.' Trixie drank some water.

'Agreed. We need as much money as we can get to set up in London.' Caroline nodded to Lizzy who brought in plates and bowls on a tray.

'Can we take the dogs for a walk after breakfast?' Bertha piped up.

'We'll do that when we go to the post office.'

As promised, after breakfast, Caroline took the girls and the dogs for a walk, she'd written a brief letter to Mr Bent and asked Lizzy where the post office was situated. Fortunately, it was only two streets away as the grey skies sent down a light drizzle. They hurried to the post office on Priory Place and then hurried back again, rushing around to the back of the inn and entering through the scullery.

Lizzy was washing up in a large stone sink. 'Did ye find the post office, madam?'

'We did.'

'Nasty day out there. There's a cloth under the sink here if ye want to dry off.' Lizzy took two bowls of food scraps and placed them on the floor for Prince and Duke.

'You'll make them fat, Lizzy,' Caroline gently admonished.

'Nay, they're beautiful boys. They can keep me company.'

Caroline pressed a shilling into Lizzy's hand. 'I appreciate your help.'

Upstairs, Caroline opened the door, listening to Elsie chatter about one of her boots that had a hole in the sole.

'We'll take them to the cobblers,' Caroline said, stopping at the sight of Mr Cavendish sitting in the chair by Mussy's bed. Cavendish had said he'd call, but it still sent her pulse racing seeing him in the room. Trixie was sewing by the fire and gave her a small smile as though to say, keep calm, everything is all right.

Cavendish rose and bowed. 'Mrs Lawson, Elsie, Bertha.'

'Good day, Mr Cavendish.' Caroline's heart thumped a little faster, but she turned from him and pulled off her gloves. 'No Thomas?'

'He has caught a train to Oxford. After some persuasion, he is resuming his studies.' Max went to stand by the window, giving Caroline the chair but she remained where she was.

'The three of us have had a lovely talk, Caro,' Mussy said, wheezing slightly.

'Perhaps it's time you had a nap,' Caroline said. 'You mustn't overtire yourself.'

'I will, in a moment.' Mussy waved her closer. 'We have something to discuss with you.'

Trixie stood and placed her sewing back in the basket. 'You don't have to decide anything just yet, we were just discussing a plan.'

Caroline stared at her. 'You've been discussing something important without me?' she accused.

'Now, Caro, do not fire yourself up,' soothed Mussy, his voice low. 'Listen, I cannot talk for long before it exhausts me.'

'Exactly, so whatever it is can wait. You need to rest.'

Mussy held up his hand to silence her. 'Mr Cavendish has kindly offered us a place to stay, at his farm north of Lincoln.' Mussy began to cough.

Cavendish quickly passed him a glass of water.

Caroline watched how he carefully helped Mussy settle back against the pillows and was touched by his gentleness. But that he had a farm, and he didn't tell her about it disturbed her. They'd had so many conversations since they met, and not once had he mentioned a farm. What else hadn't he told her?

Did he know what his cousin had done to her? The thought horrified her.

Trixie came to stand beside Caroline. 'We thought that by going to Mr Cavendish's farm, we could stay for the winter, so we'd have a roof over our heads while Mussy recovers his strength.'

'We could do that in London,' Caroline argued. The idea of being dependent on Max Cavendish didn't sit well with her. Besides, his horrid swine of a cousin could show up at any time. She folded her hands in front of her. 'You wanted to be down south, Mussy, where it's warmer.'

'Lincoln is south of York. It's south of Doncaster even.' Mussy grinned weakly. 'The climate is a little milder. We can have day trips to the coast…'

Trixie touched Caroline's elbow. 'Staying at Mr Cavendish's home would save us trying to find a place of our own in bad weather, and buying furniture and getting settled when Mussy isn't well enough to handle it.'

'And what about finding work?' Caroline focused on Trixie. 'Our money won't last for long.'

'I would not expect you to pay for anything while staying with me,' Max told her.

She'd been avoiding looking at him but did so now. 'You would be staying there with us?'

'Yes. I have only recently inherited the farm and I plan to make it my home.'

So, that cleared up one question. 'What about the abbey's estate, your responsibilities to your cousin?'

'Both are no longer any of my concern. I have resigned from my position.' He tapped the top on the chair as if in frustration.

This news shocked her that he had left the estate. Then she noticed the bruising on his knuckles. Their gazes locked, hers full of questions, and his full of tenderness and apology.

Caroline stepped to the fire, uneasy in mind and heart.

Could she stay at Cavendish's home with him there? Confined to sharing his house throughout a long cold winter?

'For Mussy's sake, I think we should do it, Caro,' Trixie whispered, coming to stand close to her. 'We'd have a roof over our heads, be warm and fed. Safe. The other option is roaming the streets of London by ourselves. It'd be like the Water Lanes all over again. No decent work, money running out, worrying about the girls…'

Caroline saw the fear in Trixie's large eyes. The fear of returning to the streets, of earning pennies from unsavoury work. She would do anything for Trixie and the girls, even if that meant living with a handsome man who gazed at her with such warmth and wanting, emotions she wasn't certain she could return.

'What are your concerns, Mrs Lawson?' Cavendish asked, coming closer when Trixie moved to sit on the bed with her sisters.

'My concerns are many, Mr Cavendish, but the main one is your cousin. We… we don't get along.' She touched the cut on her cheek. 'Would he be a regular visitor?'

'No, not at all,' Max said firmly. 'We have had a disagreement. I very much doubt I will ever see him again and I hope that I never do.'

Her eyes widened at his vehement vow. Caroline wanted to ask why but something held her back. Had they fallen out over something? Did it matter? As long as Wayland never came to visit, she could do it, she would do it for Trixie, the girls and Mussy.

She glanced at Mussy and Trixie, then back to Cavendish. 'We'd only stay for the winter, if that's agreeable? Once spring arrives, we'll take our leave.'

His smile was immediate and joyful. 'As you wish.'

'We are thankful for your kind offer.'

His blue eyes were warm, his expression happy. 'I shall make arrangements.'

Mussy stirred from his bed. 'Give me two days, my good man, and I shall be able to travel.'

'Two days?' Caroline glared at him. 'Doctor Gibb will be the one who decides when you are able to travel.'

'Don't argue, Mussy,' Trixie said, chuckling. 'We've won this one, let's not push it.'

'Aren't we going to London now?' Elsie asked quietly.

'No, pet,' Trixie answered. 'We're to live at Mr Cavendish's farm for a bit.'

'On a farm!' Bertha sighed happily. 'I didn't want to live in a city again.'

'Will Annie visit us?' Elsie asked.

'Mrs Aspall is welcome to visit and stay any time she wishes,' Cavendish said, smiling at the girls. 'Perhaps you both can learn to ride a pony as well?'

Elsie and Bertha looked at each other, then squealed in rapture. Caroline watched as Trixie's face transformed to pure bliss at seeing her sisters so delighted.

How could Caroline wish for the unknown streets of London when they had the chance to be content at Max Cavendish's home? Yet, the winter months would be difficult for her spending so much time in his presence. Was she strong enough to remain distant from him? Then she thought of Wayland and knew he'd always be a secret between them.

CHAPTER 17

$\mathcal{O}$n a windy, cold October day, Mussy was declared well enough to travel. They all rejoiced, except for Doctor Gibb, who'd become a friend, calling on them every day, usually with treats for Mussy and the girls.

'I shall miss you all a great deal,' Doctor Gibb said as they all stood on the train platform, ready to board the Lincoln bound train.

Jacob had arrived the previous day after spending time with his sister. He and Max had secured the three dogs and Queenie into the stock transport carriage and had all their luggage stowed on board. Jacob had offered to stay in the stock carriage to care for Queenie and the dogs.

Dressed in a dark-brown suit, Cavendish checked their tickets he'd bought. 'You are welcome to visit any time, Doctor Gibb. You have the address.'

'I shall look forward to it.' Gibb shook hands with them all, lastly Mussy. 'Take care of yourself, my friend.'

'You will write?' Mussy prompted, although weak, he was

standing and walking. Eight days of bed rest and good food had given him some colour and energy.

'I will.' Doctor Gibb waited for them all to board and then waved, before strolling down the platform and out of sight.

'We can never repay him for his dedicated attention,' Mussy said, puffing slightly as he sat on the seat by the window.

'I meant what I said, he is welcome at Grange Lea any time.' Cavendish placed a few of their smaller bags in the overhead racks.

'That's a nice name, Grange Lea,' Trixie said, ushering the girls to sit.

'The land once belonged to one of the Bishops of Lincoln, apparently,' Cavendish said.

'Your aunt is very generous to gift it to you while she's still alive.' Caroline tucked a blanket around Mussy's lap and sat down as the train jerked forward.

Cavendish nodded. 'Aunt Lucille is a wonderful woman. Grange Lea was, is, special to her, my uncle bought it for her because she was missing Lincoln and her family. However, becoming Lady Stockton-Lee, she did not have the time to visit as much as she wanted to. Her last visit was some twenty years ago. I look forward to writing to her and describing the farm as it is now.'

'Perhaps I could sketch her a few drawings?' Mussy offered. 'I have not used my art skills since I left university, but I used to be quite good at it.'

'I could think of no greater gift for my aunt.'

'A snow scene, perhaps? When the snow arrives,' Caroline said. 'Living in India she may miss the feel of snow on her face, the whiteness of the landscape.'

Cavendish's smile showed his enthusiasm for the idea. 'Perfect.'

'You'll have to draw it from inside, mind, no going out and getting a chill,' Trixie reminded Mussy.

Caroline relaxed with the rocking motion of the train. The passing countryside would be bright or dull as they flashed by depending on the clouds covering the sun. Mussy dozed and Trixie pulled out her knitting. She was teaching Elsie and Bertha to knit and while Elsie was good at it, Bertha soon lost interest and watched the scenery.

While Cavendish read a newspaper, Caroline could study him without his noticing. The last eight days had been an indication of what living the winter with him would be like. Cavendish was kind and considerate. Nothing was ever too much trouble to him. He'd called at the inn each day, but never overstayed his welcome. He and Mussy would talk of current world affairs, discuss politics and books, and from those times, Caroline was able to be at ease in his company. Yes, one smile from him made her blood race, but she also found a sense of calmness from him. He was a man content in his own skin. He didn't need to be loud, to show off, to peacock about the place believing in his own importance, and she admired that.

Cavendish was comfortable talking with Mussy about foreign countries or being silly with the girls. He treated Elsie and Bertha as little sisters, buying them small gifts to make their time in the inn more pleasant. He'd even started calling Bertha, Bertie-Bear, as a nickname. Trixie adored him, Jacob respected him and Mussy thought him to be a true gentleman. Caroline was grateful to him but shied away from delving any deeper into her thoughts about him.

They alighted the train at Lincoln during a brief rainstorm. Protected in the station's booking office, they waited for their luggage, the dogs and Queenie to be unloaded. Cavendish went out onto the street to look for the manager of Grange Lea, who'd he'd written to asking him to come to the station with the farm cart and a carriage if there was one at the property.

Jacob came into the booking office with the three dogs and gave the leads to Elsie and Bertha. Rain dripped off his hat. 'I'm told to take the horse down to the holding yard on the other side of the station.'

Caroline made a fuss of the dogs. 'Take Queenie there and Mr Cavendish will come to you. He expects to ride Queenie beside the carriage.'

A few minutes later, Cavendish, his expression one of annoyance, entered. 'I cannot find anyone from Grange Lea. I have asked every coach driver out on the street.'

'The rain might have held your man up?' Mussy said, wearing a thick coat and a woollen scarf around his neck.

'Jacob has taken Queenie to the holding yard,' Caroline said. 'We can't stay here.'

'No, you can't.' The stationmaster appeared, eyeing the group with disdain. 'Get those dogs out of my booking office immediately.'

'Shall we go to an inn?' Caroline suggested as they filed out.

'Yes.' Cavendish ushered them out of the station. He pointed to a red-brick building opposite. 'The Albion Hotel. Go in there and wait for me. I shall hire us a carriage if need be. We might meet the manager on the road.'

Scurrying out of the rain, Caroline worried for Mussy. In the Albion Hotel, they found seats by the fire and Caroline ordered tea for them all. A large woman served them, glaring at the three dogs.

'We are only staying a short time,' Caroline promised her.

'I don't want the smell of wet dog in my hotel, thank you very much, You can pay extra for having them in here,' she announced before flouncing off.

'We won't be staying the night here, that is for certain, not with that old hag.' Mussy grinned.

It took half an hour before Cavendish returned, soaking wet and frustrated. 'I have hired a carriage and a wagon. Jacob is loading the luggage onto the cart. He'll go with that driver and take the dogs. I shall ride Queenie, leaving the five of you to travel in the carriage.' He looked a little irritated. 'I will be having words with the manager once we reach Grange Lea. This is not good enough.' He turned to Mussy. 'I apologise. I never wanted you to be out in this weather.'

Mussy pushed himself to his feet. 'Please do not worry, my good man. I am sure there is a simple explanation about why your transport did not arrive and soon we will all be sitting around a warm fire in your home.'

Cavendish grunted some response, but Caroline could tell he was annoyed.

The rainy weather didn't ease as they journeyed through the busy Lincoln streets, climbing slowly up the huge hill, circling the mighty Lincoln Cathedral, always climbing, straining the horses.

'Imagine walking up and down this hill every day carrying shopping?' Trixie said as they looked out of the carriage's rain-streaked windows.

'We must find the chance to visit St Mary's Cathedral,' Mussy said. 'It is one of the grandest cathedrals in the country.'

'Grander than York Minster?' Trixie touted. 'I think not.'

Caroline saw Cavendish riding beside them every once in a while. Sometimes he had to drop back to allow other vehicles to pass on the narrow roads.

Eventually they made it to the top of the high hill and caught a glimpse of the sprawling town below them, including the old castle walls and prison.

Rain fell harder as they continued, drawing the day in early, shadowing the landscape as they headed away from the township and into the countryside.

Max had told them the farm was three miles from Lincoln, situated between Ermine Street, the old Roman Road as the locals called the long straight road from Lincoln to the River Humber, and the small village of South Carlton. The countryside was all farming, level fields on the top of a plateau, the Lincoln Ridge. As they headed north, the land to the west gently descended to the River Till. It was very different to the area north of York which Caroline knew so well. This road was straight and narrow with ditches along each side and the farms dotted on the flat landscape could easily be seen stretching for miles.

Caroline looked out at the darkening light. Low thick clouds covered the rising moon and the stars. Cavendish trotted past them and turned left into a drive between open iron gates that hung drunkenly off stone pillars. As the carriage turned into the gates, Cavendish rode ahead and Caroline lost sight of him in front of the carriage.

The drive was not long, but old trees lined it and the rain dropping from them hit the carriage roof like pebbles being thrown. Caroline's first sight of the house shocked her. She'd been expecting a farm cottage, similar to the one she had lived in at Hopewood Farm, but this house was a small manor.

Even in the murky light and hidden in deep shadows thrown by enormous trees, the stone house rose two storeys high with a third storey of dormer windows jutting from the slate roof. Decorative white stone edged the corners of the house, contrasting against the limestone. White painted windows were equal in size and number on each side of the double-front black door.

From inside the carriage, they watched Cavendish dismount and stare at the house.

'Are we at the wrong place?' Mussy asked.

'The house is huge,' Trixie whispered.

Cavendish went to the front door to find it was locked. He rang the bell hanging beside it before coming over to the carriage and opening the door.

'Is something wrong?' Caroline noticed the look of concern on his face.

'There is not one light lit inside.' Cavendish's forehead creased.

'Is this the right house?' Mussy asked.

'Yes. Grange Lea was inscribed on a plaque on the gate post.'

'No one has come to the door.' Caroline glanced back at the house. 'Does the manager live elsewhere?'

'I wish I knew. He never replied to my letter while we were in Doncaster. I should have come before now. Forgive me for not having visited before today to make sure the house was ready for us. It was stupid of me to wait, but I assumed the manager was busy getting the place prepared for our arrival.' He strode back to the door and banged hard on it. 'I shall go around to the back,' he called.

Caroline closed the carriage door to keep the chill out as much as possible.

Within minutes Cavendish returned. 'Every door is locked, but there was a small window I could open which looks like a scullery room. Only I will not fit through the window.'

'Our Bertha might?' Trixie volunteered her sister. 'Come on let's try as we can't sit in the carriage all night.'

They all scrambled out except for Mussy and followed Cavendish through muddy grass around to the back of the house, which seemed bigger than the front with added extensions. Cavendish pushed up the window as far as it would go and then hoisted Bertha in head first.

'How brave you are, Bertie-Bear,' he joked.

Bertha scrambled over a counter and dropped to her feet. She went to the door. 'There's a key in the lock,' she said. 'It's stiff.'

'Keeping trying,' he coached her through the window. 'Take the key out and try again. Good girl.'

'I did it!' Bertha yelled, pulling the door open a wedge until it caught on an uneven flagstone.

'Well done, Bertie-Bear.' Cavendish used his shoulder to barge the door open. He took Bertha by the shoulders and kissed the top of her head. 'You are an angel.'

They followed him from the cold scullery into a large kitchen that was just as freezing as the scullery and just as unused. One wall was dominated by two black cooking ranges and a door leading down into a cellar. A wide wooden table stood in the middle of the flagged floor. Iron hooks hung empty across another wall and beneath them a large fireplace held a fallen bird's nest sitting on a bed of ashes. By the window a wooden counter ran the length of the wall. The fourth wall was broken up by three doors. Cavendish opened each one, the first revealed a larder, the second led into a little room with a desk and shelving and the third opened into a corridor.

'This kitchen hasn't been used in a long while,' Caroline said, spotting a lacework of cobwebs in the corners. She touched the range, and it held no heat. Dead ashes filled each of the fire boxes.

'We'll not be having a meal any time soon then.' Trixie pulled a face at the dust coating the table.

'Let us go through into the house.' Cavendish led them through the dark corridor, past other doors he didn't bother to open, and a narrow servants' staircase until he reached a wider door than the rest, and opened it.

Another hallway, tiled in black and white, took them past a central staircase and into a spacious hall at the front of the house. Cavendish unlocked the front door and went out to assist Mussy from the carriage. The cart with their luggage, Jacob and the dogs arrived, but the rain kept Caroline, Trixie and the girls inside.

'No one has been in this house for a long time,' Trixie said, then promptly sneezed.

Caroline gazed about the hall, noticing the dead flowers in a vase on a table in the middle of the floor. Open doors showed a library opposite.

Cavendish came in with Mussy, the blanket wrapped over Mussy's head. 'I sincerely apologise for the state of the house, that we have no welcome and nothing is ready for us. This is not what I expected.' His eyes flashed furiously, his temper barely under control. 'I am embarrassed and only hope you can forgive me. I shall pay for you all to stay in an inn until I can find out what is happening here.'

'It's cold, dark and wet out there, going back to Lincoln wouldn't be good for Mussy,' Caroline stated, looking around.

'Nor is staying here with the house in this state,' Cavendish fumed. 'I shall dismiss the manager the minute I see him.'

'Now, old chap, let us not get into dramatics,' Mussy soothed. 'All we need are a few fires lit and some lamps.'

'What about food and the beds?' Cavendish glanced up the wide staircase. 'I dread to find out what condition the upstairs rooms are in. Good God, what a nightmare!'

Caroline didn't like to see him so agitated. None of this was his fault. He looked tortured.

Jacob found them still standing in the hall. 'There's no fresh hay for Queenie, Mr Cavendish.'

'*Of course there is no fresh hay!*' Max shouted in annoyance.

Stunned, they all looked at him. They'd never seen him angry.

Abruptly, Caroline burst out laughing. Suddenly, a strange sense of hysterics filled her, and she found it hilarious that the house Max Cavendish had spoken so excitedly about for a week was nothing but an empty cold shell. They stood in a circle in damp clothes in the dark and nothing couldn't have been funnier at that moment.

Mussy chuckled and then laughed uproariously. Trixie and Jacob began to laugh and the girls giggled, mainly laughing at Caroline until finally Cavendish grinned.

Caroline held her side and fought for control, until Mussy started coughing and she sobered instantly and went to pat his back.

Cavendish held up his hands. 'Please forgive me, Jacob, everyone. I am mortified by all of this. I wanted you to be welcomed and comfortable.' His eyes softened as he gazed at Caroline. 'I have failed you.'

'Nonsense!' She took a deep breath and smiled widely at him. He wasn't perfect, but then life wasn't perfect. 'We are all devoted friends, Mr Cavendish, and as friends we shall work together to get through this.'

'As friends then, I beg you to call me Max.'

'I agree.' Mussy coughed again, breathing carefully to stop another spasm of hacking up phlegm. 'First names only from now on. We are family.'

'Right, let's get sorted.' Caroline unpinned her hat and placed it on the centre table in the hall. 'Trixie can you see if there is anything edible in the kitchen and start the fire in the range so we can have hot water, if nothing else.'

'Yes, the girls can help.' Trixie and her sisters went back down the corridor.

'Jacob, could you bring in some wood, as much as you can find that is dry.'

'Aye, I saw a pile in the smaller barn where I've tied up Queenie and the dogs. The stables are full of stale mouldy straw and I didn't want them in there.'

'Thank you,' Max said, taking off his wet coat.

Caroline marched into a large room on the right of the hall. A drawing room by the look of it. It still held some furniture, a red velvet sofa and an old leather wing-backed armchair. The enormous fireplace was tiled in green and white and topped with a marble mantlepiece, but the grate was full of ashes. She found a flint, twists of newspaper and some wood in a box to the side.

'Any matches, Caro?' Mussy said, lifting a lamp from an ornamental table beside the sofa.

Max found some on the mantel.

Once Mussy lit the lamp, the room brightened with a golden glow, revealing the dusty appearance, the neglect. 'I shall light some more.' He coughed a little as he moved around the room, finding candles in brass holders and another lamp on the wall. In the hall, he lit two lamps mounted on plinths on either side of the front door.

Max knelt and using the poker cleared out the fire grate and while he did that, Caroline closed the thick damask curtains, shutting out the rainy night, but covering herself in dust. She sneezed.

'Caroline?' Max looked up from the fire he was building. 'Please come and stand by the fire. I could not forgive myself if you caught a chill.'

'I'm stronger than I look,' she reminded him.

'That I know, but still…' Max worked to encourage the small flames to grow, giving more light to the room.

Mussy came in carrying a lamp. 'Shall we venture upstairs?'

'Yes. We need to bring down some blankets, if there are any, and air them in front of the fire. Though I think you've done enough and should rest.' She gestured to the armchair and Mussy didn't protest, which indicated he was tired.

'You can tend to this fire if you want? I'll go upstairs.' Max passed Mussy some sticks and took the lamp from him.

Following Max up the grand staircase, Caroline watched the shadows dance on the walls.

'I can light fires in each bedroom to start banishing the cold and damp,' Max said when they reached the central landing, which was long and wide with six doors, four on the left side of the landing and three on the right side. The narrow servants' staircase that they'd passed downstairs was at the end and went up to the next storey.

'Are these all bedrooms?' Caroline went to the first door and opened it. A four-poster bed dominated the large room. It was still made up with pillows, sheets and blankets. Two tall sash windows faced the drive, not that they could see much as darkness had fully descended. The room boasted a decent-sized fireplace, a chest of drawers and an ornate wardrobe in dark wood. A door lead into a smaller room filled with more wardrobes.

'A dressing room,' Max commented, closing the adjoining door.

The rest of the bedrooms were very similar to the first one. Their windows either facing the drive or the back of the house.

Back in the first bedroom, Caroline touched the blankets on the bed and pulled back the sheets. They smelt musty. 'We'll have to wash all the bedding before we can sleep in it. Let's hope the rain stops by morning.'

'I shall employ staff to do all of that. You are a guest here, not a maid.'

'Mr Cavendish—'

'Max.'

She paused, it would feel odd to call him by his first name. 'It will take time to find competent servants. In the meantime, me, Trixie and the girls will do what is needed. Jacob, too.'

'Then you must be paid.'

'No, you're giving us a home for the winter. We are simply earning our keep.' She smiled.

He took a step closer to her, one hand holding the lamp, encircling them in a soft glow. 'Downstairs was the first time I have heard you laugh, properly laugh. It was delightful.'

'It felt good to laugh, it feels like forever since I have done so,' she said honestly.

'I wish to hear it often.'

Caroline dropped her eyes, his intense gaze unsettled her.

'I only want your happiness, Caroline,' he murmured, taking her hand. 'I will do anything for you.'

Her heart swelled, and she suddenly ached for him to hold her, but she remembered what had happened to her, what his cousin had done, and he'd find her repulsive if he ever knew.

She turned to strip the blankets from the bed. 'If we air these in front of the fire, we can wrap them around us for the night.'

'Caroline…' Max took the blanket from her, dropping it back onto the bed. 'Let me say what is in my heart, please?'

'No, don't,' she begged. 'I'm not ready.'

'Do I have hope that one day you might be?'

'I can't answer that, not at this moment.'

He softly cupped her cheek, his eyes taking in every detail of her face. 'I will wait.'

Desire and yearning curled inside her like a coiled spring, but she fought the craving to touch him. Now wasn't the time. Would there ever be a right time? But how could she keep Max out of her heart when he was so kind and generous to those she loved? She wasn't ready to acknowledge his importance in her life, not yet. Besides, how could she tell him about what Wayland did to her, his own cousin? It would shame them both. The humiliating situation with Dolan had been bad enough. Caroline had caused Max to be shot, for heaven's sake, but being attacked by his own cousin because she'd stood up to him was another matter. Her independence, her stubbornness and single-mindedness was her downfall. No man would accept that in a woman, in a wife. Max would want a lady, genteel, abiding, without independent thoughts of her own. Caroline was anything but that. No, she was better off remaining a widow and save them both from heartache.

'Caroline?' Jacob called for her from the landing.

'Coming!' She grabbed the blankets and left the room.

Downstairs, Jacob helped Max carry in another sofa from the library on the other side of the hall and an armchair. Elsie and Bertha had dragged Mussy into the library to look at the enormous collection of books, while in the kitchen Caroline lowered the herb drying rack above the table to hang a couple of blankets on to air them, the rest she hung over chairs in front of the fires Trixie had lit in both the range and the large open fireplace that warmed the kitchen.

'I found a few spoonsful of tea leaves in the bottom of a box in the larder but nowt to eat.' Trixie boiled a large black kettle on the range. She'd found cups and saucers, some matching some not. 'There's not a grain of sugar in any of the tins in the larder. It's like someone used everything up and then walked out of the house and didn't come back.'

'So strange.' Caroline added more wood to the fire. 'We aren't going to be very comfortable tonight. Sleeping on chairs with empty stomachs.'

'We've slept with empty stomachs before,' Trixie snorted. 'Even on chairs we'll be warmer than we were in that damp room in the Water Lanes.'

'Have we made the right choice?' Caroline asked her, adjusting the blankets on the chairs.

'Did we really have a choice? Mussy isn't strong enough to trek the streets of London looking for rooms to rent. We'd have gone through our money quickly staying in nice inns.'

'But we can't stay here for ever. This is Max's home, not ours.'

'It is your home, too,' Max said, coming into the kitchen, 'for as long as you want it to be. If you leave, it will be because you wish it, not me.'

'But there are six of us,' she argued, looking for an excuse to go, to be away from the temptation of Max Cavendish.

'This house is big enough to home a dozen people.' He smiled. 'I could not imagine living here alone now I see the size of it.'

Caroline focused on the blankets, knowing the argument was lost, at least for the time being. Come the spring, she'd convince Trixie and Mussy to leave, they had to, before she became too happy here and before she fell in love with Max so completely, it would ruin her to leave him.

CHAPTER 18

Trixie woke on the sofa, Elsie slumped against her side and Bertha against Elsie. Caroline was asleep on the other sofa with Mussy. A blanket remained on the armchair where Max had slept but he wasn't in the room, neither was Jacob, who'd fallen asleep on the floor in front of the fire.

For a moment she sat and watched the flames of the fire, a new log had recently been added so someone, Jacob or Max, had attended to it before leaving the room. What an odd night it had been. The seven of them chatting about nothing much, all hungry until one by one, everyone fell asleep. Wealthy and poor together.

The house could be returned to its former beauty, and with it so could Caroline. Trixie knew that. She also understood how Max felt about Caroline. He'd make her his wife tomorrow if possible. Trixie easily saw Caroline being the mistress here, she was born to the role. Although Caroline didn't confess her feelings about Max to Trixie, she knew her friend was attracted to him. It worried Trixie that if Caroline finally, one day, gave into Max, Trixie and the girls would no longer fit into her world. They would have to move on, which upset Trixie more than she thought possible. But staying wasn't an option. Thomas, being Max's brother, would visit often and Trixie didn't imagine she'd cope seeing him regularly. Come the spring either they'd all leave this farm, or it'd be just her and the girls.

She slipped out from Elsie's warm body and, adjusting her shawl, left the drawing room and made her way to the kitchen. She'd never lived in a house this size. The enormity of it, the large rooms, the distance between the service areas and the main rooms was a trek in itself.

Someone had lit the range fire, probably Jacob, not that there was anything to cook, but Trixie heated some pans of water so they could all have a wash if nothing else. She lit a lamp and carried it down into the black cellar. She was slightly scared of the dank underground room, but she needed to relieve herself and this was the most private place until she had a bedroom of her own. After using the pot, she covered it with a rag and carried it upstairs. There had to be a midden somewhere on the farm.

Outside, she glanced around the cobbled yard between the back of the house and the outbuildings. They'd arrived in the dark and now, in the morning light, the yard was revealed. The outbuildings created a square with wide openings leading to other parts of the farm. Each building was solidly made of limestone with contrasting brickwork on the corners and around the windows, similar to the house and capped with grey slate roofs, not like the wooden barns of Hopewood.

Trixie carried the pot through an opening between two buildings and followed the path to more buildings behind.

Only birdsong could be heard as the morning sun rose in a pink sky. The rain had cleared, but streaky clouds lingered.

She found the waste midden hidden behind an unused pig pen and tipped out the pot. The farm was silent, all the animals had gone, devoid of life and just how Hopewood had been when she and Caroline first arrived there. Caroline had soon filled it with animals and Max would do the same here. However, the size of this farm was impressive. It was a gentleman's manor farm, despite its current air of abandonment, and with some work it would be a lovely place to live.

Strolling back through the quiet buildings, finally some noise reached her, and she took a different turn and found the stables, a long line of buildings with a flag-stone yard with stone walls surrounding it.

'Morning, Jacob,' she called, entering the giant open barn door where an old carriage stood. Next to it was a smaller pony gig.

'Along here,' Jacob replied from the right.

Trixie walked through into the stable block. The three dogs all came to greet her, tails wagging, tongues licking. She placed the pot on the top of a stall rail and stroked their heads in turn, before going to the first stall. 'You're at it early.'

Jacob straightened from forking out old straw from the horse stall into a wheelbarrow. Dust mites danced in the streaks of sunshine coming through the windows. 'Morning, Trix.'

Trixie looked around the high ceiling, the rows of horse stalls, the red-tiled floor. 'This place is big.'

'The whole farm is big.' Jacob chuckled. 'I took the dogs for a walk when I first got up and even with the neglect, it's remarkable.'

'And we get to live here for a while.' She wasn't sure how she'd adjust. Living with Max Cavendish, a gentleman, would be difficult. She wasn't of his class.

'We're lucky, for certain.' Jacob forked up another load of mouldy straw, the fusty smell filling the stall.

'It's only for the winter.'

'Does it have to be?' Jacob placed the fork against the wooden partition dividing the next stall. 'I don't see why we'd need to leave.'

'Because we need a home of our own.'

Jacob grabbed the handles of the wheelbarrow. 'Mr Cavendish spoke to me this morning while he was saddling up Queenie. He wants us to stay. He's offered me a job, Trixie.'

'Doing what?'

'Helping him to get this place sorted. He's gone to find the manager and give him his marching orders. Mr Cavendish wants me to take the position.'

'Manager?' She blinked in surprise. 'You know nowt about managing a farm, you were born in a city.'

'I've learned a lot in the last nine months living at Hopewood.' He frowned at her. 'I might not have the experience like a proper farmer, but what do you think I've been doing all summer?'

'You've been a labourer. There's a difference between a labourer and someone in a manager's position.'

'Don't treat me like an idiot,' he said sadly. 'I've been learning skills all year from Caroline, from Mr Cavendish when he called. I've asked questions of the old farmers when having a pint at the inn or at the market in the village. You know I've been having reading lessons with Mussy and Caroline to teach me to read so I can understand the farming manuals.' He pushed the barrow into the yard. 'Anyway, thanks for the support.'

'Jacob, I didn't mean owt by it,' but as she spoke, he walked away.

Sighing, Trixie returned to the house and entered through the scullery and placed the pot into the large sink. A pump-handled tap flowed water into the sink.

Caroline came to the doorway. 'How did you sleep?'

'Fine. Have you seen this? A tap in the house.' Trixie stared as clear water gushed out.

'Yes, I've seen it before. In Greenleigh House, where I was a scullery maid for a few weeks. They had a tap in the scullery, too, for all the washing-up I had to do.' Caroline rolled her eyes. 'It seems a lifetime ago, doesn't it?'

'Yet it was only this time last year.' Trixie walked with her into the kitchen.

'What's wrong?'

Trixie put another log into the range's fire box. 'I've just had words with Jacob.'

'Why?'

'Mr Cavendish has offered him a position here.'

'What's wrong with that?'

'Jacob's getting above himself, imagining he'd be Mr Cavendish's manager or something.'

'He could be.'

'We aren't staying here once spring comes.'

'Jacob might stay, if he wants to. He doesn't always have to come with us.' Caroline frowned. 'He's a single man who is free to do what he wishes.'

'He grew up in the slums of a city, he's not a farmer!'

'He was at Hopewood and enjoyed it. The country life suits him, he's told me as much.'

'Fine. I don't care.' Trixie stormed back outside, hurt and betrayed by Jacob. He was like her, a city person, or at least that's what she thought.

She walked around to the front of the house, ignoring the expanse of lawn, the overgrown garden beds. If she admitted the truth to herself, she no longer wanted to live in a city. York had done her no favours. Elsie and Bertha had thrived at Hopewood in the clean air, the fresh food. Their plan to go to London made sense, they could find work, but she wasn't keen to be back in the damp city streets with the grey smoke from hundreds of chimneys blocking out the sun.

Where did she fit now? In York she'd lived an ugly life, struggling to survive in the disease-ridden, poverty-stricken backstreets, always poor, always hungry, selling her body to provide for her sisters in any way she could. She understood that world, and she'd been frightened to find herself in the country, on a farm, surrounded by animals and strangers. But she had risen to meet those challenges, and had, weirdly enough, come to relish her new life. Only now, she felt adrift. Caroline could adapt, her sisters and Jacob could adapt, but she found it difficult. She was a working-class lass living in a gentleman's home, neither his servant nor his friend. How was she to adjust to that?

CAROLINE FLUNG OPEN THE BEDROOMS' windows, going from room to room as she and Bertha stripped the beds. Mussy slowly followed them lighting fires in each bedroom. Trixie and Bertha had lit the copper boiler in the outbuilding used as a laundry. They didn't have time to soak the sheets and instead gave them a quick wash with the washing soda they'd found in a cupboard in the laundry, before rinsing them in a wooden tub of clean water and then hanging them out to dry in the weak sunshine.

Without breakfast, or a meal the evening before, their energy soon flagged. Caroline made Mussy sit in the library and rest. He took a book from one of the stocked shelves to read but was soon asleep and it was only mid-morning.

From an upstairs bedroom window, Caroline watched a cart turn into the tree-lined drive. She'd not seen Max at all that morning. He'd left early and not returned. 'There's a cart coming,' she told Bertha, placing a fire guard around the little fireplace. 'Let's go out and meet it, we'll take these last sheets with us.'

'I like this room.' Bertha ran her hand along the rose-patterned wallpaper. 'Could me and our Elsie sleep in here? It's got two beds.'

'I'm sure you can.' Arms full of sheets, Caroline went downstairs and using a shortcut through a dining room which had French doors leading outside, she took the path around the side of the house into the yard just as the driver was slowing his horse. The cart was loaded high with crates and trunks.

'Good day, madam.' The driver climbed down from the seat. 'Mr Cavendish told me to ask for a Mrs Lawson.'

'I'm Mrs Lawson.'

'Grand.' He untied the canvas covering the load. 'This is all for ye.'

Jacob and Trixie joined her as the driver unveiled numerous crates and sacks. Caroline stepped closer. 'What is it?'

'Food supplies.' The driver turned as another cart rolled into the yard. 'There's more. So, where do ye want it all?'

'In the kitchen.' Caroline stared at Trixie as they approached the cart. Sacks of potatoes, carrots and onions were only the start of it. Wooden boxes were stamped with tea, salt, sugar and flour. There were tins of molasses, jars of pickles and chutneys, jams and marmalades. Caroline watched the driver unload smaller bags of green beans, pea pods, radishes and small turnips.

'I'll give them a hand,' Jacob said, helping to lift off a large crate.

Caroline, with Trixie and the girls' help, began to sort out the goods as the men piled them on the kitchen floor.

'Do we hang the meat in the cellar?' Trixie asked, holding up a leg of ham.

'Yes. Though the larder needs cleaning first before we use it.' Caroline unwrapped a parcel of beef, another parcel of pork chops and three trussed chickens. They hung the meat down in the cellar on iron hooks hanging from the ceiling. Pats of butter, a churn of milk and a round of cheese were added to the cellar.

'That cellar needs a good whitewashing,' Jacob said, coming back up the stairs.

'Like a good many other things,' Caroline remarked. 'Everywhere is coated in dust and grime. It's been years since anyone cleaned this kitchen.'

While they unpacked, Elsie boiled the kettle to make tea for them all. Fruit cake and loaves of bread were found in another box.

'Look at this.' Caroline opened the lid of a straw-lined crate. Inside was a white porcelain tea service edged in gold and decorated with painted pink roses.

'It matches these plates.' Trixie held up matching plates and bowls from another crate.

'This is fun!' Bertha grinned, unwrapping silver candlesticks, while Jacob found a case full of cutlery. Another large chest was filled with copper pots and pans.

After a cup of tea, the cart drivers disappeared down the drive, leaving Caroline and Trixie standing in the middle of a sea of crates in the kitchen.

'We need to eat,' Trixie said, wiping the hair out of her eyes. 'There are the sheets to finish as well.'

Caroline collected a couple of the empty crates. 'I'll go to the laundry and finish all that if you want to set out some food? Elsie, you help Trixie and, Bertha, you can keep going upstairs and checking the fires in all the rooms are still burning well.'

'Is that another cart?' Jacob glanced out of the window before walking out of the kitchen.

'Gracious! Another one.' Caroline followed him.

An elderly couple sat on the cart and in the back of it was some cages holding chickens.

'Good day to you,' Caroline greeted them.

The couple climbed down, Jacob helping the old woman.

'That's kind of ye,' the white-haired woman said to Jacob. 'We're Mr and Mrs Todd. We live over in South Carlton. Mr Cavendish spoke to us this morning. He asked to buy some of our chickens and if we knew 'owt about Mr Platt's whereabouts.'

'I'm Mrs Caroline Lawson and this is Mr Jacob Adams.' Caroline shook their hands.

'Aye, he said ye'd all moved in.' Mr Todd gazed about the yard. 'We're happy to see the place be lived in again. It was rotten to see this farm left to ruin. As I said to Mr Cavendish, that Roger Platt, the former manager here, was a bad 'un and no mistake. Drunkard.'

'Enough, Husband.' Mrs Todd waved her husband into silence. 'We don't want folk thinking we're gossips.'

Mr Todd grumbled and walked around to the back of the cart. 'Give us a hand, Mr Adams. I've got the chickens and rooster Mr Cavendish bought this morning. He was knocking on the door not long after dawn. Keen as mustard he is, but there's nowt wrong with that.'

'There's a hen house behind the outbuildings.' Jacob took one side of the cage and Mr Todd the other.

'Would you care to come inside, Mrs Todd?' Caroline asked, aware she was wearing an old apron she'd packed in her luggage and that her clothes had been slept in.

'Nay, not this time. I can see that ye busy.' She gestured to the empty crates. 'Did Roger Platt leave ye anything?'

'Furniture mainly. He's stripped the house bare of paintings, ornaments and such like. Luckily, some lamps were left, but we've run out of oil. The kitchen was completely empty.'

'Thief,' Mrs Todd spat. 'We're not all of his ilk, I assure ye. Nobody liked the man. We had to put up with him for years, lording it about the villages. He ran this place down, did as he pleased.'

'Where is he now?'

'Who knows? He disappeared about a year ago. Before he left, he sold the animals. We've been waiting for someone to mention that the farm's been sold.'

'Is South Carlton close by?'

'Aye, a mile away.' Mrs Todd pointed over the fields. 'Our farm is off School Lane.'

'May I call on you one day once we're settled?'

The old woman, her white hair coiled in plaits about her head, gave Caroline a deep look. 'Ye call on me? I'm a farmer's wife, madam. We don't put on tea afternoons for the gentry.'

'I'm not gentry, Mrs Todd. I'm a widower of a farmer.'

'Mr Cavendish is a gentleman, his aunt is Lady Stockton-Lee. Aren't ye his kin?'

'No, just his friend staying for the winter.'

Mrs Todd gave that some thought. 'We don't usually take to strangers, as there's some odd folk about, but ye seem decent enough.'

Caroline took this as a compliment. Jacob and Mr Todd returned deep in conversation, the three dogs plodding beside them.

Mrs Todd glanced up at the house. 'This manor needs a family in it, some life brought back to it. Lady Stockton-Lee should've never bought it. A manager won't look after it like a proper owner would've done living here and being a part of the village. Mr Cavendish promises things will change. I hope I live long enough to witness it.' She hobbled back to the cart and waited for her husband to assist her up onto the seat. 'I'll see ye at church on Sunday.' She raised a hand and told her husband to hurry up and turn the cart around.

'She's a right one, isn't she?' Jacob chuckled, watching them leave.

'But genuine I feel.'

Jacob rubbed Prince's ear. 'I'm meeting Mr Todd for a drink tomorrow night. There's no inn at the village but some of the locals make their own beer and meet once a week in each other's houses.'

'That's one way to make friends. One thing is for certain, the whole village will know about us now.' Caroline grinned. She knelt and made a fuss of the dogs, feeling guilty that she'd not spent much time with them lately. 'I should take them for a walk but there's so much to do inside.'

'They're fine.' Jacob patted Duke's head. 'They can be with

me as I wander about. I'll get the chicken coop tidy and check the foxes can't get in. I'll chop more wood as well.'

'We'll have some food ready shortly. You must be hungry.'

'Aye, my stomach reckons my throat's been cut,' he joked. He waved as he walked away, the three dogs happily going with him.

Max didn't return until dark. He looked exhausted when he came into the kitchen. Throughout the day two more wagons arrived sent by him. Hay and feed for Queenie and farming tools.

'Tea?' Trixie offered, holding up the teapot she'd just mashed.

'That would be very welcome, thank you.' He sat down on a bench by the door and took off his mud-coated boots and then hung up his mud-splattered coat and hat on a hook in the scullery.

Max gazed about the warm kitchen. Fires had been blazing all day, banishing the cold and dampness. The smell of freshly cooked chops and vegetables wafted in the air. The copper pots hung on the hooks along the wall. The double range was black-leaded, the floor swept and washed. 'You have been busy, ladies.'

'Excuse us for eating without you.' Caroline ached from all the heavy work. 'We weren't sure what time you'd return, or even if you'd be staying in Lincoln for the night, but we kept a plate of food for you. It's warming in the oven.'

'I am pleased you did not wait for me. I ate in town earlier, between meetings, but I am happy eat again.'

Caroline passed him the teacup and saucer.

Trixie brought out his plate. 'The dining room isn't clean, Mr Cavendish.'

'Trixie, please, it's Max, and I am fine to eat here.' He looked at the food. 'It smells delicious. Did you cook it?'

'I did.' Trixie blushed. 'I'm not a great cook. But I'm getting better all the time. Annie taught me a lot, and Caro, but most of the time it's instinct.'

'You have a talent, Trixie. Your bread I have tasted before has always been excellent. I am sure this meal will be just as pleasant.' He cut a piece of pork. 'Thank you for cooking it for me.'

'Well, it's your food and we're all eating it. The least I could do is cook for you as well.' Trixie glanced at Caroline as if to silently beg her to step into the conversation.

'Do you wish to continue cooking for us all, or I can hire a cook?' Max asked, forking up some carrots.

'I don't mind, sir, er...' Trixie struggled to speak comfortably.

Max smiled putting her at ease. 'I can assure you, Trixie, I am content with plain wholesome food. After a busy day, that is good enough for me. I do not need fancy jellies or sauces. If you are agreeable, I will employ you as cook for Grange Lea?'

Trixie's eyes widened. 'Employ me as a cook? But I can't read properly.'

Caroline tilted her head in thought. 'Then perhaps you can take lessons with Elsie and Bertha. Mussy has been teaching them and Jacob all through summer. He wants to continue their lessons here now he's a little brighter in spirit.'

Trixie tapped her fingers together. 'I'm not bothered about the worldly things he's talks to them about. I just want to be able to read cooking books or a newspaper the same as Jacob is trying to do. I can write my name, Elsie taught me,' she confirmed to Max.

'There is no pressure, Trixie. This food is exactly what I need,' he said between mouthfuls. 'We shan't be holding dinner parties just yet,' he teased.

Trixie's face paled slightly. 'I need more time for that.'

Caroline chuckled. 'I'll inform Mussy he has another pupil.'

'I'd best get our Elsie and Bertha to bed.' Trixie touched Caroline's shoulder as she passed. 'See you both in the morning, and thank you, Mr Cavendish, for believing in me.'

Alone with Max, Caroline pushed herself up off the chair by the fire where she'd been resting and started to wipe down the table, even though it had been wiped only minutes earlier. Max's kindness to Trixie made her stupidly emotional. Seeing Trixie's eyes light up at the offer was worth everything. No one had believed in Trixie before, and her friend felt honoured by the confidence Max had shown.

She glanced at him, eating his meal. He was a good man. 'Did you have a successful day?' she asked.

'My day was interesting, tiring, and one I shall be repeating for weeks to come until Grange Lea is organised.' Max placed his knife and fork down. 'I spoke to Jacob before I came inside. He said four wagons arrived today.'

'Yes. You ordered so much. We were very grateful to see the food.'

'The market was on in town, and I bought up as much as I could think of and paid the stallholders extra to deliver it immediately to you. But I apologise for giving you so much work to do.'

'We're used to hard work.'

'True, but hopefully, not for much longer. Two maids are coming tomorrow for you and Trixie to interview.'

'Us?'

'Well, as women, I am certain you identify what you need around the house more than I.' He fought a yawn. 'I've also employed a youth of about sixteen years to help Jacob. I shall hire more men for outside once the animals arrive. But that is a thought for another day.'

'You must be ready for your bed.'

'My head is pounding. I have had so much to think about and organise today. I have visited my aunt's solicitors in town and set up a bank account.'

'We have made up the bed in the master suite and a fire has been going all day. The room is warm and comfortable for you. Mussy unpacked your clothes in the wardrobe but left your personal belongings for you to arrange.'

'I shall go and thank him in a minute.' He sipped his tea. 'How is he feeling?'

'Weak. He saw to your clothes and then slept for an hour.'

'He should not have tired himself with it. I would have done it later.'

'Well, I did try to dissuade him. However, he wanted to be useful, and Trixie didn't want him in the kitchen under her feet and he couldn't work in the laundry with me. Or out with Jacob.' She smiled.

'I do not want you working in the laundry, Caroline. You are my guest.'

'Sheets had to be washed and dried or we'd have no beds to sleep in tonight.' She put away the tea things.

Max stood and took her hands, running his fingers across the calluses on her palms. 'No more will these hands toil.'

'Nonsense.' She pulled away and headed for the door. His touch sent tingles up her arms. 'Come and see Mussy before he goes to bed. Oh, and Mr and Mrs Todd seem a nice couple.

They came with the chickens,' she babbled as they walked through the house to the drawing room where Mussy sat reading by the fire.

They sat and spoke about Roger Platt, who'd apparently taken himself off to America along with the profits of Max's aunt's belongings and all the animals he'd sold.

'You shan't hear from him again,' Mussy murmured.

'No.' Max sighed. 'I have engaged solicitors, Dobbs and Clarence, in town to handle my affairs as needed. They will investigate him as much as they can but if he has gone to America, then that is the last of it. I will not write to my aunt and tell her for she would be devastated to hear of it.' Max poured two glasses of Irish whiskey for himself and Mussy, a crate of bottles had been included in the deliveries. He looked at Caroline. 'I understand a house of this size needs more servants, but two who are coming in the morning were all I could manage to secure at such short notice.'

'We'll cope.' She yawned behind her hand.

'Which bedrooms have been allocated?' Max asked, sitting down.

'Elsie and Bertha are in the room with the rose wallpaper. We're calling it the rose room. The girls consider they are near enough princesses now.' She chuckled. 'Trixie is next to them in the yellow bedroom and I'm next to her in the blue room. Mussy is on the right side of the landing in the green room and you are in the master room.'

'And Jacob?' Max sipped his drink, looking tired.

'He has tidied up the grooms' sleeping quarters above the stables.'

'He did not have to stay out there. I doubt it is fit for a person to sleep in those quarters.' Max shook his head. 'There is, I trust, a small cottage near the grove of trees behind the stable wall. That was where Platt lived, well it was where he was meant to live, I believe he stayed in the house.' Max shrugged in a gloomy way, showing his apathy regarding the former manager. 'Anyway, Jacob must have the cottage.'

'He will be excited by that.' Caroline fought another yawn.

'You must rest,' Max said, his tone gentle, thoughtful.

'Yes, I'm away to bed. Goodnight.' She kissed Mussy's cheek. 'Sleep well.' She glanced at Max and gave him a small smile before taking a lamp from a side table to light her way up to bed.

In her new bedroom, she glanced around at her few possessions. She didn't own much, for all her spare money had been spent on the farm. The dressing table held her brush and a few hair ribbons and combs. A jug and bowl stood beside them, the water still warm from when she'd brought it up an hour ago. The fire flickered behind the guard, and she moved it to one side to add another log onto it for the night.

Undressing, she washed herself using the lavender-scented soap that had arrived in the deliveries. Max had thought of nearly everything. Once in her nightgown, she slid into bed, pushing the hot stone bottle with her feet further down the mattress.

Although tired and achy, Caroline laid in the semi-dark, watching the fire cast flickering shadows on the wall. The heavy drapes closed out the cold night. Somewhere a fox barked, but other than that there was silence. She missed the presence of Prince and Duke on her bed, but this wasn't her house, and she couldn't assume they'd be allowed inside. However, she would talk to Max and ask if they, and Princess, could have beds in the kitchen. She didn't like them sleeping outside, though she suspected they'd be with Jacob tonight, keeping him warm.

Her mind drifted to Max. He wanted her to interview maids as though she was the mistress of the house. It wasn't her role. She'd have to speak to him in the morning, but she was too tired think anymore about it now and snuggling into the warm bed, she closed her eyes. Her last thought was that he'd be sleeping just down the hallway from her…

CHAPTER 19

*C*aroline combed her hair neatly and rolled it up to pin behind her head. She teased out tendrils to hang down around her ears. She smoothed the camel-coloured dress and slipped her stocking-clad feet into house shoes. Ready, she left her bedroom and descended the staircase.

From the library, she heard Mussy instructing Elsie and Bertha in a lesson of arithmetic. She glanced into the drawing room to check the fire was still a cheery blaze and then carried on down the hallway past the staircase and into the service corridor. She'd had little chance to explore the rooms leading off this passageway and was keen to see what they revealed, and the same could be said for the rest of the house. Caroline had merely peeped into the study beside the dining room, or the sweet corner room painted apple green that buttered up against the drawing room and captured the morning light.

But first the interviews.

Max had left after breakfast, off to purchase plough horses, carriage horses and a cart. He'd told her the wage amounts he wanted to pay, but other than that she had his full support on whatever she decided to do with the maids.

Entering the kitchen, Caroline stopped as Trixie darted between range and table, pots were steaming, the table itself was covered with mixing bowls, different ingredients, spoons and other utensils. Trixie's hair was falling out of its pins and her apron was covered in stains.

'Gracious, Trix.' Caroline stepped forward to tidy the table. 'Breakfast is finished. What are you cooking?'

'No, don't touch anything.' Trixie picked up a large cookbook. 'I found this in the cupboard at the top of the larder. What does this word say?'

Caroline looked at the word in the recipe title. 'Mutton. The recipe is for mutton in beer.'

'We have mutton, it came yesterday.' Trixie chewed her fingernail. 'Do we have beer?'

'I think a few bottles came in with the case of whiskey.'

'Then that's what we're having for dinner.' Trixie squinted at the recipe, her finger on the words as she tried to read them. 'B... bone... th... the... me...me...at, meat!'

'Sweetness, we don't have time for this. I know you're trying but the two girls Max spoke about will be here shortly,' Caroline said kindly. 'I promise after the maids' interviews, I will help you read the whole recipe and cook it with you.'

Trixie sighed in frustration. 'I need to be able to read, Caro.'

'And you will, I will help you, or Mussy will.'

A knock on the kitchen door sounded. Trixie quickly took off her apron and, at the sink, washed her hands in a bucket of water while Caroline opened the door to the scullery and welcomed in the two girls waiting. Both were well dressed in dark serviceable clothes, wearing black bonnets and one had a green shawl and the other girl wore a ruby-red shawl.

'We're here for the maids' positions,' said the tallest of the two girls, the one with the green shawl.

'Come in, please.' Caroline waved them into the kitchen. From the side dresser, she took a pen and piece of paper. 'I'm Mrs Lawson and this is Miss Trixie Wilkes. Follow me. I thought we'd sit in the dining room.' Caroline led the girls, with Trixie following behind, along the corridor and into the hallway near the stairs, turning sharply into the dining room.

'Take a seat.' Caroline sat on one side of the long table with Trixie beside her and the two girls sat opposite. She'd never interviewed someone before and had to remember how she'd been questioned when she searched for work in York. 'Now, you're both here to work as housemaids, yes?'

The girls nodded.

'Your names and ages?'

'I'm Rosanna Smith, seventeen, madam,' said the girl with the green shawl. She nudged the girl next to her. 'Go on.'

'I'm Jeannie Booth, sixteen, madam,' the younger one said nervously, immediately putting her head down.

'Have you both worked in service before?' Trixie asked.

'Yes,' they chorused.

'Do you both have references?'

Dutifully they passed over pieces of wrinkled paper. Caroline read them quickly. Each piece of paper was written nearly identical to the other and signed by the same person, a Mrs Granger, housekeeper to Mrs Orville in London. The address was at the bottom, but Caroline didn't have the time to write and wait for a reply, not that she'd tell the two girls that. 'I assume Mrs Granger and Mrs Orville will testify to your good characters such that is written in these references?'

'Mrs Orville has died.' Rosanna spoke clearly and directly to Caroline. 'That's why we're out of work. We all had to leave.'

Caroline frowned. 'So, I couldn't write to these women?'

'We don't know where Mrs Granger moved to,' Rosanna supplied. Although she wasn't a beauty, she had something about her that was appealing, yet also Caroline sensed a toughness to her.

'Why have you come so far from London?' Trixie asked.

Again, Rosanna spoke. 'We heard there's more work in the country. That too many people head to the cities. We thought to try somewhere different.'

Caroline made notes. 'What were your duties at Mrs Orville's establishment?'

'Jeannie was a chambermaid, and I worked in the kitchen and served in the dining room when needed.'

'You're a cook?' Trixie's shoulders sagged a little.

'No, I was just a kitchen maid. I did some cooking but mainly only prepping the food.'

Caroline made more notes. 'Can you read and write?'

'I can,' Rosanna said, and Caroline wasn't surprised. 'Jeannie only enough to get by.'

'These are live-in positions. You'll receive room and board and a wage of ten pounds a year. Half a day off every second Saturday and one full Sunday off every month. You'll be expected to attend church every Sunday morning. There is to be no drinking of alcohol or unbecoming behaviour. Both of you will be on a trial for one month. We expect you to work hard and diligently and you both to be honest and polite at all times. You will answer to me, or Miss Wilkes. Mr Cavendish is the owner of Grange Lea. We are staying with him for the winter, along with Miss

Wilkes' sisters, Elsie and Bertha, and a gentleman, Mr Septimus Casey.'

Rosana visibly relaxed. 'Thank you, Mrs Lawson.'

'Now, we have only recently moved into the house after it was... closed for many years. The attic rooms where you'll be sleeping haven't been cleaned. That will be your first task. We shall do it now.' Caroline rose. 'Oh, and we have to order your uniforms. Take your measurements this evening and let me know, until then wear your own clothes and I'll see that Mr Cavendish reimburses you for the wear and tear.'

Trixie headed for the door. 'I'll get back to the kitchen. I'll get our Elsie and Bertha to help me.'

'Help you?' Rosanna's eyebrows rose in surprise. 'Are your sisters servants as well, Miss Wilkes?'

'No,' Caroline put in quickly. 'We are all guests of Mr Cavendish, however, he is understaffed, and we are very happy to do whatever activity is needed to make the house comfortable again.'

Rosanna nodded but Caroline could tell she thought it an odd set up and who could blame her?

The afternoon was spent tidying up the attic rooms which were once split between sleeping quarters and storage space. There were four small bedrooms at one end of the house, and a large open space at the other end packed with old dusty trunks, spare bed frames, an old cradle and various other items long forgotten.

The maids were content to share one room and Caroline helped Rosanna and Jeannie to make up the two single beds and wash the floor. The chimney from the fires downstairs was on one wall making the room warm, but Caroline found extra blankets in a trunk under one of the beds in the other room.

'When summer comes, we can give the room a proper good clean,' Rosanna stated, looking around at what they'd achieved.

'Yes,' Caroline murmured, not wanting to mention that she won't be here in the summer. 'Now, a tour of the house.' For Caroline the tour was for her benefit, too. She opened doors to rooms she'd barely glimpsed in. A study occupied once of the rooms along the corridor, situated between the butler's pantry and the gun and boot room. She imagined Max would soon want to use the study.

'The dining room needs a good clean,' she told the maids. 'Your task for this afternoon, Jeannie.'

'Yes, madam.' Jeannie barely raised her head.

'Tomorrow, we'll give the drawing room a proper going over and work our way through the downstairs rooms before starting on the bedrooms. Elsie and Bertha will help, don't think you have to do it all by yourself.'

'Yes, madam,' Jeannie whispered.

Caroline felt sorry for the poor girl, she looked worn out and terrified. 'A cup of tea is in order, I think.' Caroline smiled at them. 'Hopefully, Miss Wilkes has made something delicious to go with it.'

'I can make a decent pastry, madam,' Rosanna said as they entered the kitchen. Rosanna's confidence was the opposite to Jeannie's shy manner.

'Can you?' Trixie looked up from kneading dough.

'My favourite is a cheese and leek pie. Cook used to get bad arthritis in her hands and when she had a flare up, she'd make us girls do more for her.'

'Then that'll be your job in the morning after breakfast. It'll be what we feed everyone for the midday meal.' Trixie sighed in relief.

'I'm happiest when I'm cooking, not that I did much of it.' Rosanna washed her hands in the sink.

Trixie gave her an admiring glance. 'I feel the same, though cooking is only something I've started to do properly this year. Perhaps you can give me some advice?'

Rosanna faltered. 'I don't know that much, miss. I was just a kitchen maid, not a cook.'

'I'm guessing you'll understand a gentleman's menu more than me,' Trixie joked. 'We'll work together, yes?'

'Aye, miss.'

Caroline left them to it and went out into the yard as the sun slowly dropped in the sky. Most of the leaves had fallen from the trees around the farm, casting them as stark silhouettes against the pale sky. She wandered over to the side of the house given to gardens and parkland. However, the years of neglect had altered the neat garden beds into overgrown tangles of weeds and self-seeded flowers. The untended lawn was riddled with rabbit holes and the grass was overlong and wild.

'Out exploring?' Mussy came out of the front of the house.

'What are doing out at this time? It's getting cold.' Caroline slipped her arm through his, pleased to see he wore a thick coat and a scarf.

'I need some fresh air, dearest. I have been teaching all morning and sleeping all afternoon. Without some fresh air now, I shan't sleep tonight.' Mussy stared out over the flat fields. It was terribly quiet. 'I thought Hopewood was serene, but here... I cannot explain, the land seems ancient.'

'It's very different to York or Hopewood.' Caroline watched a formation of geese flying south.

'Apparently, this flat land falls gently away beyond those fields towards South Carlton, and keeps rolling down towards the River Till, and on further until you reach the River Trent. We are on the Lincolnshire Escarpment.'

'Did you read about the area?'

'No, Max told me. As a boy he rode for miles, exploring.'

This news made Caroline smile, and she tried to picture him as a boy riding over the countryside.

Mussy paused, wheezing.

'We should go back inside,' Caroline said. 'It's too cold out here for you.'

They turned and faced the house, which stood forlorn amongst an untidy and unloved garden.

'This will be a beautiful home once again, Caro. Max will make a difference here.'

'I've no doubt he will.'

'He'll need you by his side to achieve it.'

'He doesn't need me.'

'He *wants* you by his side.'

Caroline sighed deeply. 'I realise that.'

'This would be a wonderful home for you all.'

'And for you.'

He stopped, his eyes sad as he gazed at her. 'My dearest Caro, we both know I won't make old bones.'

'Don't say that.'

'If I can face it, so can you. There is a letter in my diary for my parents. Will you send it when the time comes?'

'Of course.' She didn't ever want to send such a letter.

They started walking again. A cock pheasant at the edge of the park crowed in its choppy way, echoing across the open fields.

'I want you to be happy, Caro,' Mussy said as they reached the house. 'You need to be settled.'

'Happiness is something other people have, Mussy. I just

want to be safe with a roof over my head, food on the table and a few coins to pay my way.'

'That is a poor view of your future, darling girl.'

'I had my time, with my husband.' She rubbed her finger where her wedding ring used to be. 'Two short years but they were happy ones, and I took them for granted.'

'Allow Max to make you happy again.'

'How can I? Once he knows about what Wayland did to me, he'll see me differently. My actions caused him to be shot. He forgave me for that and I've no idea why, but all that happened with his cousin?' She shook her head, reliving that terrible moment in the barn. 'He mustn't find out. I couldn't bear to see him look at me with pity or revulsion.'

'Why would he? Max would never think of you that way.' Mussy started coughing and taking that as the end of the conversation, Caroline took him inside to sit by the fire in the drawing-room while she went to make him a cup of tea.

In the kitchen, she found Trixie and Rosanna busy cooking and a youth sitting by the door, looking as poor and ragged as any who lived in the Water Lanes of York. He was eating a buttered piece of bread and held a cup of tea in his filthy hands.

'Who is this then?' Caroline approached him.

The boy stood immediately, a lock of light brown hair falling over his gaunt face. 'I'm Dickie Lowe, miss.'

'I'm Mrs Lawson, Dickie. Pleased to meet you.' Caroline smiled warmly and when the boy grinned back, revealing two dimples, something clicked inside her chest. 'How old are you?'

'Me grandpa told me I've lived through fifteen summers and…' he paused for dramatic effect, 'I've not ever had a sniffle,' he boasted proudly.

'Where are you from?' Rosanna asked before Caroline had a chance and Caroline frowned at her.

'Lincoln, of course,' he replied as though everyone was from Lincoln.

'Mr Cavendish isn't at home,' Caroline told him. 'But come with me and I'll take you to Jacob.' She led him out of the house and across the darkening yard. 'Do you have any belongings?'

'No, miss, er, madam. I own nothing but the clothes I'm standing in. Me grandpa needed new boots, so I sold me ferret and nets to get him some, that's why I was looking for work when I heard Mr Cavendish asking for labourers at the Hare and Hound yesterday. I told him I could work for him, but me grandpa was moving into the alms-houses this morning. I needed to get him settled before I came here. He, Mr Cavendish, was kind enough to let me do that. He seems a decent fellow, a gentleman.'

Caroline listened to the boy's monologue as they took the paths between the outbuildings looking for Jacob. They found him in the end barn which had once been a piggery.

'I've brought you a helper,' Caroline said to Jacob.

'Is this young Dickie then?' Jacob asked, sweeping out the dried muck from a pig stall by the light of a lamp.

'Aye, it is, Dickie Lowe.' The boy shook Jacob's hand like an equal, not shy or overconfident but just as a sensible young man.

'Jacob Adams. Mr Cavendish told me you'd be here today.' Jacob leant the broom against the wall. 'I'll show you where you can put your things. You can sleep in the grooms' quarters with me until I can get the cottage sorted, then you'll have the quarters above the stables all to yourself until more men are hired.'

'I don't have anything, Mr Adams.' Dickie took the broom. 'I can help you straight away.'

'Nay, lad, it's getting late. Time to wash up ready for something to eat.' Jacob took the lamp from the hook. 'I'll show you where you'll be sleeping. Oh, and call me Jacob.'

'I'll send Elsie and Jeannie over with jugs of hot water.' Caroline left them listening to Dickie chattering away asking a dozen questions and Jacob's quiet responses. She smiled, those two were like chalk and cheese.

In the kitchen, Trixie seemed a bit frazzled as she stirred two pots at once. 'Oh, Caroline, check that meat in the oven.'

Caroline took a cloth and did as asked, the smell of roasting chickens filled the kitchen. 'They look fine.'

'I did all three.' Trixie pulled a face. 'Did I do right? There's so many of us now.'

'I'm sure it'll be fine, but maybe for tomorrow's meal, make a big pot of stew, it'll go further.'

'A stew for Mr Cavendish?' Trixie's eyes widened. 'He can't have a stew.'

'I'm certain he'll enjoy it. Don't worry.' Caroline took the kettle and found it full and hot. She filled two tin jugs with it as Jeannie and Elsie came in from the corridor carrying empty wood baskets. 'Girls, take these jugs out to Jacob and Dickie.'

'Dickie?' Elsie asked.

'The new lad,' Rosanna supplied, draining some boiled potatoes. 'He needs a good wash. Was he living rough?'

'That's Dickie's business, Rosanna,' Caroline reprimanded. She'd have to watch that girl, for Rosanna was quick to have an opinion and voice it whether it was required or not.

'The dining table needs checking, Caro.' Trixie tasted the gravy she'd made. 'Elsie and Jeannie have set it and lit the fire in there. Does this gravy taste right?' Trixie offered the spoon to Rosanna.

Caroline was amazed by the quick and easy rapport that'd developed between Trixie and Rosanna and felt a little put out by it. She walked along to the dining room wondering at it. Why hadn't Trixie offered the spoon to her? And why was Trixie doubting herself? Annie had taught her how to make gravy months ago. Annie had taught Trixie an enormous amount about cooking while Caroline worked in the fields. Why was she suddenly unsure of her abilities?

Caroline missed Annie, missed the older woman's quiet counsel, her gentle presence. Elsie and Bertha missed her greatly, too.

In the dining room, she was surprised to see the long room so well lit. A candelabra was centred on the wooden table, both polished to a high shine. The candles added to the glow from the lamps on the sideboard, which had also been polished. The dinner service was neatly placed and set for three people. Three?

Caroline returned to the kitchen. 'Only three settings, Trixie.'

'Yes, you, Mr Cavendish and Mussy.'

'Where is everyone else going to eat?'

'Here, in the kitchen.' Trixie gestured to the big table in the middle. 'The seven of us will fit around this easily.'

'We eat together,' Caroline hissed, pulling Trixie aside.

'Not anymore. I'm employed by Mr Cavendish now. I can't eat at his table.'

'Then I'll eat with you like we've always done since we met.' Caroline didn't like this change or the new Trixie who'd taken her temporary role far too seriously. 'We are family.'

'Yes, we are, but I'm a member of the staff now. It's my

kitchen, and it's only right that I eat in here with the other staff.'

'Elsie and Bertha aren't maids.'

'But they might as well be,' Trixie reasoned calmly. 'They've worked all day alongside Rosanna and Jeannie. What makes them any different? Learning these skills will be useful for the future when they go out to work.'

'They're being educated so they can rise above being simply maids,' Caroline argued.

'*You* wanted them educated, Caro, not me.' Trixie shrugged. 'We aren't of Mr Cavendish or Mussy's class. Me and the girls haven't risen up, Mussy has come down to our level while living at Hopewood, but the fact remains I don't belong at a gentleman's dining table, and neither do my sisters, even if they can read and write, and we don't belong to sleep in bedrooms on the same floor as him either, so I'll look into setting up more bedrooms in the attics for us.'

'Nor am I of their class!' Caroline strove for patience.

'Who are you fooling? Just accept it. You were raised and educated in a respectable convent paid for by the inheritance in your parents' will, and you were the niece of a man from the church, a man who also had an inheritance, didn't he?'

'Yes, so?'

'If your parents hadn't died when you were so young, you'd have lived a very different life, wouldn't you?'

Caroline had often thought of what her life might have been if her parents survived beyond her babyhood. Her father had been a solicitor in Harrogate. She couldn't remember him or her mother, but Trixie was right, she'd have lived a very different life to the one she had so far.

'You belong at that table, Caro,' Trixie said gently. 'Don't fight me on this and, to be bluntly honest, I think all the staff would be more at ease if you didn't sit with us.'

That hurt Caroline more than she cared to admit. Since coming to this house just a few days ago, a division had been created between her and Trixie. Tears rose hot in her eyes. 'I wish we'd never come here,' she murmured. 'We should have gone to London and lived together as a family as we have been doing.'

Trixie's expression became thoughtful. 'We are together, but perhaps fate brought us here because it knows better?'

'To separate us, after all we've been through?'

'Nothing will separate us, not truly, but things change. I feel this place might be our destiny.'

'It isn't,' Caroline denied stiffly. 'We're all leaving in the spring, remember that.'

Trixie squeezed Caroline's arm softly. 'A lot can happen in a few months. Look how much has happened in just a few days? I have a job. Jacob has a job. The first morning here I thought I would have to leave because I wouldn't fit in, have a place, but I do. Mr Cavendish has allowed me to think I might have a future here.'

'What about me?' Caroline challenged. 'What is my place?'

'That's for you to decide.'

'I'll be leaving in the spring, Trixie. Will you be coming with me?' Caroline didn't wait for her answer and stormed out.

CHAPTER 20

October turned into November, and it seemed in a blink it was December. They'd quietly celebrated Caroline's twenty-sixth birthday in October and Mussy's birthday in November and Jacob's at the beginning of December.

Trixie became more confident and busier in the kitchen, thriving on the responsibly of cooking for them all. Christmas was only days away, and she'd been working frantically in the hope of making it the best one ever. It amazed Trixie how assured she'd become with her new skills after the first few days of nerves. The kitchen was Trixie's domain, the heart of the house, always filled with warmth and tasty smells. She didn't envy Caroline dining with Mr Cavendish and Mussy, for in the kitchen, the staff could relax and laugh and talk. They grew closer, worked as a team and Trixie welcomed it. Elsie and Bertha flourished, which only gladdened Trixie's heart further.

Outside the winter weather caused havoc, weeks of rain and early snow falls turned the farm into a quagmire. Mr

Cavendish had spent countless hours visiting markets to buy sheep and cattle, milking cows, pigs and plough horses. With Jacob and Dickie's help, they sowed acres of seed, cursing at the sodden state of the fields.

Trixie cooked basic but filling meals for them, constantly trying to learn more from the cookbooks Caroline bought for her, and from Rosanna. Although she worked closely with Rosanna, she kept their relationship strictly a working one, so Rosanna understood who was in charge. Caroline insisted the two maids called Trixie, Miss Wilkes, and she was glad that rule had been followed when she might have relaxed it and asked them to call her Trixie. Roles needed to be defined, Caroline was right. Besides, Rosanna was a bit mouthy, Trixie couldn't deny it. The maid rubbed Caroline up the wrong way most days with her constant opinions, but the harmony of the kitchen was something Trixie had become proud of, and she was content in her role working for Max Cavendish.

It worried her though that Caroline still spoke of leaving in March. Trixie had thought, as the months went by, her dear friend would settle, but Caroline prowled the house and grounds like one of those caged tigers Trixie had seen in one of Mussy's books, always looking outwards.

Trixie understood Caroline was bored and not in control of anything. Max had given Caroline full run of the house to do with as she pleased, but apart from keeping the rooms clean, she took no interest in the house. Caroline was biding her time, ready to leave the minute the new leaves appeared on the trees. And as Caroline became more unsettled, Trixie grew more content, which surprised her greatly. She never expected to find somewhere that was truly a home and which made her happy, even more so than Hopewood Farm. She hoped Caroline wouldn't make them leave.

Trixie stepped into the larder to put away the bacon, hearing Rosanna and Jeannie coming in from outside where they'd taken dirty clothes to the laundry shed across the yard.

'You'll never get him,' Jeannie said.

'Be quiet,' Rosanna hushed the other girl.

'There's no one in here,' Jeannie said. 'All I'm saying is Jacob is too old for you and he's shown no interest in you.'

Trixie, still in the larder, stiffened at their conversation. Rosanna was after Jacob?

'Only because I've not made my feelings clear,' Rosanna taunted. 'If I start to show him some attention, he'll soon get the idea that I could warm his bed in that cosy little cottage of his. He's not bad looking, and he's got a good position here and a cottage that goes with it. We'd be set for life.'

'You want to stay here then, for years?'

'Well, why not? There's worst places to be, isn't there?'

'What about me?'

'We'll find you a lad from one of the villages, or there's always Dickie!' Rosanna burst out laughing.

'No, not Dickie, he talks too much, and he's Mrs Lawson's pet, and I don't want a lad from any village. I don't want any man,' Jeannie's voice became hard.

'Forget all that happened in the past. We're safe here. I'll always look out for you.' Rosanna's tone was comforting.

'I'd best get on and get the rest of the clothes or Mrs Lawson won't be pleased,' Jeannie said. 'She's waiting for me.'

'I'll go up and get them,' Rosanna said. 'You go back out to her. It's mad that Mrs Lawson scrubs clothes when she's got you to do it for her.'

'She says it's too much for one person,' Jeannie replied. 'I like Mrs Lawson. She's kind.'

'She's crazy more like. Mr Cavendish is wild for her,

anyone can see it, and she keeps him at arm's length. I can't figure out it.'

'Not that it's any of our business,' Jeannie tutted. 'You need to keep quiet sometimes, Ros, or we'll be out on our backsides.'

Doors closed and Trixie waited a moment before coming out of the larder. Thoughtfully, she took the bread dough that had been proving near the range and tipped it out on the floured table. She kneaded, trying to sort out her feelings. After all that she'd overheard, the main thing that affected her was Rosanna having set her sights on Jacob. She didn't enjoy how that felt in the pit of her stomach. Jealousy rose up, burning in her chest. Did Jacob have his eyes on Rosanna? The girl had a fine figure and held some claim to looks. Would Jacob be tempted?

Trixie pounded the dough and paused. Caroline often mentioned in the past how she believed Trixie was blind to Jacob, that he cared for her. She saw Jacob as a brother type. He'd always looked out for her in the Water Lanes, had even been beaten to near death for helping her escape Dolan. Only, Trixie had thought herself in love with Thomas Cavendish, more fool her. She'd heard nothing from Thomas, which showed his feelings hadn't run deep.

Had she missed her chance with Jacob? Did she even want him?

Suddenly, she realised that if she had to watch Jacob marry Rosanna or any other woman, it would be a kind of torture. She'd been secure in always having Jacob by her side as he had been for years when they lived side by side in the tenement house in the Water Lanes. To think of him as belonging to someone else frightened her. It didn't feel right.

How had she been so stupid to take him for granted, to

think he would forever be a single man, someone without needs and wants? Of course, he'd want to marry and have children. Only who did he want that with?

She kept a tight smile on her face as Rosanna came through the kitchen, carrying a basket of washing.

'I'll be back shortly to help you, Miss Wilkes,' the girl called on her way out through the scullery.

The corridor door opened again, and Elsie stepped into the kitchen. Her and Bertha's morning duties were to dust all the rooms of the house, then she and Bertha would have lessons with Mussy in the afternoon.

'All finished?' Trixie forced a smile.

'Yes.' Elsie placed her box of dusters on the side counter. 'Mr Cavendish has just arrived.'

Trixie glanced out of the kitchen window, she hadn't heard the cart. He'd gone to Lincoln to buy roof slates for the damaged roof on one of the barns. 'He's back early from Lincoln.'

'Not Mr Max but his brother, Mr Thomas. I opened the front door to him. Mussy asked for a tea tray when you have time, I said I'd do it.'

A tingle ran over Trixie's skin. 'Mr Thomas?' She didn't think he'd turn up. As far as she'd been told by Caroline, Thomas would remain in Oxford over Christmas, and she'd been thankful to hear it.

'He's brought us all gifts.' Elsie was excited. 'But not to be opened until Christmas Day after church.'

'That is a surprise.' Trixie put the kneaded dough back in the tin. She felt the blood heat her cheeks at the humiliation of their last meeting. Lord, how would she cope? Thomas was *here*, she'd be *cooking* for him, but with that thought she calmed a little. Her defined role meant she'd stay in the kitchen and Thomas would spend his time in the main part of the house. He had no reason to come into her kitchen. Still, she silently prayed his visit wouldn't be long.

Jacob walked in from the scullery, holding a dead cock pheasant. 'My aim is getting better!' He lifted the bird higher with pride.

'Can I have its feathers for my bonnet?' Elsie peered closer to it.

'I'm sure you can, but it needs to hang for a few days in the cellar.' Jacob stopped near Trixie. 'Mr Cavendish is partial to a bit of pheasant.'

'He'll be well pleased then.' She couldn't look at him, not after hearing Rosanna's conversation and now Thomas turning up. Her mind and heart were at war.

'What's wrong?'

'Nowt.' She turned to Elsie. 'Make that tea tray.'

'Trixie?' Jacob persisted.

'I'm just a bit thrown. Mr Thomas Cavendish has arrived, and I wasn't expecting to cook for another person,' she lied.

'Thomas Cavendish?' The light faded from Jacob's eyes. 'You must be pleased he's here?'

'Not really.'

'Are you lying to yourself?'

Before she could answer him, Rosanna and Jeannie entered the kitchen with Caroline not far behind.

Trixie busied herself at the stove, her hands a little unsteady and she winced when Rosanna made a fuss of Jacob's good shot.

* * *

IN THE BLEAK grey light of late December, Max leant against the fence separating the gardens from the fields and watched the flock of sheep graze at the untilled field. Within a few weeks, the field would be cleared of most of the grass and weeds that grew, and he could start ploughing. A good farmer knew that fields needed to be left to fallow in rotation, but Grange Lea had been left in a state of neglect and the fields were not in great shape. Ditches needed to be dug and cleared for drainage and the weeds gone before sowing. It would take him years to see a return on the money he was spending.

The stress from his financial woes gave him a headache. He'd overspent on first arriving, desperate to bring the house and farm alive, to make it appealing for Caroline so she'd stay, but he could tell she wasn't interested in making the house her home. She organised and worked alongside the maids to make the rooms presentable, the house efficient, but it was done because it had to be not because she cared. He didn't know what else to do. She understood his feelings about her but gave nothing back.

He thought that maybe his present for her would break the uncomfortable tension between them. He'd bought everyone presents and thoroughly enjoyed watching them open their gifts after church on Christmas Day. He'd selected each gift with care: Mussy, an atlas; Trixie a new shawl; Elsie, a pretty bonnet; Bertie-Bear, a doll; and for Caroline, he'd bought her a small sapphire brooch in the shape of a forget-me-not flower.

Caroline had gasped with surprise on opening the velvet box and thanked him sincerely, but quickly put it away and barely said a word to him since, unless it was in general conversation with others present. Just once he wanted her to come to him, speak to him alone, share with him her thoughts on anything. She lived in his house but moved around like a ghost, untouchable.

Christmas had been celebrated, church attended, and work continued around the farm. Max spent the days visiting other farmers in the area with Thomas, learning about the farming community. He'd visited some of the wealthier manors, leaving his card. He, along with Thomas, Mussy and Caroline had been invited to the reverend's home for dinner, but only he and Thomas attended as Mussy felt unwell and Caroline stayed behind to care for him.

'There you are.' Thomas walked up from behind.

'Here I am.' Max kept his eyes on the sheep.

'I have decided to leave in the morning.' Thomas adjusted his scarf around his neck.

'I shall miss you, but your studies are important.' He'd liked having his brother stay for the Christmas festivities. Another person to talk to, one more person to sit at the dining table. Yet he was conscious of the unease in Thomas. Trixie's presence made any meeting in the kitchen or yard awkward. She'd stayed away from the main rooms and Thomas did not linger in the kitchen after taking his boots off.

'Come June I will be finished at Oxford.'

'Then what will you do?'

'Apply for some positions. There is a land agent's position at a large estate in Cumbria and a few in Ireland. I shall apply for them all.'

'So far away?' The news saddened Max.

Thomas leaned his arms on the fence post. 'I cannot be close to Lincoln, Max, as much as I would want to. Not yet. I need to forget Trixie first.'

'I understand, and you will in time. Perhaps you will meet a pretty young squire's daughter.'

Thomas chuckled. 'I shall aim higher I think, a princess?'

Max grinned. Thomas was one to lighten his mood. 'Any lady would be lucky to have you.'

'And what about you? Caroline talks of moving on soon.'

Max's heart twisted. He was so tired of feeling rejected.

'You need to talk to her, Max.'

'I have done, many times.' A raw emotion filled him. 'She does not love me.'

'I think she does,' Thomas declared. 'Often, I have seen how she looks at you when she thinks no one is looking. When we used to take her to stock auctions last spring, she used to hang on your every word. Smile at you, appreciate your company.'

'Yes…' Max began walking, walking off the pain. 'Then Caroline changed. She grew cold and hard and turned away from me, from our friendship.'

'Because of that bastard Dolan and because of Wayland.' Thomas strode beside him. 'She has suffered. Is it any wonder that she turned her back on becoming closer to you, after our cousin's attack?'

A spark of anger flared in Max's chest. What could he have done to prevent any of that?

'Caroline has no idea that you know what Wayland did, does she?'

Max huffed. 'How am I to mention such a delicate subject in conversation? I would embarrass Caroline. I shan't do that.'

'I believe you must. Before she leaves here, you need to tell her that you have knowledge of what happened.'

'Why? What would it do but drive a wider wedge between us. She hates Wayland and who would blame her? Her trust in our family is slim indeed. Your behaviour towards Trixie only added to that.'

Thomas jerked to a halt. 'What do you mean? My reaction to Trixie's past is justifiable! You yourself said I should not marry her!'

'And I stand by that because I feel you are only infatuated with Trixie.'

Thomas swore and turned away, hands on hips.

Max sighed deeply, his breath misting in the freezing air. 'Come, let us not quarrel on your last day.'

'No.' Thomas continued to walk by his side. 'Have you heard from Aunt Lucille or Wayland?'

'I have written to our aunt a few times, but the post takes so long to travel to her in India and then an answering letter must make its way back again. Months go by.' Max turned from the fields and towards the house through the ugly gardens.

'I would like to visit Aunt Lucille,' Thomas said.

'You should. I may do so should Caroline leave…' He'd been pondering on such a journey. Without Caroline, living here would be difficult. Now he'd seen her in every room, he would continue to picture her there. A journey to another country would help him flush Caroline from his mind and heart.

'Really? I am surprised you would go to India.'

'I would like to see our aunt, it has been too long. She would be extremely delighted to see us.'

'Agreed. Poor Aunt, living out there by herself. She should come home.'

'To Wayland?' Max scorned. 'He cares nothing for her or anyone but himself.'

'If you did go to India, what about this place?'

'I shall employ a manager if I go. A better one than the previous man!' Max scoffed.

'And no news from Wayland?' Thomas lowered his voice as they reached the house.

'We have no reason to communicate,' Max replied harshly. 'He can live his life in London or the depths of hell as far as I am concerned.'

They stopped as a horse and rider came up the drive. Max recognised the village reverend, Mr Trott. Max welcomed the older man, helping him down from his horse and ushered him inside as a misty rain began to fall.

'You do not mind me calling unannounced?' Reverend Trott asked, taking off his cloak to hand it to Jeannie.

'Not at all, please come in by the fire.' Max led him into the drawing room where Mussy sat with a blanket over his knees. Caroline was serving him a cup of tea with a worried look on her face. In the last two days Mussy had developed congestion in the nose, throat and chest.

'Ah, Mrs Lawson, Mr Casey.' The reverend bowed.

'It's a pleasure to see you, Mr Trott.' Caroline glanced at Jeannie. 'Another tea tray please, Jeannie.'

Max watched Caroline, admired the way she took to instructing Rosanna or Jeannie with ease. She would make a wonderful mistress of Grange Lea.

The reverend sat opposite Mussy, pulling from his inner coat pocket a small black leather-bound book. 'I thought you might welcome reading the works of Henry Alford. We spoke about him after church last week and I promised you I'd find the book I had of his hymns.'

'Thank you.' Mussy took the little book. 'That is most kind of you.'

'I have heard him speak at Cambridge. An excellent man.'

Mr Trott gave his full attention to Mussy and spoke to him in a calming way, even when Mussy had a coughing attack that left him breathless.

'Should we send for a doctor?' Thomas whispered to Max and Caroline.

Caroline looked at Max. 'Forgive me, but I have sent Jacob to post a letter to Doctor Gibb, asking him to come. I know there are doctors in Lincoln, but Mussy liked Doctor Gibb, and they got along well, became friends.'

'You did the right thing,' Max assured her, wishing he could take the anxious expression from her beautiful face. 'We must do all that we can to improve Mussy's comfort.'

'I will give up my room for the doctor and sleep in with Trixie.'

'No need, Caroline. I shall be leaving in the morning. The doctor can take my room.'

Caroline squeezed Thomas's arm in gratitude. 'We shall miss you.'

'Then I expect long letters from you.' Thomas grinned.

Coughing drew them apart and Caroline hurried to Mussy's side, offering him a glass of water to sip.

Jeannie entered with a tray of tea things and Elsie followed, carrying a tray of cakes and tarts. Max smiled at the girls, stepping aside so they could place the trays on the side tables. His house was well run, efficient in every way, but he couldn't forget the fact that money was running short.

'You seem out of sorts, Brother,' Thomas murmured as they stood to one side of the room. 'Last night you spent a good deal of time in your study.'

'My financial situation needs serious thought,' he finally admitted to Thomas.

'Has aunt's gift of Grange Lea become a noose around your neck?'

'Somewhat, but I shall overcome any difficulties.'

'Yes, you will, and I will help you.' Thomas accepted a cup of tea from Jeannie.

'There is no need.'

'There is every need. You have taken care of me since our parents died. I can return the favour easily. My inheritance from uncle is sitting in a bank. I shall invest it in Grange Lea, in you.'

'No, Thomas.' Max shook his head, guilt nearly swallowing him whole. 'That money is yours for your future.'

'I do not need it yet. I shall obtain a position on some estate and earn a wage, besides I have my townhouse in Oxford that I intend to lease out and that will provide me with extra income. I want to invest in you, in this place, unless you go to India?'

'You're going to India?' Caroline had come upon them without them realising, a teacup and saucer held out to Max. The shock on her face silenced Thomas.

'No,' Max said quickly.

Caroline blinked rapidly, as if absorbing the news. Mussy's coughing drew her back to him, but not before she gave Max a soulful look.

'Sorry,' Thomas muttered.

Max shrugged. 'Perhaps India is my best option.'

CHAPTER 21

Caroline stood by the window in Mussy's bedroom watching as Doctor Gibb examined Mussy who laid on the bed, flushed and weak.

Behind her, outside the window, fog covered the landscape, blotting out the world beyond the garden. Snow had fallen overnight turning to slush when rain fell as the day progressed. She was aching to feel the warmth of the sun again, to see flowers and smell their scents, to be able to sit outside and watch butterflies and bees, the birds swoop and sing.

'Are you hungry?' Doctor Gibb asked Mussy as he had done numerous times since he arrived three days ago.

Mussy shook his head slowly.

'What about some beef bone broth?' Doctor Gibb glanced up at Caroline.

She stepped forward eagerly. 'Yes, Trixie has a pot of it keeping warm for you.'

Mussy's glassy eyes closed gently. 'Half a cup…'

'I'll get you some immediately.' Caroline dashed from the

room and down the staircase, but at the bottom she stopped and took a breath. A wave of despair flowed over her. She wiped away the tears gathering, refusing to give in to them, and strode down the hallway and into the service corridor nearly bumping into Max as he came out of his study.

'Caroline?' He held her arms.

His tender gaze nearly brought her undone.

'Is it Mussy?'

She shook her head, but he drew her into his study and closed the door.

'What is it? Tell me?'

'It's nothing, I'm being silly.'

'I very much doubt that,' he chided softly.

Caroline bowed her head, desperately wanting him to hold her and as if reading her mind, suddenly she was in his warm embrace, her cheek pressed against his chest, breathing his scent of soap and the tweed of his clothes.

'My darling,' he breathed so lightly Caroline thought she'd misheard the endearment but looking up at him she saw it there in his blue eyes. His love for her was always there, waiting.

She pulled away. 'I must fetch Mussy's broth.'

Max let her go, reluctantly.

Caroline glanced around the small bare room, painted in dull brown, the square window without any coverings, his plain wooden desk and chair, the mean little fire smoking in puffs back down the chimney. 'I don't like this room,' she abruptly told him. 'You need to redecorate it.'

He smiled. 'This room is last on my list of things to spend my money on.'

Caroline left him, thinking it was a strange thing to say. Max never spoke to her about money, but she'd noticed that less of everything was being bought for the farm. It suddenly occurred to her that he might be running out of capital. After all, he had no income coming in while the farm was in such a state. Was he in financial trouble?

In the kitchen, she paused on the step. Trixie, Rosanna, Jeannie, Elsie and Bertha were all working various jobs in the room. Jacob and Dickie were working in the outbuildings, Mussy and Doctor Gibb upstairs and herself. Ten people. Max was providing meals and lodging to ten people, and wages to five, all while the farm was in hibernation. How was he affording it?

Elsie laughed at something Jeannie said, distracting Caroline from her thoughts. She went to the pan of broth and ladled some out into a cup.

'Mussy is feeling hungry?' Trixie asked. 'That's good.'

'I think he's only humouring us,' Caroline murmured. She took Trixie to one side. 'Can you eke out the food a bit more?'

Stunned by the request, Trixie stared at her. 'What do you mean?'

'I'll talk to you later about it, but can you?'

'Aye, of course. It wasn't so long ago we'd make one loaf of stale bread last a week, remember?' Trixie grinned at their shared memories of living rough in the Water Lanes.

'I'd better take this up before Mussy is asleep again.' She cradled the cup.

'I can make him some poached eggs later, if he's feeling up to it.' Trixie went back to cutting up cubes of ham for the pea and ham soup.

It was gone nine o'clock that night before Caroline found Trixie alone in the kitchen. Everyone had gone to bed, except Max who was in the library reading with a glass of whiskey.

Trixie poured them a cup of tea and they sat on chairs next

to the large fireplace. Around them, the kitchen shone with its daily scrubbing, the copper pans hanging on the wall reflected the flames.

'How long do you think Doctor Gibbs will stay for?' Trixie wondered.

'Until the end I feel.' Saying the words felt like an act of betrayal to Mussy, as though she'd given up on him.

'The end. I can't imagine it,' Trixie whispered tearfully.

'Nor I. Doctor Gibbs told me he's taken extended leave from his position at the hospital and his practice.'

'He must think highly of Mussy to leave all that and travel from Doncaster to here to be with him.'

'Yes…' Caroline had only admiration for Gibb's dedication to Mussy. 'They became good friends while we were in Doncaster. Mussy is pleased Doctor Gibb is here.'

They sat in comfortable silence for a few minutes. Caroline realised it had been a long time since she and Trixie had spent any time alone, just the two of them, not since they were living at Hopewood.

'What else is worrying you?' Trixie asked quietly, sipping her tea. 'I can see it on your face. I know you too well, Caro. And what's this business of eking out food?'

'I have no proof, but I think Max is having some money issues.'

'Really?'

'He's spent a lot of money on the house and farm since we arrived.'

'He *may* have a lot of money.'

'I don't think so, at least not anymore. He spends so much time in his office when not out ploughing the fields. His desk is cluttered with invoices, and he's not bought anything new for the farm in the last couple of weeks.'

'Max Cavendish is one of the cleverest men I've ever known, Caro. He wouldn't get himself into money troubles. He's too sensible for that.'

'I overheard him and Thomas discussing Max going to India.' Ever since she'd heard those words, she'd been unable to sleep.

'India? To his aunt?'

'Yes.'

'Why?'

'Maybe he's going there because this place isn't working out as he expected? The farm needs years of dedication to make it profitable again.'

'Jacob would be sad and disappointed if he went to India. He thinks the world of Mr Cavendish. When would he go?'

'He'd wait until we'd left, I'd imagine.'

'We are still leaving then?' Trixie frowned.

'I thought you wanted that as well? Because of Thomas?'

Trixie blushed. 'Thomas visiting his brother was my fear, but I faced it, didn't I when he suddenly turned up at Christmas?'

'You handled his arrival well, but I could see how uneasy you were the whole time he was here.'

'Thankfully, I was too busy to worry about him.'

'Do you still love him?'

Trixie took another sip of her tea. 'No, I don't think I do. I feel... something, but is it love? Attraction, yes, I can't deny that.'

'Would you marry him if he asked again?'

'No. He wouldn't ask again. We are too different. His reaction to my past hurt me deeply. I know my place, Caro.' She looked about the kitchen with warmth in her eyes. 'I'm happiest in here, this kitchen, and that's the truth. I never thought I would be content to be someone's cook, but I find pleasure in it, take pride in it. I've never felt like that before.'

Caroline nodded, her tea cooling as she thought.

'Our Elsie and Bertha, and Jacob are all glad to be here, too.' Trixie paused. 'But all of us will follow you when you leave.'

Guilt flared in Caroline. 'I don't want to take you all away from where you're comfortable.'

Smiling, Trixie raised her eyebrows. 'As if we could not be together? I'd never let you go anywhere without me.'

A lump of emotion clogged Caroline's throat. 'I can't stay here, but nor do I want to take you all away. That's not fair to you. I want you to be happy, all of you. I could easily get a position as a lady's companion, or work in a hotel by the seaside…'

'Aye, you could,' Trixie replied matter-of-factly. 'But do you really want to?'

'I don't see any other choice.'

'You could marry Max Cavendish and let the poor man love you.'

'We've been through this.'

'Aye, we have, and we don't agree on it.' Trixie stood and put their cups on the table. 'I'm dead on my feet.' She yawned.

Caroline put the guard around the fireplace. 'Maybe I can run this house for him if he goes to India?'

Trixie looked at her. 'Or maybe you could give yourself a chance of happiness.'

SITTING BESIDE MUSSY'S BED, Caroline sewed a darn in Bertha's stocking by the light of the lamp on the bedside table.

Over the weeks of January, since the doctor's arrival, Caroline and the lovely doctor had created a routine where Doctor Gibbs stayed by Mussy's bed at night, and Caroline in the evenings. During the day Elsie or Bertha, sometimes Trixie and Jacob, and often Max would take turns in spending time with him. Every day, Reverend Trott would spend an hour in prayer with Mussy.

Caroline found peace in those long evenings sitting beside Mussy who slept most of the time. After each day of seeing to the house and the people in it, she felt herself relax the minute she closed Mussy's bedroom door and sat beside him.

She always did something with her hands, sewing, embroidery, folding towels, reading the newspaper or unpicking old woollen garments. The evenings gave her plenty of time to think about those concerns she pushed away during the day, but mainly she thought of the future.

Since her talk with Trixie weeks ago, she refused to consider taking them with her when she left. They had created a life here, a good, decent life, and it would be selfish of her to ask them to give that away for her. She wouldn't do it. Although it would hurt her considerably to leave Trixie and the girls, she knew she must.

'What day is it?' Mussy whispered, his head not moving on the pillow.

'Sunday, the twenty-ninth of January.' She smiled at him, her needle plying in and out.

'Eighteen fifty-four,' he croaked.

'Yes.'

'I missed celebrating... the new year...'

'I'm afraid you slept straight through it.' She continued to darn, upset that he was talking about something that happened weeks ago. Lately his mind had started to wander and for the last three days he'd refused anything to eat.

Mussy laid staring at her, too weak to leave his bed now, his body had wasted away. Nothing remained of the old Mussy, his flamboyant clothes were packed away in the wardrobe, his clever brain too tired to utter a witty word, his body too exhausted to rock with laughter. 'Where's Matthew?'

'Our dear doctor is taking a nap. Will I fetch him for you?'

'No.' His voice was barely above a whisper. 'I want this time with you, dear Caro…'

She lowered her darning to her lap and took his hand closest to her. 'Would you like me to read to you?'

'No… You are not as… good at it as Matthew…'

'Hey, you cheeky beggar!' She laughed.

A broken smile appeared on his withered face before it fell away as though he didn't have the strength to hold it. 'The letter…'

Caroline leaned closer. 'Letter?'

'To my… parents…'

She tried to understand his meaning. She thought he wanted her to send the letter after his death. 'Do you want me to write to them now, ask them to come and see you?' She moved, ready to find paper and pen.

'No…'

She listened intently, his voice barely heard.

'Send the letter…'

'I will. I will send it to them I promise you.' She gripped his hand tighter, emotion welling up.

'Tell them… I am sorry…'

'I will.' She could barely breathe.

His eyes, the only part of him that was still Mussy stared at her with his last bit of passion. 'Daffodils…'

'Daffodils?' She was confused.

'Favourite…'

She blinked to clear her blurred vision. 'Daffodils are your favourite flower, yes, dear one, I know. You've told me that before. You made me buy bulbs and put them at Hopewood when I really wanted to use that money on other things,' she teased, bringing his hand up to kiss it.

'Plant daffs… on my grave…'

A cold shiver went over Caroline. 'Yes, darling Mussy.' Silent tears ran down her face. 'I'll plant dozens of them everywhere, for you. Every spring I will see them and think of you and smile and remember all our times together.'

'Love you… thank you… for being my friend…' His eyes closed and his breathing changed.

She watched the long pauses between each breath. She was losing him, this sweet, gentle man, her friend, Septimus Casey.

Some time later, Matthew Gibbs put his hand on her shoulder. Caroline looked up at him. Words weren't needed. They both watched a chest that wasn't moving anymore.

Gibbs left her and when he returned with jugs of warm water, Max was behind him.

'Do you want to help me lay him out, Caroline?' Doctor Gibbs inquired with concern.

She nodded. She'd helped wash and lay out the body of her husband, Hugh, a heartbreaking task. She would do it again for Mussy, another man she'd loved and lost.

Max stood quietly and helped them when required. Trixie, her eyes red from crying, kept the jugs coming, more than they needed, but no one told her to stop.

'What shall we dress him in?' Gibbs asked.

Caroline went to the wardrobe. The flash of colours, the

extravagant array of suits and cravats brought on fresh tears. She selected a grey and white pinstriped suit, a purple waistcoat, one of Mussy's favourites, and a gold silk cravat. From a drawer she selected a gold cravat pin with a ruby stud that she knew had once belonged to Mussy's grandfather.

When they'd finished, Caroline and Matthew Gibbs sat on either side of Mussy and stayed with him until the new day dawned.

CHAPTER 22

*T*hey buried Mussy a week later on a biting cold February day. The skies were a clear blue, the sun shining weakly when the coffin was lowered into the ground. Reverend Trott's voice carried across the graveyard. Behind him, the pale stone church of St John the Baptist had been full of parishioners, many hadn't known Mussy long, but they'd seen and spoken to him at Sunday church services until he became too ill to attend.

Caroline, her arm linked through Trixie's, thought it ironic that the village people of South Carlton, most of them strangers to Mussy, had taken time to pay their respects, yet his own parents hadn't even replied to her letter informing them of their son's death.

Max and Thomas and Matthew Gibbs stood on the other side of her and as people came up to speak to her, the three men moved away a little.

Finally, Caroline walked over to two men standing under a tree. She smiled with sadness at Mr Charles Bent and Mr Bob

Warburton, who'd arrived together from York just before the service.

'Caroline.' Mr Bent kissed her cheek. 'Our train was delayed.'

'Thank you both for coming. Mussy would have appreciated that.' She was glad to see them.

'It's a sorry day for certain.' Mr Bent nodded.

'You'll come back to the house before you catch your return train?'

'Aye, lass. We've a few hours yet before we need to be at the station.'

She smiled at Bob Warburton, the pub landlord in York who'd been Mussy's friend, and also hers. 'You, too, Mr Warburton? You'll come back to the house for refreshments?'

'I will, thank you.' Bob gazed at the coffin as the gravediggers began throwing soil over it, the thud echoed hollowly. 'I feel like I'm burying Douglas all over again.'

'At least they are together now.' Caroline hoped it would be true. Douglas Warburton had been Mussy's great love, a hidden sweetheart, a secret burden both men carried.

Trixie came to Caroline's side and nodded to the two men. 'I'll get everyone on the cart and start back to get the kettle boiled.'

'You came in the carriage,' Caroline whispered.

'And I'll return in the cart with Jacob and the girls. One carriage ride sitting opposite Thomas is one too many,' Trixie whispered back.

Caroline understood and said no more as Max came to her and offered his arm. She took it with a smile but hesitated as a large black carriage rolled up the church lane. They all watched an elderly man open the carriage door from inside and emerge to assist an equally elderly lady down the carriage steps.

'Mr and Mrs Casey, I presume?' Max muttered for Caroline's ear only.

Caroline didn't know what to think or feel now finally meeting Mussy's parents, the two people who had shunned him and pushed him out of their lives because he was different.

The old man, dressed in severe black, nodded slightly but didn't remove his tall top hat. 'Mrs Lawson?'

'Yes.' She glanced at the wife, a short thin woman of fading beauty, also dressed in all black with a large gaudy diamond brooch at the base of her neck which flashed in the sunlight. Caroline touched her delicate brooch that Max had bought her and wouldn't have swapped it with the woman's jewellery for anything.

'Is that our son's grave?' Mrs Casey's voice was small, insignificant.

'Shall I take you to it?' Caroline offered.

At their nod, she walked back to the grave with them. The dirt was now halfway up the hole.

Mrs Casey wept into her handkerchief.

'Pull yourself together, Margery,' Mr Casey snapped, though his chin quivered a couple of times.

'He was my dear friend,' Caroline told them.

Mr Casey turned away. 'I shall thank the reverend and make a donation to his church. He will need instructions for the headstone.'

Caroline watched him go, then gave her attention to Mrs Casey who continued to sob. 'As I said in my letter, Mussy loved you.'

'I gave him that name, Mussy,' the woman said, wiping her wrinkled face. 'He was my little Mussy once, not for long, of course, boys never are. Nannies care for them, then they go to boarding school and they never really come home again, not to a mother's embrace, not like when they are born. He would never settle for his nannies, but he would calm down the minute I walked into his room. My boy, Mussy.' Mrs Casey's voice drifted away, lost to her memories.

Caroline wanted to ask why she hadn't been more of a mother to him when, as a grown man, he needed comfort and understanding, but she didn't say a word. None of it mattered now.

From under her cloak, Mrs Casey pulled out an envelope and darting a look at her husband whose back was turned, placed the letter in Caroline's gloved hand. 'Hide it, quickly.'

'What is it?' Caroline tucked it up her sleeve.

'Mussy wrote to me when he was released from prison. He told me he was living with you at your farm. He said if anything were to happen to him, I was to give you this letter.'

'What does it say?'

Mrs Casey, eyes bloodshot from crying, lifted her head regally. 'Mussy wanted you to have whatever money he had left when he died. His solicitor's details are in the letter.'

'I don't want Mussy's money.'

'Where else will it go?' Mrs Casey wrung her handkerchief in her hands. 'I doubt it is very much, for my son lived a hedonistic life, but whatever there is, he wanted you to have it, not his father. Good day to you, Mrs Lawson, and thank you for being Mussy's friend.' She turned on her heel and walked back to the carriage to wait for her husband.

Caroline stayed where she was until the Casey carriage disappeared down the lane.

'Ready?' Max asked, coming to her.

She nodded and went with him to the carriage, the letter crinkling in her sleeve.

It was days later before Caroline could talk to Trixie without other people present. She'd asked her to come upstairs and help her sort through Mussy's belongings.

'What are we to do with them?' Trixie pulled out several suits from the wardrobe.

'Max doesn't want any of the clothes, but said he'd like a few of Mussy's cravat pins.' Caroline placed shoes and boots in a trunk. 'I need to speak to you about something.'

'Oh?'

'Mussy left me some money, not a lot, three hundred pounds.'

Trixie's eyes widened. 'Heavens!'

'I now have the means to go somewhere and start again.'

'What?' Trixie threw down a shirt. 'You? *Just you?*'

'Yes. You're not coming with me.'

Hands on hips, Trixie glared at her. 'Did I hear right? You're leaving me and the girls?'

Caroline closed the lid of the trunk. 'The three of you are content here. Why should you want to change that?'

'We'd be happy wherever *you* are. We've *talked* about this!'

'But I've decided to go alone.' Caroline was adamant. 'The girls need stability. They have that here and I know, deep down in your heart, you don't want to leave either and Jacob certainly doesn't. So, I'll go alone.'

Anger glowed from Trixie's eyes and her cheeks reddened. 'If you want to leave, then go! Go and be damned with you, Caroline Lawson. I don't need you!' Trixie ran from the room.

Caroline sighed and folded a shirt. Mussy's money had helped her make a decision to leave and start again somewhere new, but it had also created a wedge between her and Trixie and that was the last thing she wanted. Saying goodbye to them would break her heart.

She went to the window seat and sat down. She rested her head against the cold pane and spotted a few daffodils defiantly spearing up through the dirt and weeds in the garden beds. Spring was coming.

'Look down, Mussy,' she whispered. 'Daffs. You'd have seen them if you'd stayed…'

'I shall plant the whole garden with daffodils for him.' Max stood in the doorway.

Caroline didn't have it in her to smile or say thank you.

Max came and sat beside her. 'I just saw Trixie running past the office, crying. When I asked her what was wrong, she said to come and ask you. She also swore like a sailor, but I'll forgive her for that.' He grinned with questioning eyes.

'I am leaving.'

He bowed his head and Caroline wanted to touch his dark hair.

Max glanced up at her, his blue eyes desperate. 'Can I beg you to stay?'

'If you love me, like I think you do, then you'll let me go.'

'I absolutely love you, I have done since I first met you.' He grabbed her hands. 'Why would I let you go?'

'Because there are things you don't know about me.'

'Did you have the same occupation as Trixie did in York?'

She reared back. 'No!'

'No, I didn't think you would lie to me about that.'

'But there are other things that happened to me, which rule me out as a potential wife to you.'

'Do you mean what Wayland did to you?'

Caroline jerked to her feet in utter shock. 'You know he attacked me? That he raped me?'

'Yes.' Max stood, his expression serious, intense.

'How?'

'Thomas told me.'

'When?'

'Months ago. I gave Wayland a beating for it and resigned my position at the estate.'

'All that time?' Caroline couldn't think straight. 'You've known for months?'

'I have.'

'You knew and still offered for me to live here, to help me, and my friends?'

'Definitely. Why would I not?'

'What must you think of me?' Caroline cried, horrified, needing to hide from him.

'Think of you?' Max scowled in confusion.

'Your cousin defiled me! You must think of me as ruined, unclean.' Sobs caught in her throat.

Max looked appalled. 'God, no! No, never, Caroline. You are not to blame for his perversion. Christ, is that what you think? That in my mind you would be damaged goods, unworthy? That I would hold you in low esteem because of a despicable act that happened to you? None of that could be further from the truth.'

'I brought it upon myself. I riled him, disrespected him, your cousin, a lord!'

'I refuse to believe that you are anything but an innocent. Whatever you said to him gave him no right to do what he did to you.'

'But he did do it.'

'I am so very sorry, but it changes nothing. I love you. You are *not* at fault for his disgusting actions, Caroline. *He is.*'

They stared at each other, Max trying to convince her, and Caroline mortified that he knew what Wayland did to her.

She backed away, finding it hard to breathe. She ran from the room, down the stairs and out of the house. She ran across the gardens, through the fields, not knowing where she was going. Suddenly, she heard a sound. She turned and tripped over the uneven ground and fell hard in the cold wet dirt as Prince and Duke bounded up to her, licking her face, nuzzling her neck and whimpering, knowing she was in pain and needing them.

She hugged her dogs, her glorious dogs to her and sobbed without control. Pain and fear and hurt welled up inside her and she howled out the anguish she'd been carrying deep in her heart for months.

Max found her and pulled her up into his arms and held her tight as she cried. 'There, my darling, you cry it out. Let me be strong for you. You are no longer alone. I love you and will never let another person hurt you again.'

She raised her face to his, seeking his mouth, hungry for his kiss and when his lips touched hers, she melted against him, and the sobs lessened as his touch began to heal her.

'I shan't let you go, Caro.' He smiled. 'Not this spring or any spring in the future.'

'I don't think I want to go.'

'Good.' He wiped the tears from her cheeks with gentle hands. 'So, you will become my wife?'

She placed both her hands on either side of his face and kissed him, finally accepting his love and giving her own back to him. 'If you'll have me. I don't come alone, you know.'

'I have gathered that by now.' Max grinned and kissed her

again. He lifted her from the ground and swung her around. Prince, Duke and Princess barked and pranced about, eager to play.

At the edge of the field, Trixie stood smiling with Jacob by her side.

CAROLINE AND TRIXIE'S stories continue in book 3, *The Summer Bride,* coming soon.

AFTERWORD

Hello readers,

Thank you for choosing *Whispers of Spring*. I hoped you enjoyed reading it. I thoroughly loved writing the book, and continuing Caroline and Trixie's stories from book 1, *The Winter Window*. It was so satisfying seeing Dolan come to his rightful end, and introducing Wayland, who I don't think we've seen the last of yet! It was exciting to introduce new characters and find a new setting in Lincoln. Though, I cried writing Mussy's last scene, he was such a great character!

With luck, I will be continuing Caroline and Trixie's stories in book 3, *The Summer Bride,* hopefully to be released in 2025.

Some notes: St Dennis' Church in Walmgate, York, still stands. At some point since the 1850s the spelling of the name changed to St Denys, including the street next to it. However, on my 1852 map of York, the spelling was St Dennis' Church. The church is very old, thought to be built on the spot of a

Saxon church and a Roman temple and is dedicated to the French saint Denis of Paris.

Sadly, Doncaster's Guild Hall on French Gate was demolished to make way for shops in the 1960s. How such a lovely building could have been bulldozed is beyond me. It's appalling, really. White Hare Inn did exist opposite the Guild Hall but was also demolished.

I would like to sincerely thank all the lovely readers who leave comments on Facebook author page or send me messages or who write emails to me via my website. I really appreciate it and I try to reply to everyone when I can. Having people connect with me about my books is such a joy and one I'll never take for granted.

As always, I would like to seriously thank my family, especially my husband, who puts up with me living in the past all the time and having our TV planner filled with historical documentaries and history books left around the house. He is the best of men, and to the rest of my family who are patient when I'm deep in edits or writing a new story and live like a hermit, only to emerge once a story is finished. I love you all.

Take care and keep safe,
AnneMarie
2024

ABOUT THE AUTHOR

Author of over thirty-five novels, AnneMarie Brear has crafted sweeping historical fiction with atmosphere, emotion, and drama aplenty that will surely satisfy any fan of the genre. AnneMarie was born in a small town in N.S.W. Australia, to English parents from Yorkshire, and is the youngest of five children. From an early age she loved reading, working her way through the Enid Blyton stories, before moving onto Catherine Cookson's novels as a teenager.

Living in England during the 1980s and more recently, AnneMarie developed a love of history from visiting grand old English houses and this grew into a fascination with what may have happened behind their walls over their long existence. Her enjoyment of visiting old country estates and castles when travelling and, her interest in genealogy and researching her family tree, has been put to good use, providing backgrounds and names for her historical novels which are mainly set in Yorkshire or Australia between Victorian times and WWII.

A long and winding road to publication led to her first novel being published in 2006. She has now published over thirty historical family saga novels, becoming an Amazon best seller and with her novel, The Slum Angel, winning a gold medal at the USA Reader's Favourite International Awards. Two of her books have been nominated for the Romance Writer's Australia Ruby Award and the USA In'dtale Magazine Rone award and recently she has been nominated twice as a finalist in the saga category of the UK Romantic Novelists Association RONA Awards.

AnneMarie now lives in the Southern Highlands of N.S.W. Australia.

To subscribe to AnneMarie's newsletter, please visit her website.

http://www.annemariebrear.com

Printed in Great Britain
by Amazon